PLAGUE AND POWER

DRAMA AND DESPAIR AMIDST THE PLAGUE: A 1665 ENGLAND TALE OF LOVE, SURVIVAL, REDEMPTION AND POWER BULLETIN IN THE SHADOW OF DEATH AND WAR.

MASON MARLOWE

MARCYMICHAEL.COM - SIGNUP FOR FREE ADVANCED COPIES OF OUR

NEWEST KINDLE EBOOKS

Visit MarcyMichael.com for FREE advanced copies of our newest Kindle ebooks.

Again, that is MarcyMichael.com

CONTENTS

1. Chapter One   1

2. Chapter Two   10

3. Chapter Three   20

4. Chapter Four   33

5. Chapter Five   50

6. Chapter Six   62

7. Chapter Seven   74

8. Chapter Eight   81

9. Chapter Nine   86

10. Chapter Ten   97

11. Chapter Eleven   106

12. Chapter Twelve   119

13. Chapter Thirteen   133

14. Chapter Fourteen   142

15. Chapter Fifteen   151

16. Chapter Sixteen   170

17. Chapter Seventeen   181

18. Chapter Eighteen   189

19. Chapter Nineteen   198

20. Chapter Twenty   205

21. Chapter Twenty-one   212

22. Chapter Twenty-two   221

23. Chapter Twenty-three   229

24. Chapter Twenty-four   239

25. Chapter Twenty-five   246

26. Chapter Twenty-six   255

27. Chapter Twenty-seven   266

28. Chapter Twenty-eight   276

29. Chapter Twenty-nine   288

CHAPTER ONE

Times were turbulent, but Martha Quinn didn't let it bother her. She had a knack for sticking to the basics: keeping life going and ensuring it continued. She didn't waste time wrestling with life's complexities or debating the mysteries of the afterlife—questions that have driven men to push each other into uncertain journeys. Nor did she get caught up in the political turmoil splitting the nation or even the looming war with Holland that had everyone else on edge. Not even the scare about the plague reportedly inching closer from the outskirts could rattle her calm demeanor. The decadent misconduct of the Court, which spiced the town with juicy gossip, caught her attention more. As did the latest fashion trend of yellow bird's-eye hoods sweeping through the high society ladies and the city's infatuation with Sylvia Shallmont's stunning beauty and talent as she performed with Mr. Betterton at the Duke's House in the role of Katherine in Lord Orrery's "Henry the Fifth."

But to Martha, the capable keeper of the Paul's Head Inn in Paul's Yard, these were mere adornments on the main course of life. She focused her efforts on life's core essentials. When it came to food and drink, her skills, befitting the hostess of such a prosperous establishment, were probably unmatched. She didn't just understand the secrets of bringing a goose, turkey, or pheasant to mouth-watering perfection; a chine of beef roasted in her oven was like no other. She could work wonders with marrow bones and disguise venison umbles in a pasty so well that it would be fit for a prince's table. These culinary talents were the foundation of her solid success. Additionally, as the mother of six robust children, each with different fathers, she had a sharp eye for a handsome man.

I'm willing to bet she had the same sharp intuition for people that she claimed to have for knowing the weight and age of a chicken just by looking at it. Because of that keen sense, though Colonel Dempsey had no clue, he'd been living in luxury for the past month without anyone bringing up the matter of payment or even asking about his financial situation. Whether this worried him, I can't say. But he had reason to be concerned. Despite his solid build, his appearance wasn't the kind to inspire financial trust.

Mrs. Quinn had generously reserved a snug little parlor behind the main room solely for his use. There he lounged now, while Mrs. Quinn, despite being past the age or habit of doing such tasks herself, cleared away the remains of his hearty breakfast. The old-fashioned window, made of small, round leaded panes of greenish, warped glass, stood open, letting in the sunlight and the splendor of cherry trees that were unusually late in blooming. From one of these trees, a thrush filled the air with a joyful song, celebrating spring. Both the bird and Mrs. Quinn focused on the basics of life, relishing simply being alive. Colonel Dempsey, however, was deeply entangled in life's complicated webs. You could see it in his slumped posture, the deep furrow of worry etched between his brows, and the faraway wistfulness in his gray eyes as he lounged there, poorly dressed, with one leg stretched out along the leather-cushioned window seat, idly puffing on a long clay pipe.

Mrs. Quinn, accustomed to observing people discreetly, continued her work without disturbing his reverie. She was a woman just shy of middle height, curvaceous but not overly so, moving between the table and sideboard with a practiced grace.

You could have coined the phrase "plump as a partridge" just for her. Pushing forty, she had a sort of homely charm, but anyone sensible would know she wasn't what you'd call beautiful. Her eyes were strikingly blue, cheeks perpetually rosy—like she was the picture of health, which wasn't unappealing. But if you looked closer, you'd see the greedy curve of her full lips and the sly glimmer of her sharp eyes, hinting at a cunning born from a lack of intellect.

Still, she had enough allure and wealth to catch the eye of Coleman, the bookseller from Paul's Yard, and Appleby, the mercer from Paternoster Row. Either man would have married her in a heartbeat. But she wasn't interested. Appleby's knock-knees and Coleman's bow-legs disgusted her. Plus, the glimpses she'd had into the upper crust of society, thanks to her various "associates," had made her picky. She wasn't about to demean herself with a bookseller or a mercer.

Lately, though, marriage had been on her mind. She realized her days of adventure were winding down—time to find a life partner and settle down. But not just any partner. Martha Quinn was in a position to be choosy. Fifteen years of shrewd management and thrift at the Paul's Head had made her a wealthy woman. She could leave Paul's Yard anytime she wanted, buy a modest estate in the countryside, and reinvent herself as one of the landed ladies, a role she felt she was born to play.

Whatever her birth had failed to give her—a genteel upbringing or refined connections—a husband could. Lately, she'd been narrowing those cunning blue eyes, imagining her future and the man who would help her secure it.

What she needed was a gentleman—one born to privilege but down on his luck—who would keep his expectations in check when it came to marriage. He had to be a proper man, too. And finally, she had found him in Colonel Dempsey. From the moment he walked into her inn a month ago, followed by a street urchin lugging his bags, and spelled out his immediate needs, she knew he was the husband she was looking for, the one she had set her sights on.

With a single look, she had taken his measure: tall and solidly built, with the bearing of a soldier. Broad at the shoulders, tapering down to lean, strong legs, he had a face as smooth-shaven as a Puritan's, framed by thick golden- brown hair that could have belonged to a cavalier. Dangling from his right ear was a long, pear-shaped ruby, likely a relic from better days. His left hand rested with habitual ease on the pommel of his sword. His stance, his air of command, and his voice—pleasant yet authoritative—made her certain he was the one.

Yet she didn't miss the signs of his hardship: the frayed edges of his tall boots, the drooping, faded feather in his hat, the heavily worn leather jerkin that likely hid a threadbare doublet. What might have made another innkeeper wary only made Mrs. Quinn more eager. She metaphorically opened her arms to him, preparing to do so literally when the time was right. She knew at once that this man was her destiny, brought to her by Providence, to whom she already owed so much.

He said he had business in town—at the Court, no less. It might keep him there for a while. Could she put him up for perhaps a week? Maybe longer? She assured him she could—no problem at all. She could house him for a week, and if need be, even longer.

She made up her mind it should last longer—maybe even forever. She knew him and herself well enough to think that at least. This rugged, charming man had won not just the best bedroom upstairs but also her own private parlor, draped in grey linsey-woolsey and gilded leather, overlooking the garden. Normally, she kept that room for herself. The Paul's Head was alive with activity upon his arrival, as if they were welcoming royalty. The hostess, servers, and maids bustled to anticipate his every need. The cook had been unceremoniously fired for overcooking the marrow-bones that marked his first breakfast, and the chambermaid got a smack for forgetting to warm the Colonel's bed. It had been a full month since he arrived, and in all that time, he had been treated to the best Paul's Head could offer. Yet, in all that time, there was neither talk of payment nor questions about his ability to settle the bill.

At first, he objected to all the indulgence. But his protests were brushed off with good-natured laughter. His hostess assured him she knew a true gentleman when she saw one and knew exactly how a gentleman should be treated. He didn't suspect the truth—that this warm hospitality was a trap. The debt he was racking up was her way of binding him to her.

After finally wrapping up her household tasks, which she had stretched out as long as possible, she decided to break into his reverie. His face suggested his thoughts were as dark as the storm clouds gathering outside. She approached him with a deft touch, based on her knowledge of the Colonel's legendary thirst. After all, that morning's grilled herrings must have made his thirst even worse.

As she spoke to him now, she held the long pewter pitcher from which he had taken his morning drink.

"Is there anything you need, Colonel?"

He shifted and turned his head to face her, pulling the pipestem from between his lips.

"No, thank you," he replied with a gravity that had grown on him over the last couple of weeks, overshadowing the cheerfulness he once carried.

"Nothing at all?" The buxom woman's rosy face creased with an alluring smile. She raised the tankard, tilting her still-golden head. "Not another sip of October before you head out?" she coaxed. As he looked at her, he smiled. It has been noted by those who knew him best that his smile was irresistible, a smile that could charm anyone he bestowed it upon. It appeared suddenly, like sunshine breaking unexpectedly through a cloudy sky.

"I swear, you spoil me," he said. She beamed at him. "Isn't that what a proper hostess is supposed to do?"

She set the tankard on the laden tray and carried it out with her. When she returned with it refilled and placed it on a small table beside him, he had changed his position, but his thoughtful mood remained. He stirred himself enough to thank her. She lingered nearby until he had taken a deep drink of the brown October.

"Are you going out this morning?"

"Yes," he answered wearily, as if burdened with hopelessness. "They told me I'd find his grace back today. But they've said the same thing so many times now that..." He sighed, trailing off, his doubts hanging in the air. "I sometimes wonder if they're just mocking me."

"Mock you!" Her voice was filled with horror. "When the Duke is your friend!"

"Ah! But that was a long time ago."

"And people change... sometimes in ways you wouldn't believe."

He brushed off the weight of his dark thoughts. "But if there's going to be war, surely someone with my skills will be needed—especially someone who knows the enemy from the inside." His voice trailed off, almost as if he were talking to himself. She frowned at that. Over the past month, she had slowly pieced together fragments of his story. Though his confessions were far from complete, she had gathered enough to convince herself that there was a reason he shouldn't reach the duke, who held the key to his military dreams. That thought comforted her because, as you might guess, she had no intention of letting him march off to war again, risking his life and separating from her.

"I don't see why you're worrying about all this," she said, perplexed.

He met her gaze. "A man's got to make a living," he replied.

"But that doesn't mean he has to run off to war and probably die. Haven't you had enough of that already? At your age, a man's thoughts should be elsewhere."

"My age?" He chuckled softly. "I'm only thirty-five."

Her eyebrows raised in surprise. "You look older."

"Maybe I've lived more. I've had a busy life."

"Busy trying to get yourself killed. Doesn't it occur to you that it's time to consider other things?"

He shot her a slightly bewildered look, his brows knitting together.

"Other things?" he echoed.

"It's time you thought about settling down, finding a wife, building a home, and starting a family."

She spoke with a casual kindness, but her breathing grew a bit quicker, and her normally vibrant face paled slightly. The sudden rush of confronting him with her true feelings had her nerves tingling.

He stared blankly for a moment, then shrugged and let out a laugh.

"That's great advice," he said, still chuckling, a note of derision aimed at himself. "Find me a lady who's both well-off and not too picky, someone who'd settle for a husband like me, and we're set."

"Now there, you're not giving yourself enough credit."

"I learned that trick from watching others."

"You know, you're a fine man."

"Sure, but fine for what?"

She pressed on, ignoring his flippant question. "There's plenty of women out there with means who need a man like you—a man who can protect her and navigate this world, a man with standing."

"I have standing, do I? You're telling me news about myself."

"If you don't have it, it's only because you lack the resources. But those resources are rightfully yours."

"Rightfully mine? How do you figure that?"

"By birth, by breeding, and by your military rank. It's all evident. Why do you keep selling yourself short? A wife with the right fortune could put you in your proper place."

He shook his head and laughed again.

"Do you know of such a lady?"

She paused before answering, her full lips pursed as she pretended to think it over, masking her hesitation. That hesitation carried more weight than either could have guessed. It was the crossroads of his destiny. Human fates often hinge on such delicate moments; had she taken the plunge and offered herself then and there—rather than ten days later—the entire course of his life might have shifted. Even though his eventual answer wouldn't have changed, his story might never have been worth telling.

At that pivotal moment, her nerves unraveled, guiding her into the web of uncanny events that twisted together before her eyes. Destiny nudged her forward, and the uncanny chain of consequences it summoned fell into place, link by eerie link.

"I think," she said slowly, almost hesitantly, "that finding her won't be so difficult. I... I don't believe she's too far away."

"Such confidence," he replied dryly, his smile as sardonic as ever. He made it clear he wasn't convinced; to him, it was nothing more than fodder for snide remarks and dark humor. Rising from his seat with a wry grin, he added, "I'll place my bets on the Duke of Northridge. Those might be bleak odds, but not nearly as dim as hoping to tie the knot." As he spoke, he slung his baldric over his shoulder, securing his sword. Mrs. Quinn watched him with a mix of yearning and uncertainty, momentarily frozen before finally sighing and snapping herself out of it.

"We'll see; we'll see. Perhaps we'll revisit this conversation."

"Please, spare me, oh matchmaker extraordinaire," he said with mock despair, turning to leave. Her worry for his welfare overrode everything else.

"You won't leave without fortifying yourself with another drink, will you?"

She grabbed the empty tankard, determined. He paused and chuckled. "I might need that boost," he admitted, thinking about all the failed attempts to meet the elusive Duke. "You always think ahead," he said, genuinely appreciative. "You're not just Mrs. Quinn of Paul's Head; you're Lady Luck herself, showering us with her boundless generosity."

"Ah, flattery will get you everywhere!" she laughed, bustling off to refill his drink. It would be mistaken to assume she didn't fully grasp his compliments; no, she understood every nuance. His flowery praise was what she craved most, a promise of better things lurking on the horizon.

CHAPTER TWO

Through the chaotic throng of Paul's Yard, Colonel Dempsey moved with a swagger that was somehow both arrogant and worn. His old, tattered finery looked almost comical, but his air of grim determination kept the laughter at bay. The noisy bombardment of "What d'you need?" from the shouting apprentices in front of The Flower of Luce, The White Greyhound, The Green Dragon, The Crown, The Red Bull, and all the other shops punctuated the air. Among them, the booksellers were the most numerous, their stalls cluttered with yellowing pages and the smell of ink.

Colonel Dempsey walked with an audacious confidence that seemed to dare the world to challenge him. His hat, a Flemish beaver, was jauntily tilted, almost as if to declare to anyone watching, "Go on, underestimate me." The long sword thrust up behind him by a gloved hand, resting on the pommel, spoke of battles past and battles yet to come. His spurs, polished to a reflective gleam by a hopeful boy at the Paul's Head, clinked with every step, providing a metallic soundtrack to his journey.

The grim air around him seemed to part the sea of bustling citizens, making sure no one jostled him unnecessarily. In this crowd of busy, peaceful city dwellers, Colonel Dempsey wasn't just another man; he was a wolf moving through a field of sheep. People hastened to give him space, even if it meant shoving others into the muck and mire of the street. Below Ludgate Hill, in that dismal valley nourished by the foul waters of the Fleet Ditch, hackney-coaches were abundant. The thought of covering the distance in comfort, arriving with clean boots, tempted him momentarily.

Like a rare moment of clarity cutting through a drunkard's haze, he resisted the urge. For a man who had never truly mastered the survival art of frugality, this was no small feat. He sighed as he thought of his worryingly light purse and the heavy tab he'd run up at the Paul's Head, where his self-restraint had been sorely lacking over the past month. Luxuries had flowed freely in those days, and he indulged himself with reckless abandon, knowing that if Northridge didn't come through, he had no clue how he'd settle his debts.

While he contemplated his dwindling resources, his thoughts kneeled to a nugget of hope: the ruby in his ear. It was a jewel that, if sold for gold, could afford him comfort for almost a year. This contemplation of his dire financial straits served to highlight his exaggerated sense of doom. There remained, after all, the ace up his sleeve.

For fifteen years, through all the ups and downs, it had hung there, glowing amid his tousled gold-brown hair. There were times when hunger clawed at his insides, urging him to sell it to fill his stomach. But every time, that stubborn reluctance held him back. That shiny gem meant more to him than just its physical worth; it was a symbol, a superstition he couldn't shake.

In his mind, this jewel—a gift from a stranger whose life he had saved on the verge of death—was a talisman. It was entwined with his destiny and somehow, he believed, it was connected to that unknown person's fate as well. The conviction was iron-clad: this ruby would guide their paths to cross again, no matter the obstacles. And when they did, it would be a moment of profound significance for both.

Sometimes, in a more rational state, he mocked his own foolish belief. Strangely, those were never the moments when dire desperation led him to think seriously about selling it. As soon as he considered it, the old superstition seized him, commanding him to hold on to it, to endure everything but death itself before trading it for survival.

So it was that, as he trudged up Fleet Hill, he didn't factor the jewel into his bleak calculation of his meager resources. Westward he moved, through the Strand's muck, his soldierly stride carrying him to Charing Cross, and finally into Whitehall. He passed through the crowded street, filled with anxious energy, the fresh war with Holland stirring up a frenzy.

As he approached the checkered, embattled Cockpit Gate, linking the two sides of the palace, the weight of his situation pressed on him. It was nearly noon, and the curial thoroughfare was unusually bustling, the war casting its restless, feverish pall over everything.

A line of carriages rolled slowly down the road, heading towards the crowded Palace Gate, nearly blocking the street from one row of posts to the other. Across from the Horse Guards, Colonel Dempsey paused on the edge of a group of onlookers, who were watching workmen on the palace roof installing a weather- vane. When he inquired, a gentleman explained that it was for the convenience of the Duke of York, the Lord High Admiral. His grace wanted to keep an eye on the Dutch fleet, which was expected to sail from Texel any day now, without wasting precious time on the quarter-deck.

Colonel Dempsey continued on, glancing up at the windows of the banqueting house. Sixteen years ago, as a young cornet of horse, he'd watched the late King step out into the crisp January sunlight to face his execution. Maybe he remembered then that his father, dead long ago and safely out of Stuart reach, had been one of the men who signed the death warrant.

He walked on, from sunlight into the shadow of Holbein's grand gateway, and then turned right, past the Duke of Monmouth's lodgings and into the courtyard of the Cockpit, where the Duke of Northridge resided. Any doubt he had about whether the Duke had returned to London was resolved by the hustle and bustle around him. But another doubt lingered: would the Duke receive him now? Over the past month, he had tried six times to gain an audience. Three times he was told the Duke was out of town; once, more specifically, that his grace was in Portsmouth on fleet business.

Twice he showed up, and twice he had plenty of proof that the Duke was home and receiving guests. But the Colonel's ragged appearance triggered the ushers' suspicion, and they blocked his way, asking in a haughty tone if he had been summoned by the Duke. When he admitted he hadn't, they curtly informed him that the Duke was far too busy to meet anyone not specifically commanded to appear and suggested he return another day. He hadn't expected George Monk to be so hard to reach, remembering his approachable and informal manner from the old days. But after getting turned away twice at the door, he decided to write a letter before showing up again, pleading with the Duke to give orders for his admission, assuming he still remembered him. This visit, therefore, held tremendous weight. A denial now would be final, leaving him to curse the whim that had dragged him back to England, where starvation seemed a likely fate.

A doorman with a halberd stopped him at the threshold. "What's your business, sir?"

"It's with His Grace of Northridge." The Colonel's voice was sharp and self- assured. This confidence eased the next question from the doorman.

"Were you summoned, sir?"

"I have reason to believe I'm expected. His Grace knows I'm coming."

The doorkeeper gave him another scrutinizing glance, then stepped aside. He passed the outer guard, and his spirits lifted. But at the end of a long gallery, a stiff-faced usher blocked his path, and the questioning began anew. When Dempsey explained that he had written ahead to request a meeting, the usher asked his name.

"Randal Dempsey." He said it softly, with a pang of internal dread, fully aware that a name like his would hardly serve as a golden ticket in Whitehall. It was the name of his father before him—a regicide and much more. An abundance of wild, sensational, and mythical tales had bloomed in the public imagination around the execution of King Charles I.

The execution of a king was always a dark omen, and with such omens came a parade of rumors, each one more outlandish than the last. One such tale claimed that the royal headsman had vanished on the day of the king's beheading, his courage failing him at the thought of striking down a divine ruler. The story went that the headsman's mask had hidden the face of a last-minute substitute—a volunteer with the steel to do the unthinkable. Speculation about the identity of this deputy ran wild, with many well-known figures caught in the tangled web of gossip. But no name was whispered more persistently than that of Randal Dempsey. His vocal support for the republic had been twisted by the public into a personal vendetta against King Charles. Consequently, in the days of the restored monarchy, Randal

Dempsey's name carried a taint of infamy that clung to him like a leech.

Not that Dempsey cared. As he repeated his name to the usher, his calm demeanor remained unshaken. The usher, eyes scanning a crumpled sheet of paper, found what he was looking for, and a visible shift occurred in his stance. Obsequiousness replaced aloofness as he pushed open the studded door before him.

"If you would kindly enter, sir," he murmured.

Colonel Dempsey strode in with a swagger, the usher trailing behind like a shadow.

"If you would kindly wait, sir," the usher added, leaving Dempsey in the antechamber. The usher then moved across the room, presumably to pass on Dempsey's name to another attendant—a clerk with a wand, guarding yet another door.

Dempsey surveyed the room, ready to bide his time. The antechamber soared high above him, sparsely furnished but commanding in its austerity. He was one of many clients waiting their turn, all of them dressed in finery that spoke of their importance. Some turned to glance at Dempsey, their gazes questioning the presence of such a rough figure. But their scrutiny was fleeting. The steely gleam in Colonel Dempsey's grey eyes had a way of silencing the most arrogant stare.

He knew his world and the people in it too well to be impressed or scared by anyone anymore. Those emotions simply had no effect on him. Every person he met seemed as insignificant as a tavern boy cleaning tables. With a confident stride, he made his way to an empty bench against the intricately carved paneling and sat down with a noisy thud. The clamor caught the attention of two gentlemen standing nearby, deep in conversation.

One of them, facing away from Dempsey, turned around. He was tall and elderly, with a friendly, ruddy face. The other, roughly Dempsey's age, was short and stocky, his face dark and set off by a heavy black wig, meticulously styled. His demeanor mixed friendliness with a hint of self-importance. He shot Dempsey a look with bright blue eyes that held no trace of hostility or disdain. Though he didn't know the Colonel, he gave a slight nod, a formal and dignified gesture, as if seeking permission to continue their lively discussion within earshot of the newcomer.

Fragments of their conversation drifted to Dempsey.

"... and I tell you, Sir George, his grace is utterly fed up with all this delay. That's why he rushed off to Portsmouth, to take matters into his own hands..."

The pleasant voice trailed off, rising again after a moment.

"The need is dire for officers, men trained in war..."

Dempsey's ears perked up at that, but the voice dipped again, and listening more closely would have been too obvious. He had to wait until the conversation's volume lifted once more.

"These eager young men are commendable, and their enthusiasm is admirable, but in war..."

The speaker lowered his voice yet again, much to the Colonel's frustration. His companion's muted reply left Dempsey straining to catch more of their exchange, a torturous wait before another snippet would reach his ears.

By that time, their conversation had taken a new direction.

"...and now everyone's talking about the Dutch fleet being out," the stocky, dark-haired gentleman said. "And the rumors about the plague spreading through the Town—God help us—are nearly the only topics these days."

"Nearly, but not quite," the older man interjected with a chuckle. "There's something else I didn't expect you'd forget—the Shallmont girl at the Duke's House."

"Sir George, you're right to correct me. I shouldn't have overlooked that. The fact that she shares the public's attention alongside war and plague shows just how much of an impact she's made."

"Deservedly?" Sir George asked, with the air of someone who knew these things inside and out.

"Oh, quite deservedly, I assure you. I was at the Duke's House two days ago and saw her play Katherine. She amazed me. I don't remember seeing anyone as good in that role, or any role, really. The whole Town feels the same. I arrived at two in the afternoon, but the pit was already packed, so I had to shell out four shillings for a spot in one of the upper boxes. Everyone loved her, especially His Grace of Buckingham. He praised her loudly from his box, saying he wouldn't rest until he'd written a play for her himself."

"If writing her a play is the only way His Grace will show his admiration, then Miss Shallmont is lucky."

"Or maybe unlucky," said the stout gentleman with a mischievous smile. "It all depends on how she sees things. But let's hope she's virtuous."

"I never knew you to speak ill of His Grace before," replied Sir George, and both men laughed. Then the other man lowered his voice to a whisper, saying something that made Sir George laugh even harder, until it shook his whole body.

The laughter in the room was still echoing off the walls when the door to Northridge's office creaked open, and a slight man with flushed cheeks emerged, folding a piece of parchment as he walked. The man scurried across the antechamber, quick-stepping and nodding at those he passed, before disappearing out another door. As he vanished, the usher with the wand appeared in the doorway, his presence commanding attention.

"His Grace will now see Mr. Pepys."

The sturdy, dark-skinned gentleman wiped the last traces of laughter from his face, adopting a serious demeanor.

"I'm coming," he said. "Sir George, you're with me." His tone was both inviting and commanding. Sir George bowed slightly, and together they moved towards the Duke's room.

Colonel Dempsey leaned back against the wainscoting, puzzled. With war looming and the plague threatening, he couldn't fathom why the town was abuzz with the scandal of some playhouse floozy. It seemed absurd that, in the heart of power, Mr. Pepys of the Navy Office could lose himself in such sordid distractions, ignoring the grave issue of the navy's lack of officers and overall unpreparedness for the Dutch threat or the pestilence.

Lost in thought about the peculiar workings of the human mind and the strange governance of the restored Stuarts, Dempsey barely noticed when Mr. Pepys and his companion emerged. He snapped back to reality only when the usher's voice called his name.

"Mr. Dempsey!"

Dempsey, still partly in a haze and caught off guard by the lack of his military title, didn't react until the usher called again. Realizing it was his turn, he stood up. As he did, the room's occupants, who had eyed him with suspicion earlier, now looked on with a mix of resentment and curiosity, wondering why this rough-edged intruder was given precedence. They shared sneers, exchanged jabs, and muttered discontentedly. But Dempsey ignored them. Fortune had, at last, thrown open a door for him. His hope, bolstered by some overheard snippets from the ever-voluble Mr. Pepys, grew into an unwavering certainty.

Cops were in short supply; seasoned fighters, even rarer. Men like him, forged in the crucible of blood and battle, were an endangered breed. Northridge, the one holding the power to dispense such coveted roles, knew damn well what this man was worth. That's why he was ushered ahead of the rest of the polished, desperate faces cooling their heels in the antechamber. He strode forward with scarcely concealed eagerness.

CHAPTER THREE

In a high-ceilinged room bathed in sunlight, with windows looking out over St. James's Park, George Monk sat at a huge writing desk. Baron Monk of Potheridge, Beauchamp, and Tees. Earl of Torrington and Duke of Northridge. Master of the Horse, Commander-in-Chief, a member of the Privy Council, and a Gentleman of the Bedchamber. He held enough titles to make a lesser man crumble beneath their weight. But George Monk, whom his enemies called a trimmer and "honest George" by the rest of England, carried them with an almost indifferent grace. He could have even been King if he'd wanted to, and some said the kingdom wouldn't have been worse off. Instead, he chose to restore the Stuart dynasty, an act that wasn't winning him any popularity contests.

Monk was a man of average height, strong but beginning to soften around the edges in his fifty-seventh year. His complexion was dark, almost rugged, and his features had a certain handsomeness offset by the kindness in his nearsighted eyes. A heavy black periwig sat atop his large head, which rested awkwardly on a short neck, adding to his imposing frame.

When Dempsey entered the room, Monk glanced up, set his pen aside, and rose slowly, as though burdened by hesitation or maybe surprise. Indeed, surprise flickered across his face as he watched Dempsey approach with an urgency that was hard to miss. Not a word was spoken until there was only the table between them. Then Monk addressed the usher tersely, dismissing him. He followed the usher's exit with his eyes, only shifting his gaze back to Dempsey once the door had closed. Concern mingled with the lingering surprise in his expression, and he extended a hand to the Colonel, whose reception he found a little bewildering.

"God save us, Randal!"

"Is it really you?"

"After ten years, is it possible I look so different that you have to ask?"

"Ten years," the Duke echoed, his voice a slow drawl of disbelief. "Ten years," he repeated, his almost sorrowful eyes moving over the visitor from head to toe. He tightened his grip on the Colonel's hand briefly before, as though uncertain or hiding the depth of his emotions, waving toward the armchair opposite his. "But sit, man, sit," he urged. Dempsey adjusted his sword hilt and placed his hat on the floor before sinking into the chair. The Duke settled back into his seat with the same measured slowness, his eyes never leaving Dempsey.

"You look so much like your father now," he finally said.

"That's something, at least, in a life filled with loss."

"Indeed," the Duke agreed sorrowfully, shaking his head. "You wear it like a shroud."

Randal Dempsey the elder had been Monk's closest friend. Both were from Potheridge in Devon, growing up side by side into men. Political tides had their way, though; Monk was a staunch royalist while the elder Dempsey sided with Parliament's republicans. Yet their bond

endured. When Monk finally accepted a command from Cromwell
for the Irish campaign in '46, it was Dempsey's influence that sealed
the offer and Monk's acceptance. Later, when young Dempsey chose
the military path, it was under Monk's wing that he started his service,
and thanks to Monk's friendship—and his own abilities—he quickly
rose to Captain after Dunbar and Colonel after Worcester. If he had
continued following his father's friend's guidance, his fortune might
have turned out quite different. This thought weighed so heavily on
the Duke's mind that he couldn't keep it to himself.

"You know, had you stayed with Monk, your life might have taken a
very different turn," the Duke mused, unable to hold back any longer.

Dempsey let out a deep sigh. "Don't I know it? But..." He trailed
off. "The answer is a long and tiresome story. Let's not get into it.
You've read my letter. That's clear since I'm here now. So, you know
my situation."

"It pained me, Randal, more than anything I can remember. But
why didn't you write sooner? Why come knocking at my door only to
be turned away by servants?"

"I didn't realize how hard you'd become to reach."

The Duke's eyes narrowed. "Is that bitterness I hear?"

Dempsey nearly sprang from his chair. "God, no! I'd never be bitter,
no matter how low I've fallen. Everything you have, you've earned. I
celebrate your success, as should everyone who cares for you." With
a touch of dry humor to mask any deeper feelings, he added, "I have
to, because it's now my only lifeline. Without it, I might as well throw
myself off London Bridge."

The Duke studied him quietly for a moment.

"We need to talk," he said finally. "There's a lot to discuss." Then, in
his straightforward manner, he asked, "Will you stay for dinner?"

"I wouldn't turn down that invitation, even from an enemy."

The Duke rang a small silver bell. An usher stepped into the room. "Who's waiting in the anteroom?"

The usher listed off a series of names and titles, all distinguished, some even intimidating.

"Tell them, with my apologies, that I won't be seeing anyone before dinner. Those with urgent business can come back this afternoon."

As the usher left, Dempsey leaned back in his chair and laughed. The Duke frowned, curious and almost worried.

"I'm just thinking about how they looked at me earlier, and how they'll look at me next time. Forgive me for finding humor in the small things. It's one of the few luxuries I still have."

Northridge nodded somberly. If he had a sense of humor, it rarely showed, which might explain why Mr. (continued)

Pepys, always one for a joke, had noted him down as a dull fellow.

"So, tell me," he urged, "why have you come back home?"

"The war," came the reply. "Could I stay in Dutch service, even if they hadn't made it impossible? For the past three months, an Englishman couldn't show his face in The Hague without facing insults. And if he dared to retaliate, he'd find himself at the mercy of authorities all too eager to make an example out of him. That's one reason. The other is that England is in peril. She needs every sword, and in times like these, she should be ready to offer me a position. You need experienced officers, I hear..."

"That's painfully true," Northridge cut in, bitterness tinging his voice. "My anteroom is packed with young noblemen sent by the Duke of This and the Earl of That, and sometimes even by His Majesty, all wanting commissions to command men far more capable than themselves..." He paused, perhaps realizing he was letting his emotions get the best of him. "But as you say," he continued after a moment, "there's a dreadful shortage of seasoned officers. Yet that alone isn't something you can count on, my friend."

Dempsey's face was a mask of confusion. "How...?" he began, but Northridge didn't let him finish, jumping in to clarify.

"If you believe that even in these desperate times there's no place for men like you in England's ranks," he said gravely, his voice slow and solemn, "then you haven't a clue about what's been happening here while you were away. In these past ten years, Randal, I often thought you might be dead. And I wonder, given everything that's happened, if as your friend I truly have cause to celebrate seeing you alive."

To make life worth living, you have to live it with purpose. That means doing the best you can, showing what you're made of. But how do you prove yourself here, in England?"

"How?" Dempsey was flabbergasted. "Give me a chance, and I'll show you. I still have it in me, I swear. Test me, and you won't be let down. I won't disgrace you." He stood up, excitement shaking him. His face had gone a shade paler. Challenging and tense, his sharp eyes locked onto the Duke. Northridge remained unruffled, his sallow, pudgy hand gesturing for the Colonel to sit.

"I don't doubt it," said the Duke. "I'm not interested in how you've spent these years. It's clear they haven't been kind to you, even without your letter hinting at it. But that's not my concern. I know your character, and it's one I trust. I know your talents, partly from the promise you once showed, partly from the opinions I've heard abroad. Surprised? I keep tabs on the world. Wasn't it Opdam who described you as a man of great war expertise?" He paused, a sigh escaping him. "God knows I need men like you, desperately. And I would use you gratefully. But..."

"But what, sir? For God's sake, what?"

The Duke's lips parted again, his raised black eyebrows leveling out. "I can't do so without putting you in the gravest danger."

"Danger?" Dempsey laughed.

"You don't understand," the Duke said. "You bear a name that's on a very specific list—one marked for vengeance."

"You mean my father's name?" The Colonel was incredulous.

"Your father's, yes. It's a pity he named you after him. But there it is," the Duke continued in his slow, weighty tone. "The name of Randal Dempsey is listed on the warrant for the execution of the late King."

"If he'd lived long enough, they would've come for your father too," Northridge said, his eyes dark with conviction. "You served Parliament, arms in hand, against our current king. In England, the only way you'd stay alive is by fading into total obscurity. And now you ask me to give you a command, to throw you into the spotlight, under the royal scrutiny and memory that, trust me, never forgets."

"But the act of indemnity?" Dempsey's voice trembled, his dreams turning to dust before his eyes.

"Please." Northridge sneered, his lip curling. "Have you been living under a rock? Do you have any idea what happened to those it was supposed to protect?" He let out a bitter laugh, shaking his massive head. "Never force a man to make a promise he doesn't want to. Those promises are never kept, no matter how tight the legal bindings. I extracted that promise from His Majesty when he was just a throneless nomad. At Breda, I conspired with him and Clarendon for there to be only four exceptions in that bill. But once His Majesty was restored to the throne, Parliament decided the exceptions. I knew what was coming. I pleaded, argued, pushed the royal promise. Finally, we settled on increasing the exceptions to seven. I gave in, having lost the power to fight a de facto king. Yet when the bill reached the subservient

Commons, they named twenty exceptions, and the Lords went even further to include everyone involved in the late king's trial and a bunch of others. And that was their bill of indemnity! It was followed by the King's decree, demanding all involved in his father's death surrender within fourteen days. They claimed it was just a formality. Most had the sense to distrust it and fled the country."

Northridge's words hung in the air, heavy and damning. Dempsey saw the future as an abyss, his high hopes crumbling, leaving nothing but shadows and silence.

But about twenty chose to comply, thinking they'd get away with just a slap on the wrist.

He paused for a moment, sinking back into his chair. A thin smile twisted his lips, those lips that never knew humor.

"It was announced that those who hadn't surrendered were excluded from the Bill of Indemnity. Meanwhile, those who did surrender were supposed to be protected by it. Yet, a loyal jury still found them guilty. They were tried, convicted, and sentenced to death. Major-General Harrison was the first to die. They disemboweled him over at Charing Cross. More followed, and the gruesome spectacle became part of daily life until the people couldn't stomach it anymore and started to murmur. So, they paused. But only for a while. The executions resumed soon enough, and others were charged later on. Lambert and Vane weren't brought to trial until '62. And they weren't the last. Perhaps we haven't reached the end yet."

He paused again, and his tone softened, the bitterness dissipating like smoke in the wind.

"I'm not telling you this to criticize or censure the actions of His Majesty. It's not a subject's place to question the deeds of a King, especially when that King is avenging what he sees, rightly or wrongly, as his father's murder. I'm telling you all this so you understand that, despite my deep desire to help you, I can't do it the way you want. I fear that by bringing you to His Majesty's attention, directly or indirectly, I'd expose you to that ever-watchful vengeance. And it doesn't sleep."

Your name is Randal Dempsey, and...."

"I could change my name," the Colonel suddenly burst out, a glimmer of hope flickering in his eyes as he held his breath and watched Northridge ponder the idea.

"There are still people from the old days who would jump at the chance to expose you."

"I'll take that risk." Dempsey's laughter rang out, breaking the gloom that Northridge's lengthy lecture had cast over him. "I've lived my whole life on risks."

Northridge's gaze bore into him, serious and heavy. "And what about me?" he asked.

"You?"

"I'd have to be part of this deception...."

"That can be avoided. Trust me, I won't let it come to that."

"But I would still be a part of it," Northridge persisted, his tone even more deliberate. Dempsey's momentary enthusiasm faded, the familiar lines of grim hopelessness etching back into his face.

"You see?" said the Duke, his voice full of sorrow. But Dempsey refused to accept it. He shifted restlessly in his seat, finally leaning over the table towards the Duke.

"But surely... at a time like this... with England on the brink of war, needing officers with experience... there has to be some justification for...."

Northridge shook his head again, his expression graver, sadder than before. "There can never be justification for deceit, for falsehood."

They stared at each other in tense silence, Dempsey desperately trying to mask the despair on his face. Slowly, the Colonel slumped back in his chair, his gaze dropping to the polished floor. With a small sigh and a defeated shrug, he reached for the hat lying beside him.

"In that case..." He paused, his voice barely steady, "it looks like I'll be taking my leave...."

"No, no." The Duke leaned forward, placing a restraining hand on Dempsey's arm. "We won't part ways like this, Randal."

Dempsey looked at him, the struggle for self-control still raging within him.

He offered a sad yet irresistible smile. "You've got a lot on your plate, sir. The weight of a state at war is on you, and I..."

"Yet you'll stay for dinner," Northridge interrupted.

"Dinner?" Dempsey echoed, uncertain where he'd find his next meal. The looming thunderclouds of his financial woes promised a harsh storm, and the comforts of the Paul's Head would soon be out of reach.

"Yes, dinner, as you were invited, and to catch up with her grace." Northridge stood, pushing his chair back. "She'll be happy to see you. Join us. Dinner's already late."

Dempsey reluctantly stood, torn between a desire to flee Whitehall and wallow in his despair alone and the sense of obligation tugging at him. Finally, he gave in, a decision he wouldn't come to regret. The duchess welcomed him with a warmth that cut through his anxiety. A large, flamboyant woman, she stared as Northridge brought him into her orbit. Then she clapped her thighs in unmistakable glee and surged toward him.

"Well, bless my soul, if it isn't Randal Dempsey!" she exclaimed. Before he could react, she hoisted herself up by his shoulders and planted a hearty kiss on his cheek. "George is lucky you're here to excuse his lateness," she added with a wry smile. "Dinner's been waiting ten minutes, and cold food ruins good meat. Come, let's sit. Tell me what stroke of luck brought you here."

Looping her arm through his, she led him to their humble table. It was the kind that Mr. Pepys, a connoisseur of life's finer things, would have condemned for its dirty dishes and mediocre fare. Neither the setting nor the service hinted at nobility. But then again, neither did the hostess, and no amount of human effort could have conjured that illusion.

Even at the end, she remained Nan Clarges, the farrier's daughter and widow, the seamstress who had been Monk's lover while he was locked away in the Tower of London some twenty years past. Rumor had it Monk married her in a moment of madness to legitimize their children. In the grand world her husband inhabited, Nan had few friends, and those she might have had from her former life were long lost to memory. Thus, she clung fiercely to the scant handful of people she considered friends. Chief among them was Randal Dempsey.

Dempsey treated her with a respect that few others did, partly out of respect for Monk, but mainly because he was naturally kindheart-ed. From the early days of Monk's marriage, Dempsey had shown Nan the consideration due to her as a wife, even though she was scorned openly by most of her husband's acquaintances. Nan savored Dempsey's courtesy in a way only a woman starved for kindness could. The memory of his respect remained deeply etched in her mind.

Clarendon, who loathed her as many did, had damned her with a phrase: "Nihil muliebris præter corpus gerens." He believed she pos-sessed nothing womanly but her body. Clarendon failed to see the heart beneath her disheveled exterior—a heart as capable of hate as it was of love. Dempsey knew better, though he never moved in the same circles as Clarendon.

Sometimes, the little acts of kindness we scatter across our path grow into a harvest of goodwill in our times of need. Dempsey was finding this out firsthand. As she noisily devoured her meal, Nan bombarded him with questions until she'd extracted the full picture—his current state, the reasons that drew him back to England, the dreams he harbored, and how her own husband had shattered those hopes.

It sent her into a rage.

"By God's grace!" she shouted at her stoic duke of a husband. "You would have turned him away like a beggar? Him—Randal!"

George Monk, composed and steadfast all his life, the man who carved out his path with unwavering integrity and feared no one—not even the King he had helped place on the throne—lowered his proud gaze before his tempestuous wife. He was a great soldier. Once, he single-handedly faced down a rebellious regiment in Whitehall, silencing their insurrection with nothing but his commanding presence. But the boisterous, commoner of a duchess before him had a grip on his nerves stronger than any soldier's sword.

"My dear, you must understand..." he began unsteadily.

"Understand, you say?" she retorted, her voice dripping with scorn. "Your so- called understanding must be pretty dull if you can't see well enough to help a friend in need."

"I might end up helping him to the gallows," he argued. "Please, give me a moment to explain."

"I'll need all the patience in the world—God knows I shall! Well, go on, man."

He smiled gently, a sign he preferred kindness over exerting his authority. Despite her scornful interruptions, he explained the situation as he had already laid it out for Dempsey.

"Good Lord, George!" she exclaimed once he finished, her large face blank with disbelief. "You're getting old. You're not the man you used to be. A kingmaker! Ha!" She cast him a withering glance. "Where's the cleverness that brought back King Charles Stuart? You didn't get scared off by the first hurdle back then. I wonder what you'd do without me. It takes me to show you how to help a friend without putting him at risk."

"If you can find a way, my love...."

"If?" she spat. "I'd be a fool if I couldn't. I swear to God I would!"

"Isn't there anything else you could do besides sticking around here all the time?"

His eyebrows shot up, as if her words had sparked something in his mind.

"Aren't there any colonies still under England's control? What about the East and West Indies? There's a ton of those islands out there, always needing officers. Who'd remember Randal's name or past in one of those places?"

"Well, that's an idea!" The Duke's eyes lit up as he glanced at Dempsey. "What do you think, Randal?"

"Is there a job for me out there?" the Colonel asked eagerly.

"Not right now. But positions open up all the time. Men die in those faraway lands, get tired of the life, or can't handle the climate and come back. There are risks, of course, and..."

Dempsey interrupted, "I've lived my whole life taking risks. And any risk out there has to be better than what's waiting for me here. I'll take those risks without hesitation. I've got nothing holding me to the old world—I'd gladly trade it for the new."

"Alright then, we'll see. Be patient, and I might find you a position overseas."

"Patience," Dempsey repeated, his face falling.

"Of course. Positions like these don't just fall out of the sky. Keep me posted on where you're staying, and I'll let you know when something turns up."

"And if he takes too long, come and see me again, Randal," said her grace with a sly smile. "We'll hurry him along. He's decent enough, but he's getting old and slow."

And the great man, who had once struck fear into the hearts of armies, smiled kindly at his sharp-tongued wife.

CHAPTER FOUR

C olonel Dempsey leaned heavily on the windowsill in the Paul's Head parlor, staring out at the garden bathed in sunlight. Two cherry trees stood proudly in the small green space, still clinging to some of their last, late blossoms. But Colonel Dempsey wasn't really seeing these trees before him. His mind had drifted to another time, another place—a cherry orchard in Devon, years lost to the relentless march of time. It was a familiar scene, one that cherry blossoms always conjured for him. Their delicate flowers had an uncanny way of summoning memories he'd thought long forgotten.

Mrs. Quinn's modest garden, with its two trees, vanished. In its place, an acre of sunlit orchard unfolded, blossoms white and pink under the sapphire sky. Above the trees, a church spire thrust into view, crowned with a weather-vane shaped like a fish—an emblem of Christianity he'd learned about but never fully understood. His gaze shifted through an ivy-clad gap in the wall to the left, the bricks crumbling and worn. Over this wall, a boy was climbing with a stealthy grace, a lean, fair-haired boy whose features echoed Dempsey's own, if you took away the lines etched by years and hard living.

The boy dropped softly to the ground on the near side of the wall, moving with a cat-like nimbleness. His young face wore a smile, his gray eyes sparkling with laughter. He was watching a girl, blissfully unaware of his presence, swinging back and forth on a single rope tied between two of the trees. She was no more than a child, yet the lissom grace of her movements gave an impression of age beyond her fifteen years. Her complexion was not the porcelain delicacy often admired; instead, it was the healthy tan of someone who spent most of her life outdoors, far from the grime of cities.

In that moment, Colonel Dempsey stood spellbound at the window, caught in the grip of a memory so vivid, it was as if he were living it anew. Each detail of the orchard, each note of the girl's laughter, every petal of the blossoms brought him back to a time when life seemed simpler, when hope had not yet been carved away by the cruel hands of time.

One look into her deep blue eyes, the kind that seemed to hold secrets of their own, would tell you she wasn't just a country girl. Beneath that innocent surface, she carried the same shrewdness that's been passed down from Eve herself. If you were a smart man, you'd be on your guard when she looked her most demure.

The swing creaked as she flew through the air, her loose brown hair streaming behind her like a banner. As she swung back, it billowed into a wild halo around her face. She sang to the rhythm of the swing's movement, a lilting tune that filled the quiet space around her.

"Hey, young love! Ho, young love! Where do you tarry? While here I stay for you, waiting to marry. Hey, young love! Ho, young..."

Her song abruptly ended in a scream. Unnoticed and unexpected, the young man had slipped through the trees. Just as she reached the peak of her backward arc, he grabbed her around the waist with his strong arms. For a heartbeat, there was a flurry of black-stockinged legs and a cascade of petticoats. The swing pitched forward, leaving her in the arms of her mischievous captor. But only for a moment. She wriggled free from his grip, feigning outrage or perhaps genuinely furious, landing on the ground breathless, her cheeks flushed, eyes blazing.

"You're awfully bold, Randal," she snapped, giving him a sharp slap on the ear. "Who invited you here?"

"I... I thought you called me," he replied, grinning widely, undeterred by her hit or her glare. "Admit it, Nan!"

"I called you? Me?" She laughed, an indignant sound. "Oh, sure, very likely!"

"Of course, you'd deny it, being a budding young lady." He sang her line back to her, tauntingly: "Hey, young love! Ho, young love! Where do you tarry?"

"I was hiding on the other side of the wall. I came running. And all I get for my troubles and risking a brand-new pair of breeches is a slap and a denial."

"You might get more if you stay."

"I'm hoping for it."

"I wouldn't have come otherwise."

"But you might regret it."

"That's possible. But first, there's the matter of that slap. I don't take a blow from anyone. If it were a man, I'd challenge him with my sword..."

"Your sword!" She burst into laughter. "You don't even have a pocket knife, let alone a sword."

"Oh, I do. I have a sword. My father gave it to me today for my birthday. I turned nineteen today, Nan."

"You're growing up so fast! Soon, you'll be a man. So, your father gave you a sword?" She leaned against the trunk of a tree, eyeing him playfully. "That was reckless of him. You're bound to hurt yourself."

He smiled, but his confidence wavered slightly before he regained his composure.

"You're missing the point."

"The point of your sword, dear sir?"

"No, the point of my argument. It's about that slap. If you were a man, I'd have to kill you. My honor would demand it."

"With your sword?" she asked with feigned innocence.

"With my sword, naturally."

"Good grief. Jack the Giant-Killer in a cherry orchard. You must realize you're out of place here. Leave, boy. I don't think I've ever liked you, Randal. Now I'm sure of it. You've got a nasty streak for someone so young. Who knows what you'll be like as an adult... I shudder to imagine."

He swallowed the insult.

"And what you'll be when you're a woman is something I look forward to seeing. But let's get back to this slap..."

"Oh, you're insufferable."

"You're the one holding me up. I've already told you what I'd do to a man who struck me."

"But you can't really believe I take you seriously."

This time he wasn't going to be sidetracked.

"The real question is what to do with a woman." He moved closer. "When I look at you, only one punishment seems fitting."

He grabbed her by the shoulders with a grip that was surprisingly firm.

There was a sudden alarm in her eyes, eyes that had been taunting him just a moment ago.

"Randal!" she screamed, grasping his intent. Unfazed, he went through with it. He kissed her, then stepped back, bracing himself for the explosion he was sure would follow. But there was no explosion. She stood before him, limp and drained of her earlier defiance, her cheeks slowly losing their color. Then the blush returned with a rush, her mouth quivered pitifully, and her eyes glistened with unshed tears.

"Nan!" he exclaimed, unnerved by these unexpected reactions.

"Oh, why did you do that?" she sobbed. Here was meekness! If she had slapped him again, it wouldn't have surprised him at all—he had been expecting it. But for her to be so defeated, to offer nothing but that plaintive question, left him gaping in astonishment. Maybe he'd found a way to calm her wild spirit; he regretted not trying this approach sooner. Her question demanded an answer.

"I've been wanting to do it for the past year," he said simply. "And I'll want to do it again. Nan, dear, don't you know how much I love you? Don't you know even without me telling you? Don't you?"

Her trouble was replaced by surprise. She stared at him for a moment, her gaze growing sharper, a hint of her old self resurfacing.

"The declaration should have come before the... the... insult."

"Insult?" he yelled, protesting.

"What else? Isn't it an insult to kiss a girl without asking? If you were a man, I'd never forgive you. I couldn't. But since you're just a boy"—her tone turned mocking again—"I'll forgive you, as long as you promise it won't happen again."

"But I love you, Nan!"

"I've already said it," he protested.

"You're too clever for your own good, young Randal. It's what happens when you give a boy a sword to play with. I'll have to talk to your father about this. You need manners more than a sword right now."

Nan was an expert in doling out punishment. But the boy stood his ground, unflustered.

"Nan, dear, I'm asking you to marry me."

She jerked at that, her eyes widening. "My goodness!" she exclaimed. "How noble! But do you think I want a child clinging to my skirts?"

"Can't you take this seriously, Nan?" he implored. "I mean it."

"Well, you must be serious if you're thinking about marriage."

"I'm leaving, Nan. Tomorrow, very early. I came to say goodbye."

Her eyelids fluttered, just for an instant. A keen eye might have caught a flash of alarm in her blue eyes. But her voice gave nothing away.

"I thought you said you came here to marry me."

"Why do you keep teasing me? This means so much, Nan. I want you to say you'll wait for me, that someday you'll marry me."

He was close now, near enough that his presence was almost like a physical touch. She felt a tremor pass through her. Her instincts warned her he was about to take a liberty; her mischievous nature made her want to thwart him, even though part of her secretly thrilled at the thought.

"Someday?" she mocked. "When you're grown up? I'll be an old spinster by then, and I don't think I want that."

"Answer me, Nan. Don't tease. Will you wait?"

He reached for her shoulders again, but she slipped from his eager grasp.

"You haven't told me where you're going yet."

With a grave expression, he dropped the bombshell, sure it would make a difference to her. Maybe, just maybe, it would even make her see him in a new light.

"I'm going to London, to join the army."

"My father pulled some strings to get me a position as a cavalry officer. I'm going to serve under General Monk, who's an old friend of his."

That got her attention, though she hid how much the news shook her. To be fair, she saw the army as nothing more than clashing swords and blaring bugles. She hadn't yet grasped the grisly reality of war, otherwise, she might have reacted differently. As it was, she just stared at him in a new-found curiosity. He moved closer, thinking he could use her silence to his advantage. He misread the moment entirely, trying to pull her into his arms before she could react.

"Nan, my love!"

She fought against his grip. But he held on tight. The struggle only fueled her anger, and with a push against his chest, she broke free.

"Let go of me! Let go or I'll scream!"

Her fury startled him, and he backed off, looking foolishly contrite as she put distance between them, her breath shaky, eyes blazing.

"Good lord! You'll be a hit in London! They'll love your brutish ways there. I think you should go."

"Forgive me, Nan," he pleaded, desperation in his voice. He'd clearly pushed her too far this time. "Don't be so harsh. It's our last day together for who knows how long."

"Well, thank heavens for that."

"You don't mean that, Nan. You can't mean you don't care about me at all. That you're glad I'm leaving."

"You need to learn some manners," she replied, tempering her disdain.

"I will, I swear. It's just that I want you so much; I'm going so far away; after today, who knows when I'll see you again, maybe years. If you tell me you don't care for me at all, well then, I don't think I'll ever come back to Potheridge."

"But if you care even a little bit, Nan, if you'll wait for me, it'll give me the courage I need. It'll make me strong enough to achieve greatness. I'll conquer the world for you, my dear," he ended, his voice filled with the grandiosity of youthful ambition. "I'll bring it back just to lay it at your feet."

Her eyes sparkled, touched by his devotion and fervor. But the playful glint in her eyes belied her feelings. She laughed, a sound that came out mocking, lifting at the end.

"I wouldn't know what to do with it," she replied. Her laughter stung him. He had laid bare his heart, boasted in his enthusiasm, only to feel himself diminishing under the acid of her mockery. He adopted a cold, distant demeanor.

"You may laugh now, but one day you might not find it so funny. You might regret it when I return."

"With the world in tow?" she teased him. His face went pale, a white mask of barely contained rage. Without another word, he turned on his heel and stormed off through the trees. He'd only taken a few steps before he almost collided with an elderly gentleman, dressed in the humble garb of a churchman, engrossed in a book. The man lifted his eyes—blue and kind like Nancy's, but warmer.

"Why, Randal!" he greeted, nearly bowled over by the boy who was blinded by unshed tears. The lad managed to regain his composure.

"Good morning, Mr. Russell. I... I just came to say goodbye...."

"Indeed, my boy. Your father mentioned it...."

From among the trees, Nancy's teasing voice rang out.

"Father, you're holding him up. He's off to conquer the world."

Mr. Russell raised his thick, gray eyebrows slightly; a shadow of a smile played at the corners of his gentle mouth, his eyes twinkling with amusement. Randal shrugged, his shoulders heavy with bitterness.

"Nancy finds my departure entertaining, sir."

"No, no."

"She's amused by it, as you can see, sir."

She laughed, though it was a thin mask for her unease.

"Ah, don't mind it!" The parson turned, draped an affectionate arm around him, and led him toward the house. "A façade to hide her worries," he murmured. "Women are enigmatic that way. It takes an age to understand them, and even then, I'm not sure it's time well spent. But rest assured, she'll give you a warm welcome when you return, no matter if you've conquered the world or not. We all will, my boy. You're off to serve a noble cause. May God bring you safely home."

Randal found no comfort in those words and left Mr. Russell with a solemn vow that he would never return, no matter the outcome. Yet, before leaving Potheridge, he had proof Mr. Russell was right. That day, Nancy waited endlessly for his return, but it never came. That night, her pillow was wet with tears—some of annoyance, but some of genuine sorrow for his departure.

Before dawn the next morning, when the village still slumbered, Randal rode forth to conquer the world, bolstered by a full purse and a brand-new sword—the gifts that accompanied his father's blessing. Riding alongside the wall draped with cherry blossoms, he neared the grey rectory by the road. Suddenly, a lattice window above swung open, and Nancy leaned out, her head and shoulders framed by the morning light.

"Randal!" she whispered. He reined in his horse, looking up. His anger dissolved instantly, replaced by a racing heartbeat.

"Nan!" he breathed, pouring his soul into the name.

"I... I'm sorry I laughed, Randal. I wasn't really happy. I cried afterward. I stayed up all night just to see you one more time." It wasn't entirely true, but she probably believed it. "I wanted to say goodbye and God keep you, Randal. Please... come back to me soon."

"Nan!" he cried again.

It was all he could manage to say, but the words hung in the air, filled with a quiet intensity. A cool breeze swept by, and something light and soft landed gently on his horse's neck. His hand darted out, catching it just before it fell. He realized it was a small, tasseled glove.

A startled cry rang out from above. "My glove!" she called. "I've dropped it. Randal, please!" She leaned over the balcony, her hand outstretched in a desperate attempt to retrieve it. But she was too high above, making any return impossible. Besides, he knew her games too well now.

With deliberate calm, he removed his hat and slipped the glove into the band. "I'll keep it as a token until I can claim the hand that wore it," he declared, feeling a surge of triumph. He brought the glove to his lips, kissed it, and with a graceful bow, replaced his hat. The horse responded to the slight touch of his spurs, and they began to move away.

Her voice floated through the air after him, laced with a mocking edge yet quivering with emotion. "Don't forget to bring the world back with you."

That was the last sound of her voice he would hear for five long years. The next time he returned to Potheridge, the cherry trees were in full bloom again, their blossoms dancing in the breeze above the grey wall of the rectory orchard. His heart pounded as he rode forward, a servant trailing dutifully behind him.

Randal's father had moved to London soon after Randal left for Monk, and he had passed away two years earlier. Though Randal hadn't conquered the world as he had ambitiously declared, he had carved out a respected place in it. His military career had flourished, and he had become the youngest colonel in the army—a testament to both his skills and Monk's patronage. But the patronage would mean nothing if Randal hadn't proved his worth. He had become a man of remarkable stature, with expectations riding high among those who knew him.

All this was written clearly on his stern face: the commanding presence, the opulent attire, the fine leather of the saddle, the servant dutifully tailing behind. Every detail announced him as a man of significance. And he reveled in these things, not out of vanity, but for the woman who had inspired every facet of his ambition. He silently thanked God he had something of worth to offer her. What would she look like now? He mused, riding hard, with his heart racing as fast as his horse. It had been three years since he'd heard from her; but that was understandable, given the ceaseless churn of his soldier's life, making letters scarce commodities. He wrote often, but only one reply came through those years, penned after Dunbar to congratulate him on his promotion to captain, marking another step in his grand conquest of the world. How would she receive him now? How would she look at him? What would be the first thing she said? He imagined it would be his name. He hoped for it, for within that single utterance, he believed he would find all the answers he sought.

They pulled to a noisy halt at the rectory door. He dismounted without waiting for his groom, boots hitting the ground with a creak and clank as he marched up to the oak door. He rapped on it with the butt of his riding whip, the sound reverberating in the quiet.

The door swung open, revealing a lean old woman, a far cry from the well-fed Mathilda who once ran the rector's household. Her startled eyes met his; some of the eager joy slipped from his face.

"The... the rector?" he stammered. "Is he at home?"

"Aye, he's here," she muttered, eyeing him suspiciously. "Wait a moment while I fetch him." She disappeared into the dimness of the hall, her voice echoing back to him: "Master! Master! There's a stranger here!"

A stranger. Oh God, not everything was as it should be.

From the shadows emerged a young man, his steps brisk and assured. He stood tall, strikingly handsome, with a mane of golden hair. Clad in somber black and sporting the distinctive Geneva bands of a clergyman.

"You wanted to see me, sir?" he asked, his tone polite but firm. Randal Dempsey stood there, temporarily robbed of speech, staring in disbelief. Finally, he found his voice, though it trembled slightly.

"It was Mr. Russell I sought," he replied, his urgency causing him to clutch the young cleric's arm with unexpected force. "Tell me," he implored, almost desperately, "where is he? Has he left?"

"No," came the soft response. "I have taken his place." The cleric hesitated, then continued, "Mr. Russell has been with God these past three years."

Dempsey took a moment to regain his composure. "This is grievous news to me, sir. He was an old friend. And what of his daughter... Miss Nancy? Where is she?"

"I don't know, sir. She departed from Potheridge before my arrival."

"But where did she go? Where?" In a sudden, feverish panic, he shook the cleric's arm. The young man bore the assault in patient silence, recognizing the man's acute distress.

"That, sir, I cannot say. I never had the pleasure of knowing Miss Russell. Perhaps the squire might know..."

"Yes, the squire!"

With that, Dempsey made his way to the squire's residence and barged in, finding Squire Haynes comfortably dining in the hall. The squire, rotund and aged, struggled to his feet at the unexpected arrival of this distinguished yet disheveled stranger.

"God in Heaven!" he exclaimed, eyes widening in shock. "It's young Randal Dempsey! Alive!"

It soon became clear that the townsfolk of Potheridge believed Randal had perished at Worcester. That coincided roughly with Mr. Russell's death, and his daughter's subsequent departure. Under different circumstances, Dempsey might have chuckled at his vanity, imagining his name was known far and wide. Yet here, in his own native Potheridge, no whisper of his renown had reached.

He'd been reported dead, and nobody in the village, the one place in all of England where folks might actually care, had seen anything to prove that rumor wrong. Maybe later he'd chew over it and learn a bit of humility. But right now, the only thing on his mind was Nancy. Did anyone know where she'd gone? The squire had heard something at the time, but it had slipped his mind—after all, a parson's daughter wasn't a big deal to him. He strained to remember for Randal's sake, but nothing came. Then he thought maybe his housekeeper might know. Women held on to these little details.

Called into the room, the housekeeper, true to form, remembered perfectly. Nancy had gone to Charmouth to stay with a married aunt, her father's sister—the only family she had left. Her name was Tenfil, an odd name that would stick with Randal to the end of his days. He'd never forget that frantic ride to Charmouth, anxiety numbing his fatigue, trailed by a lackey who alternated between dozing and grumbling. Dead tired yet driven by suspense, they finally arrived at Charmouth. They found the house, found Mrs. Tenfil, but no Nancy.

Mrs. Tenfil was an elderly, hard-faced, hard-hearted woman, all piety and no charity, a walking sermon of damnation in her own right. She softened a bit at the sight of the handsome, elegant young stranger.

Beneath the years and the bigotry, she was still a woman. But the moment Nancy's name came up, the sourness and hardness returned full force.

"A godless creature. My brother was a weak man, and he spoiled her with kindness," she spat out, her face set in harsh lines.

It was a blessing he passed before he ever learned of the sinful ways of his headstrong, worldly daughter.

"Madam, I don't need your judgment; I need her location," said Randal, his frustration barely contained. The woman sized him up differently now, seeing something wicked in the charm and sophistication that had first impressed her. She knew a man like Randal could mean no good for her niece, yet he was precisely the kind of man her niece might welcome, to her own detriment. Her lips set in a resolute line. She would shield her niece from this man at any cost. By great fortune—and she was certain, divine intervention—her niece was away. And so, in the name of righteousness, she lied, though Randal remained unaware.

"In that case, young man, you're asking for something I cannot give you."

She would have left it at that, skirting the line between truth and falsehood. But Randal pressed on.

"You mean to say you don't know... that she has left you?"

She steadied herself for the holy lie.

"That is what I mean."

Still, he didn't relent. Gaunt and desperate, he pushed her to the brink of deceit.

"When did she leave? At least tell me that."

"Two years ago. After staying with me for a year."

"And where did she go? You must know that much!"

"I do not. All I know is she left. Probably London. She always wanted to be there, being so worldly and ungodly."

He stared at her, feeling physically ill. His little Nan in London, all alone and without resources. What could have happened to her in two years?

"Madam," he said, his voice quivering with passion and sorrow, "if you drove her out, as your manner suggests, God will surely punish you."

Without waiting for her response, he staggered out.

If Randal had asked around in the village, his life might have taken a completely different path. But as if some unspoken deity in Mrs. Tenfil's prayers decided to thwart any chance of diverting her plans, Randal left Charmouth without talking to a single soul. Why would he, based on her story? What reason did he have to doubt her? For six months, he searched for Nancy in both obvious and impossible places. Meanwhile, back in Charmouth, Nancy waited with unwavering patience for Randal to come rescue her from the iron grip of Aunt Tenfil's overzealous piety. She was convinced that one day, he would realize where she had gone and follow her. She didn't buy into the village rumors that he was dead, although she had grieved deeply when she first heard them echoing through Potheridge. Later, after moving to Charmouth, a letter from Randal reached her. Written months after the battle of Worcester, it revealed he was not only alive and well but also thriving, conquering the world, and promising to return soon to claim her.

Meanwhile, despair had settled upon young Randal. After living and striving with a single purpose, finding out in his moment of triumph that his goal was now unreachable felt like a cruel joke played by fate. For someone as loyal as Randal, this realization was devastating. It drained his life of purpose, stripped away his ambition, and twisted his very nature. His once steadfast soul turned reckless and restless. He needed a distraction from his dark thoughts; the military life at home, in peacetime, offered no solace. So he left the service of Parliament and ventured to Holland, that infamous refuge for rootless wanderers. He joined the Dutch forces, and for a while, he found success. But it wasn't the same. He no longer cared about building a position in the State.

Such a thing was unthinkable in a foreign land, where he was a mercenary—a soldier for hire, trading in weapons and lacking any genuine passion. He adopted the rituals of a mercenary like a second skin. The gold he earned easily, he squandered just as easily—blowing it on gambling, liquor, and women who offered nothing but fleeting pleasure. He became infamous, a man with reckless courage who treated his life as a trivial wager; he was a capable leader of men but also a brawling, hard-drinking, quarrelsome Englishman whom no one could trust for long.

The realization hit him after five years spent in this soul-corroding lifestyle. One day, he woke up and saw that he was over thirty, that his youth had been wasted, and the road he was on led to a pitiful old age. Something good buried deep within his soul surged up to bring him to a halt. He had to go back. Both physically and morally, he would retrace his steps. He wanted to seize this life that was slipping through his fingers and reshape it to its original purpose. For that, he would return to England.

He reached out to Monk, who was now the most powerful man in the kingdom. But Fate played its cruel hand—he wrote just a bit too late. The Restoration had already happened, only a few weeks prior. As the son of a prominent Parliament man and once a notable Parliamentarian himself, there was no place for him in the new English order. If he had sent that letter months earlier, while the Restoration was still undecided, and aligned himself with Monk to make it a reality, he might have redeemed himself in the eyes of the Stuarts, erasing his past failures with that single act.

Imagine the rest. He slipped even further into his old habits, making himself ever more unfit for any significant position. And so he languished for another five dreadful years, each day feeling like an eternity.

Then came the war, and England's silent call echoed in the hearts of every wandering son. The Dutch service no longer bound him. This was his chance. Finally, he could shed the grime of a mercenary's existence and return home with a purpose worthy of his blade. But for a sly tavern-keeper's credit and the favor of a coarse old woman who had her reasons to remember him kindly, he might have already been condemned, forced to navigate the treacherous path to hell once more.

CHAPTER FIVE

Colonel Dempsey walked through Paul's Yard, feeling a tight knot of anxiety twisting in his gut. It was the third day since his visit to the Cockpit, and the silence from Northridge was gnawing at him, unreasonable as it was to expect news so soon. Drawn partly by a preacher's voice reverberating off the stone steps of Paul's, partly by his own restless impatience, Dempsey found himself threading through the crowd that had gathered around the man.

"Repent while there's still time! The wrath of the Lord is upon you. The scourge of pestilence is poised to strike you down."

Dempsey's gaze pierced through the sea of heads, spying the preacher — a spectral figure draped in black, his face like a death's-head, eyes burning with unholy fire from deep, shadowy hollows.

"Repent!" the preacher's voice rasped, slicing through the murmurs. "Awaken! See the peril before you, and through prayer and repentance, strive to avert it while there's still a chance. Within the parish of St. Giles this week lie thirty dead of this dreadful pestilence, ten in St. Clement's, and as many in St. Andrew's, Holborn. These are merely warnings. Slowly but surely, the plague creeps upon the city. Just as ancient Sodom was destroyed, so shall this modern Sodom perish unless you rise up and cast out the evil amongst you."

The crowd was largely indifferent, even mocking. Laughter rippled through the gathering, punctuated by a single, piercing voice that jeered at the preacher. Undeterred, the preacher straightened, towering above them as he raised his arms skyward.

"They laugh! Scoffers and mockers, will you not heed my warning? Oh, the mighty and terrible God! His vengeance looms over you, and yet you laugh. 'You have defiled your sanctuaries with your multitude of sins, the iniquity of your commerce. Therefore, I will summon a fire from within you, and I will reduce you to ashes upon the earth before the eyes of all who behold you.'"

Dempsey pushed forward, blending into the throng, the preacher's words lingering in the air like black crows circling a carcass.

He'd heard of the strange plague creeping around the outskirts, with whispers branding it as a biological weapon unleashed by the Dutch. At least, that's what the paranoid ones claimed. But such rumors barely registered with him; there were always fearmongers around, blabbermouths eager to sow panic. And from what he saw, Londoners largely shared his indifference, paying no mind to the doomsayer bellowing through the streets.

Wandering through the throng, Dempsey carried himself with the confident stride of a seasoned soldier. His presence was commanding, his attire crisp and proper. A man with sharp eyes and a military bearing scrutinized him closely. When Dempsey came level with him, the stranger broke from the crowd and grabbed his arm. Dempsey halted, turning to face eyes that regarded him with an unsettling familiarity.

"You're either Randal Dempsey, or the devil's wearing your skin."

Recognition hit Dempsey like a freight train. The man before him was a specter from his past, just as he himself was a ghost to this stranger. An old comrade from the days of Worcester and Dunbar.

"McCormick!" he exclaimed. "Ned McCormick!" His face brightened, and he extended his hand. McCormick clasped it firmly.

"I'd know you anywhere, Randal, despite the years."

"Time's left its mark on you too, Ned. But it looks like you've done well for yourself." The Colonel's face was almost boyish with delight.

"I'm doing okay," McCormick replied. "How about you?"

"You can see for yourself."

McCormick's dark eyes studied him intently. A heavy silence fell, charged with the weight of countless unspoken questions.

At last:

"I last heard of you in Holland," McCormick said, his voice cutting through the autumn chill.

"Just got back," Dempsey replied, pulling his coat tighter around him.

McCormick's eyebrows shot up, a signal of his surprise. "What could've dragged you back here?"

"The war," Dempsey paused, his eyes narrowing, "and the need to find work where I can serve my country."

"Found anything yet?" McCormick's smile, dark and mocking, suggested he already knew the answer.

"Not yet."

"Didn't think so. Bit reckless to return, don't you think?" He glanced around, his voice dropping to a whisper. "Old soldiers of the Parliament aren't exactly welcome here."

"And yet, here you are," Dempsey pointed out.

McCormick's smile widened, slow and tainted with a hint of disdain. He leaned in, speaking even softer. "My father wasn't one of the regicides," he said. "That keeps me fairly anonymous."

Dempsey's excitement at the reunion dimmed, replaced by a sorrowful realization. Would this shadow always loom over him in Stuart England? Would he forever be tied to a past no one could forgive?

"Come on, don't look so glum," McCormick laughed, clapping Dempsey on the shoulder. "Let's find a place to talk. We've got a lot to catch up on."

"Let's go to the Paul's Head," Dempsey suggested. "I'm staying there."

McCormick hesitated, then shook his head. "My place is nearby in Cheapside." They turned, walking in silence, drifting together like ghosts from a forgotten time.

At the corner of Paul's Yard, McCormick stopped and turned, casting a glance at the doorway of Paul's where a preacher's voice cut through the evening air.

"Oh, the great and dreadful God!" the preacher cried, his fervent eyes wide with zeal.

McCormick's face hardened into lines of grim irony. "A passionate one, isn't he? Might wake these sheep from their stupor."

Dempsey stared at McCormick, baffled. The words seemed to carry a weight he couldn't quite decipher.

But McCormick, without saying another word, guided him onward. In a lavishly decorated room on the first floor of one of the grandest houses in Cheapside, McCormick gestured for his guest to take the finest chair.

"An old friend, bumped into by pure chance," he explained to his housekeeper, who had come to attend to them. "So, we shall have some wine... the best stuff!"

Once the woman brought the wine and left, closing the door behind her, McCormick turned to his friend, ready to hear the tale he craved. McCormick listened intently, his expression remaining somber even after the story was done. He sighed deeply and gazed at the Colonel with shadowed eyes.

"So George Monk is your only hope?" he said slowly, finally breaking the silence. Then he let out a short, sharp laugh full of disdain. "If I were you, I'd hang myself and be done with it. Far less tormenting."

"What are you getting at?"

"You actually think Monk will help you? That he genuinely intends to?"

"Of course. He gave me his word, and he was a friend to both me and my father."

"Friend!" McCormick spat the word bitterly. "I've never known a fence-sitter to be loyal to anyone but themselves. And if there ever was a master of compromise, it's George Monk. The very prince of trimmers, his whole life is testament to it. First, he was a loyalist; then he hovered between the Crown and Parliament; next, he fully sided with Parliament, betraying his former allies. And when it suited him, he switched back to the Crown, turning his back on his so-called friends in Parliament. Always choosing the side with the upper hand or whoever can pay more for his services. And look where it's got him: Baron of this, Earl of that, Duke of Northridge, Commander-in-Chief, Master of the Horse, Gentleman of the Bedchamber, and God knows what other titles. He's grown fat on his betrayals."

"You're wrong about him, Ned." Dempsey's voice held a hint of restrained anger.

"That's impossible."

"But you are."

"You forget that a person can change sides out of conviction."

"Especially when it benefits him," sneered McCormick.

"That's unfair and absolutely untrue." The Colonel's voice burned with a fierce loyalty. "You're wrong on another count as well. He would've given me all the help I needed, but..."

"But he figured that even a slight risk—no, inconvenience to himself should questions arise—wasn't worth it. He could've easily dodged any trouble by claiming ignorance of your past..."

"He's too honest for that."

"Honest! Honest George Monk!" McCormick's smile was a twisted mix of contempt and sorrow. "Usually, bad luck teaches a man to be wise to the world. But you..."

"I told you, he will help me. He's promised."

"And you put your faith in promises? Promises cost nothing. They're the bait a manipulator uses to keep the desperate at bay. Monk saw your need, just like I do. It's written all over you, in every worn seam of that threadbare coat. Forgive me, Randal!" He laid a conciliatory hand on his friend's arm, seeing the Colonel's face flush with anger. "I only mention it to make my point." With that, he continued, "Monk's income is thirty thousand pounds a year—such are the rewards for those who play all sides. He was your friend, you say, and your father's friend, owing him much, as everyone knows. Did he offer you his purse to tide you over this rough patch until he could fulfill his promise? Did he?"

"I couldn't have accepted it if he had."

"That's not what I'm asking. Did he offer it? Of course not. Not him. Yet wouldn't a real friend have stepped in immediately where he could?"

"He just didn't think of it."

"A real friend would've thought of it. But Monk isn't anyone's friend."

"I'm telling you, you're wrong about him."

"You're forgetting that he wasn't obligated to promise anything."

"Oh, he definitely was. Remember his Duchess? Dirty Bess can be really persistent, and she has him wrapped around her finger. He lives in fear of her. Pressured by her constant demands, he made a promise he'll probably try to wriggle out of. I know George Monk and his slimy crowd, feeding on England's carcass with the greed of vultures. I..."

He noticed Colonel Dempsey's eyes on him, wide with surprise at his sudden anger. He stopped short and laughed.

"I'm getting worked up over nothing. No, not nothing, for you, old friend, and against those who've duped you. You shouldn't have come back to England, Randal. But now that you're here, don't let empty promises fuel your hopes. They'll only lead to disappointment." He lifted his glass, locking eyes with the Colonel. "Here's to better luck for you, Randal."

Without a word, the Colonel raised his own glass and drank. It felt as if his heart had turned to lead. McCormick's venomous description of Monk painted a vivid picture, one that the bleak facts of Monk's life seemed to support. The likeness was disturbingly clear, even if skewed. And Dempsey, already pessimistic and worn down by his plight, saw the truth in McCormick's words, not the exaggeration.

"If you're right," he said slowly, staring at the table, "I might as well take your advice and hang myself."

"Just about the only dignified option left in England," McCormick replied.

"Or anywhere, for that matter. But why such bitterness about England in particular?"

McCormick shrugged. "You know how I feel, always have. I'm no flip-flopper. I stick to my principles."

Dempsey studied him intently. He couldn't mistake the meaning in McCormick's words, much less the sharpness of his tone.

"Isn't that... isn't that a risky stance?" he asked.

McCormick's eyes met his with a mix of amusement and sadness. "There are things an honest man should prioritize over danger."

"Oh, I agree," Randal replied.

"True honesty lies in steadfastness, Randal. And I strive to be an honest man."

"By which you mean that I'm not," Dempsey said slowly. McCormick didn't deny it, just shrugged and offered a polite, dismissive smile. The Colonel stood up, suddenly fired up by his friend's unspoken judgement.

"I'm a beggar, Ned; beggars can't be choosers. Besides, I've been a mercenary for ten years now, nothing more, nothing less. My sword's for hire. That's how I survive. I don't create governments; I don't bother with their merits; I serve them—for gold."

But McCormick, still smiling sadly, shook his head. "If that were true, you wouldn't be in England now. You came because of the war, as you said. Your sword might be for hire, but you still have a country. And the first offer always goes to her. If she refuses, the next won't go to one of England's enemies. So why diminish yourself like this? You still love your country. There are many here ready to love you back, even if they're not the ones ruling England. You returned to serve her. So serve her. But first, ask yourself how best you can do that."

"What's that?" Randal asked, confused.

"Sit down, man. Sit, and listen."

Swearing the Colonel to secrecy in the name of their old friendship and considering the Colonel's desperate state, McCormick then revealed what could only be described as treason. He started by asking the Colonel to think about the dire condition the country had been brought to by the misrule of a wasteful, lecherous, vindictive, dishonest king.

Starting with the Bill of Indemnity and its disgraceful evasion, he meticulously recounted the escalating tyranny of the past five years since King Charles was restored to power. Each act, reviewed through his own intensely critical lens, was bitter but brutally accurate. He then addressed the war that the country was embroiled in; he revealed how it was sparked by reckless decisions and made even more disastrous by the grievous, criminal negligence of the once-imposing navy Cromwell had built. And he lingered on the shocking debauchery of the Court, with a fervor only a true Puritan could muster.

"We're nearing the end," he concluded with fierce conviction. "Whitehall will be purged of Charles Stuart and his whores and cronies. They will be thrown onto the dungheap where they belong, and a commonwealth will be restored to govern this England with sanity and purity, so honest men can once again be proud to serve her."

"My God, Ned, you must be insane!" Dempsey gasped, equally shocked by the certainty of his words and the manner in which they were delivered.

"Worried about me, are you?" McCormick smiled grimly. "Better men have lost their lives for this cause, torn apart by these vampires, and if it comes to that, they can have mine too. But we won't fail. Our plans are cunningly designed and already well underway. There's someone in Holland orchestrating this—someone whose name I can't reveal just yet, but it's a name cherished by every honest soul. The time is almost upon us. Our agents are everywhere, shaping the minds of the people, guiding them towards sanity. Even Heaven has lent us a hand, sending this plague to strike fear into hearts and force people to consider how much the rulers' vices may have brought this curse upon us."

"That preacher you heard on the steps of St. Paul's? He's one of our operatives, spreading the word, planting seeds in fertile minds. And soon, the harvest will come—a plentiful, bountiful harvest!"

He paused, looking at his stricken friend with eyes that blazed with a fanatical gleam.

"Your sword lies idle, Randal, and you crave purpose. Here is a chance to fight with honor. This is the cause of the old Commonwealth, the one you'd once been so faithful to. It's a cause aimed at those enemies who still deny men like you a place in England. You fight not just for yourself but for thousands in the same plight. And your country will remember. We need swords like yours. I'm offering you both a cause and a career. Northridge gives you nothing but empty promises, favoring the sycophants of Charles Stuart's corrupt Court. I've laid my heart bare to you, even at some risk. What do you have to say?"

Dempsey stood up, his decision made, his face like granite. "What I said from the start. I'm a mercenary. I don't make governments. I serve them. There's no cause on this earth that could stir my enthusiasm."

"Yet you came back to serve England in her time of need."

"Because I had no other place to go."

"Very well. I'll take you at face value, Randal—though I don't believe you—but let's not muddy the waters. You came here and found all the doors you counted on entering firmly shut and locked. What will you do? You claim you're a mercenary, that you offer soulless service to whoever pays you. I'm presenting you with a generous taskmaster, one who will reward you well. Since you say all services are the same to you, let this mercenary give me his answer."

He, too, had stood up now, and extended a hand in earnest appeal.

The Colonel studied him intently for a moment before a thin smile crept across his face.

"Ned, you missed your calling as a lawyer," he said, his voice coated with a sardonic edge. "You're adept at staying on topic, yet somehow you manage to sidestep it completely. A mercenary serves existing governments; those driven by ideology serve the governments of dreams, and I haven't chased dreams in over a decade. Establish your government, and I'll gladly sell you my sword. But don't expect me to risk my neck to make it happen; my head's all I've got left."

"If you won't fight for love, will you at least fight out of hate? Against the Stuart, whose malice keeps you from earning your livelihood?"

"You exaggerate. While much of what you say might hold some truth, I haven't given up on getting help from Northridge just yet."

"You fool," Ned spat, his voice edged with desperation, "I swear to you, before long, Northridge will be incapable of aiding anyone, even himself."

Dempsey opened his mouth to respond, but McCormick silenced him with a raised hand.

"Don't answer now. Let my words settle in your mind. Take some time to think. We have a few days, after all. Reflect on what I've told you, and if no news comes from Whitehall—no realization of this wishful thinking—maybe you'll see things differently. Maybe you'll understand where your true interests lie. Remember, we need seasoned soldiers to lead our cause, and there's a sure welcome waiting for you. And bear in mind—for that mercenary persona you embrace—that those leading now will continue to lead when we win, and they'll reap the enduring rewards. For now, Randal, let's focus on the half-empty bottle in front of us."

"Take a seat and let's discuss other matters," he said, with an eerie calm that made the Colonel's skin crawl.

As dusk settled over the town, the Colonel's mind swirled with thoughts. What intrigued him most was the reckless honesty shown by McCormick. Revealing such a heavy secret to someone based solely on a past reputation seemed reckless. But the more the Colonel reflected, the clearer it became. McCormick hadn't revealed anything that could truly harm the conspirators. No names were dropped; he only vaguely hinted at a powerful figure in Holland, someone the Colonel suspected was Algernon Sidney, conveniently out of the Stuart's reach.

Beyond that, what had McCormick really told him? Just that there was a serious movement to overthrow the Stuart dynasty and bring back the Commonwealth. If Dempsey went to the authorities with that, what would come of it? He couldn't name anyone except McCormick, and even then, it would be McCormick's word against his own. Dempsey's shady past would be scrutinized, and any revelation would put him in danger, not McCormick.

It dawned on the Colonel that McCormick hadn't been as forthright as he seemed. He chuckled softly at his own gullibility and then laughed outright as he considered McCormick's proposal. Desperation hadn't clouded his judgment that badly. He tenderly rubbed his neck, not keen on feeling a rope tighten around it.

McCormick's words about Northridge had been layered with self-interest, yet the more the Colonel pondered it, far from McCormick's influence, the more he believed in Northridge's sincerity and good intentions.

CHAPTER SIX

When the Colonel returned to the Paul's Head after that treacherous chat with McCormick, he found an unusual buzz of excitement gripping the normally tranquil inn. The common room was packed, which wasn't particularly strange for that hour; what stood out was the uproarious chatter of the typically calm, almost somber merchants who frequented the place. Mrs. Quinn was there, listening to Coleman, her bookseller-suitor, who was speaking in an uncharacteristically shrill voice. Her normally rosy, round face, which the Colonel had never seen devoid of false jovial smiles, was now solemn and had lost some of its usual vibrancy. Nearby, the drawer was busy scraping imaginary crumbs from the table with his wooden knife, using it as an excuse to linger and eavesdrop. Mrs. Quinn, deeply engrossed in the conversation, didn't bother to reprimand him.

Despite her agitation, she couldn't help but throw a coy glance at the Colonel as he walked in with his usual air of lofty detachment and arrogant indifference, which she found so utterly charming. Not long after, she followed him into the small parlor at the back. He was reclining at ease on his favorite seat beneath the window, his sword and hat thrown aside, in the middle of loading a pipe from a leaden tobacco jar.

"Lord, Colonel! There's dreadful news," she said, her voice tinged with urgency. He looked up, raising an eyebrow.

"You haven't heard?" she added. "It's the talk of the Town."

He shook his head. "No, I heard nothing dreadful. I met an old friend over by the Flower of Luce. We've been catching up for three hours. I haven't spoken to anyone else. What's this news?"

But she was frowning now, scrutinizing him with her round blue eyes. His dismissive words made her shift her thoughts to more immediate concerns. He had met a friend, an old friend. There wasn't much in that to provoke worry, perhaps. But Mrs. Quinn...

Quinn moved through her days in a haze of constant dread, always glancing over her shoulder for signs that the Colonel might slip through her fingers. She'd carefully mined enough details from his meeting with Northridge to know the promises he'd hoped for weren't going to materialize. Northridge had fobbed him off with vague assurances, and Quinn, well-versed in the ways of the world, wasn't too ruffled by it. Nonetheless, she itched to solidify her grip on the Colonel, yet the man showed no signs of craving the chains she'd fashioned for him. Quinn was a seasoned huntress, too savvy to spook her prey with a hasty ambush.

Her only real fear stemmed from the wild card of the unexpected. She knew that chaos had a nasty habit of kicking down the door uninvited, and the mention of some old friend—the one with whom the Colonel had shared a long and candid chat—set her nerves on edge. Quinn wanted to probe deeper about this friend, but the Colonel's persistent question kept stabbing through her thoughts like a splinter under the skin.

"What's this news, Quinn?"

Dragged back to the gravity of the situation at hand, her mind pushed aside the murky worries of old friends and sly conversations.

"That the plague has broken out in the heart of the City, on Bearbinder Lane. A Frenchman from Long Acre carried it here. Tried to outrun the pestilence in his neighborhood, poor fool, but he was already infected. Now, he's brought the damn sickness to our doorstep."

The Colonel's mind darted to McCormick and his band of fearmongers. Always stirring the pot, always feeding the panic.

"Maybe it's just another rumor," he said, grasping at straws.

"No, it's true. Beyond question. Some preacher lunatic shouted it from the steps of Paul's today. At first, nobody believed him, but you know how these things spread."

They headed to Bearbinder Lane, finding the house locked up tight and guarded under orders from the Lord Mayor. Word on the streets was that Sir John Lawrence had gone to Whitehall to strategize against the plague, planning to close down playhouses and other crowd-gathering spots. This likely meant shutting down taverns and eateries too. "What's going to happen if they do that?" she fretted.

"Don't worry," Dempsey said, trying to soothe her anxiety. "It won't go that far. People need to eat and drink, or they'll just starve, and that's as bad as the plague."

"Exactly. But you know how they are in their newfound piety; in their panic and godliness, they won't consider that. They'll be blaming this on the Court's vices bringing this curse upon us. And all this happening now, with the Dutch fleet about to attack the coast, it's madness!"

She ranted on, her usual self-centered nature shaken by the broader crisis threatening her world. Her sudden verbosity covered topics she had long ignored, and her news was unfortunately accurate. At that very moment, the Lord Mayor was at Whitehall pushing for immediate, drastic action to combat the plague, including the immediate closure of playhouses. However, he made no mention of closing churches, where people gathered just as closely and dangerously. This led to whispers at Court that Sir John was merely a tool for the Puritans, who saw the plague as an opportunity to seize control. Besides, the plague mainly affected the poor and lower classes. Heaven would never be so indiscriminate as to allow such a dreadful disease to touch people of high status.

And then there was Whitehall, swamped with other pressing matters. Rumors swirled that the Dutch fleet was out and about, keeping the nation's elite on edge whenever they could break from their pleasure-seeking jaunts, following the lead of their indulgent King. Many among the nation's elite were seething over personal grievances tied to the fleet and the ongoing war. Chief among the disgruntled was the highly esteemed Duke of Buckingham. He felt the nation was shockingly indifferent to the fact that he had journeyed all the way from York, abandoning his lord-lieutenancy, to offer his indispensable services during this critical time.

Buckingham had asked for the command of a ship, a rank he believed his status and abilities rightfully deserved. The idea that such a request might be denied had never crossed his mind. Yet denied it was. Two significant obstacles stood in his path. First, the Duke of York had a deep-seated dislike for Buckingham and missed no opportunity to belittle him. Second, the Duke of York, as Lord Admiral of the Fleet, was not about to take any chances. While there were plenty of cushy positions where capable naval officers could be shoved aside for the aristocratic darlings, commanding a man-of-war wasn't one of them.

Buckingham found himself offered a gun-brig instead. Given that this offer came from the King's brother, he couldn't react as heatedly as he wanted. Nevertheless, he marked his disdain in the only way he could. He turned down the gun-brig and volunteered instead for a position aboard a flagship. Here, however, a new snag emerged. As a Privy Councillor, Buckingham claimed the right to participate in all war councils. This role, he thought, might allow him to inflict even more damage than if he commanded one of the great ships.

Once again, the Duke of York's resistance had thwarted him, and in a fit of rage, he sped from Portsmouth to Whitehall, intent on pouring out his frustration to his old pal, the King. The Merry Monarch, who cherished merriment and wit, might have felt torn. It must have irked him not to be able to appease the charming rascal who had such a knack for stirring up laughter. But faced with choosing between his own brother and Buckingham, Charles had no real choice. He couldn't help Buckingham. So, the Duke stayed at Court, nursing his wounded pride and spiraling anonymously into the tangled tale of Colonel Randal Dempsey.

You know how Buckingham was, a man with a volatile nature, never losing his liveliness even as he approached forty. Such people are easily consoled because they readily find distractions. It wasn't long before he forgot his humiliation in new, less reputable pursuits, becoming blind to both his injured dignity and even the fact that his country was embroiled in war. Dryden nailed it in a single line: "He was everything by starts, and nothing long." The phrase captures the essence of Buckingham's shifting moods and versatile talents; it defines the man from head to toe.

His buddy George Ballard, another gifted rogue who had burst into renown the previous year with his comedy "The Comic Revenge," had been incessantly praising the beauty and talent of Sylvia Shallmont, the newly hailed actress who everyone seemed to admire. At first, Buckingham had dismissed his friend's excitement.

"All this fuss for a mere playhouse floozy?" he had scoffed, yawning. "For someone of your caliber, George, I daresay you're disappointingly naive."

"You honor me by your criticism," Ballard chuckled. "To remain naive despite the years is a sign of greatness. Those whom the gods love stay forever young, regardless of their age."

"You're aiming for a paradox, I guess. God help me!"

"It's no paradox at all."

"The ones the gods love never age," Ballard murmured, his voice thick with conviction. "They don't suffer the way you do, grown weary of your indulgences."

"You might be right," the Duke admitted, a shadow of gloom crossing his features. "Got a tonic for that?"

"I do: Sylvia Shallmont, performing at the Duke's House."

"Seriously? An actress? A painted doll on strings! Maybe twenty years ago, that might have helped."

"You admit you're getting old. No surprise there. But, believe me, this isn't just any painted doll. She's the embodiment of beauty and talent."

"I've heard that about plenty of others who had neither."

"Let me add, she's virtuous."

Buckingham looked at him, his eyes narrowing with lazy suspicion. "What's that supposed to mean?"

"The key ingredient of my prescription."

"Are you sure it even exists, or are you more naive than I thought?" Buckingham quipped.

"Come and see," Ballard challenged with a knowing smile.

"Virtue," Buckingham scoffed, "isn't something you can see."

"Like beauty, it's in the eye of the beholder. That's why you've never seen it, Bucks."

Despite his disgruntlement, the Duke allowed himself to be led to the playhouse in Lincoln's Inn Fields. He went to mock and ended up mesmerized. You've probably already heard from the gossiping Mr. Pepys how, from his box, he announced to his companion and the entire house that he wouldn't rest until he'd written a play worthy of Miss Shallmont's exceptional talents.

His words reached her ears, laden with a certain flattery she couldn't ignore. She hadn't fully adjusted to the fame that had suddenly wrapped itself around her. She remained unspoiled, not yet aloof enough to brush off such praise from someone so exalted, a distinguished author, and a close friend of the King. His commendation put a triumphant capstone on the accolades she'd been collecting recently, preparing her for the Duke's imminent visit to the green room.

Mr. Ballard introduced her to the room. She already knew him, but his presence didn't ease the tension she felt as she stood before the tall, immaculate duke. His piercing gaze was unrelenting, even intimidating. With his golden wig perched elegantly on his head, he didn't look a day over thirty, despite living a hard life since boyhood. The roughness depicted in Sir Peter Lely's later portrait had not yet marked his refined features. At the court of King Charles, he still reigned as the most handsome man around, with long, dark blue eyes that sat beneath perfectly straight brows, a fine nose and chin, and a mouth that hinted at humor, sensitivity, and hedonism.

His physique and poise had a magnetism that drew every eye. Yet, Miss Shallmont found herself recoiling internally, an instinctive dislike flaring up. Beneath his polished exterior, she sensed something dark and menacing. His bold eyes seemed to probe too deeply, making her flush with an uneasy blush. But reason and ambition forced her to suppress these instincts. This was a man of influence, someone whose approval would solidify her hard-earned place in society. She had to navigate this relationship carefully, with prudence and a calculated deference.

The Duke, who had already been taken by her grace and beauty on the stage, was now spellbound by her close-up elegance. Indeed, she was a vision, and the blush that rose to her cheeks, provoked by his relentless scrutiny, only served to enhance her beauty. It almost made him believe Ballard's far-fetched claims about her virtue. Shyness can be an act, and the coquettish behavior of the unworldly is easily faked, but a genuine blush—impossible to fabricate.

With a graceful bow, his wig curls cascading like the ears of a spaniel, he spoke, "Madam, I would congratulate you on your performance. However, I find myself more compelled to congratulate myself for witnessing it, and even more so, Lord Orrery, your current play-wright."

Not only do I congratulate him, but I also envy him—a gnawing, corrosive emotion I won't conquer until I've written a role for you that matches the greatness of his Katherine. You're smiling?"

"I'm pleased with your promise, Your Grace."

"I wonder," he said, his eyes narrowing, his lips curling into a faint smile, "Is that really why you smile, or do you think I'm boasting? Do you think I can't achieve it? Honestly, I didn't think I could—until I met you. But now, my dear, you've made it possible."

"If I've done that, I must have truly earned my audience's favor," she replied lightly, laughing a little to downplay his lofty compliment.

"I hope I will have earned yours as well," he said.

"An author must always strive to give his characters the best," she countered.

"Strive, yes. But how seldom does he get what he deserves!"

"You, Bucks, have little reason to complain," jibed Ballard.

"In my case, it's entirely different," Buckingham agreed, not hiding his irritation. "You, George, are the exception. You've always found better than you deserved. I haven't—until now." His gaze lingered on Miss Shallmont, making his point unmistakable.

When he finally looked away, her sense of exaltation had vanished. She couldn't explain why, but the Duke of Buckingham's approval no longer lifted her spirits. She almost wished she hadn't received it. So when Betterton approached with good-natured smiles, offering his congratulations on her accomplishment, he found her troubled and distant.

Bemused, too, was Ballard as he and the Duke rode back to Wallingford House.

"Almost, I think," Ballard said with a smile, "that you're starting to like my so-called despised prescription. Stick with it, and it might even restore your lost youth."

"What I wonder," said Buckingham, "is why you prescribed her for me instead of yourself."

"I'm like that," said Ballard with a grin, "the embodiment of self-sacrifice."

"She's not interested in me," he said, shaking his head. "I might be ten years younger than you, just as good-looking, and almost as ruthless. But the girl's a prude, and I've never been able to handle prudes. It's a whole education in itself."

"Is it now?" Buckingham replied, a sly smile curling his lips. "Then I suppose I'll have to give it a try."

With the eagerness of a scholar diving into a new subject, Buckingham plunged in. You could find him daily in a box at the theatre in Lincoln's Inn Fields. Every day, he'd send her flowers and sweet treats as tokens of his respectful homage. He wanted to shower her with jewels, but Ballard, the more prudent of the two, held him back.

"Don't rush things," advised the younger man. "You'll just scare her off with your urgency and ruin everything. Patience is key for a conquest like this."

Buckingham took the advice to heart, reigning in his ardor and approaching her with a careful and measured charm. He paid her frequent visits after performances, showering her with praise for her acting skills. When he did compliment her beauty, it was always framed in the context of her stage presence, painting a picture of her as an artistic muse rather than an object of desire. Cleverly, he sought to dull her wariness with the sweet poison of flattery.

He discussed with her the play he was writing, promising it would immortalize both of them and forever bond them in a spiritual union. This wasn't just about physical attraction; it was about merging their artistic talents to create something eternal. He spun tales of Laura and her Petrarch set against the rich tapestry of old Italy, a theme he knew would captivate her.

And he didn't stop there. He began outlining the form this grand romantic saga would take, wrapping her tighter into his web of seductive storytelling. Little by little, she started to believe in the vision he painted, swallowing at least half the bait. The more he spoke, the more real and tempting his promises seemed.

He sharpened his mind and crafted an outline for her, a first act brimming with tenderness and power. After a week, he triumphantly declared that the first act was already written.

"I've labored day and night," he said, eyes gleaming with fervor, "driven relentlessly by the inspiration you've given me. It's so overwhelming that I must consider this work more yours than mine. But I can only truly do that once you've given it your seal of approval." He cut himself off abruptly, as if the question had been gnawing at him for days. "When will you let me read it to you?"

"Wouldn't it be better for you to finish the whole piece first?" she suggested. His face fell, a mixture of shock and near horror.

"Finish it!" he exclaimed. "Without knowing if it aligns with what you desire?"

"It's not about what I desire, Your Grace..."

"What else, then? Isn't this something I'm creating specifically for you, inspired by you? And shall I finish it while plagued by doubts about whether you'll find it worthy of your talents? Would you let a dressmaker complete your gown without a fitting to see how it suits you? And is a play less important than a garment? Isn't a role, in a way, a garment for the soul? No, I insist. If I'm to continue, I need your input. I need to know how this first act strikes you, how well my Laura showcases your strengths. And we must discuss how the rest of the play should unfold."

"So, once more, I implore you, driven by the sacred fire of art, to deny me if you can—when will you hear what I have written?"

"Since you consider me worthy of such an honor, whenever you please."

The praise was intoxicating, coming from someone of his standing—an intimate of princes, a confidant of kings. It temporarily silenced the nagging doubts she had felt about this charming gentleman. Over the past week, their growing intimacy and his consistently respectful behavior had seemed to negate her initial wariness.

"When I will," he repeated, his voice like velvet. "That's a true honor. How about tomorrow?"

"If it pleases your grace. And if you'll bring the act..."

"Bring it here?" He raised an eyebrow, his lips curling in amusement as he glanced around the drab green room. "You don't suggest I read it in this place, do you?" He laughed, the sound filled with dismissal.

"But where else?" she asked, slightly puzzled.

"Where else but in my home? What other place would be appropriate?"

"Oh!" Her heart sank. A shadow of unease crept over her once more, an instinctual alarm. She hesitated, her mind battling itself. It would be foolish to refuse him, implying mistrust and potentially offending him—a risk she couldn't afford to take. He saw the trouble flickering in her blue eyes but chose to ignore it, waiting for her to continue. After a moment, she did, her voice shaky.

"But... in your house... What would people say of me, your grace? To go there alone..."

"Child! Child!" he interrupted, his tone filled with gentle reproach. "Do you think I would expose you to the gossip of the town so carelessly? Alone? Rest your mind."

"I'll have some friends to keep you company and be the audience for what I've written. There'll be one or two ladies from the King's House; maybe Miss Seymour from the Duke's place will join us. She's got a small part in the play. And of course, I'll invite some of my own friends; perhaps even His Majesty will honor us with his presence. We'll have a merry supper party, and afterward, you'll bring Laura to life. Have you made up your mind yet?"

She had. Her head was spinning. A supper party at Wallingford House, where she'd be the guest of honor in a sense, and the King himself might attend! She would have been crazy to hesitate. It was like stepping into the big league overnight. Other actresses had done it—Moll Davis and little Nelly from the King's House—but they had taken... different routes to get there. She'd have preferred it if Miss Seymour weren't involved. She didn't think much of Miss Seymour's reputation. But the part was small, so maybe it was justified.

With a decisive push, she cast her doubts aside and agreed to be there, lighting up his grace with her consent.

CHAPTER SEVEN

That evening, after Dempsey and McCormick's fateful encounter, around the same time Sir John Lawrence was arguing in vain at Whitehall for the closure of theaters and other gathering spots due to the plague spreading through the City, the Duke of Buckingham was enjoying supper with a lively group in the grand dining hall of Wallingford House. The table was set for twelve, but only eleven were seated. The chair to the Duke's right remained conspicuously empty. Their guest of honor, Miss Shallmont, had yet to arrive. At the last moment, she sent a message saying she was unavoidably detained at home but assured them she would make it in time for the reading the Duke had planned to entertain his guests with.

Her message was partly pretense. There was nothing actually keeping Miss Shallmont; it was her gnawing intuition warning her against the intimacy that her presence at the Duke's supper might invite. Still, the performance intrigued her. So she decided to time her arrival just right—to miss the supper but arrive in time for the reading. To be extra cautious, she planned to show up at Wallingford House two hours after the time she had been invited.

The Duke found her message irritating, and while he would have preferred to delay supper until she arrived, his guests wouldn't let him have his way. The truth was, there was no act, no play, nothing prepared at all—the Duke hadn't written a single line and probably never would. Supper was the entire show. Therefore, the meal would be drawn out, so no matter how late Miss Shallmont arrived, the party would still likely be entrenched at the table. Her tardiness would hardly matter in the end.

Meanwhile, the empty chair to the Duke's right awaited her presence. This elite company was already a merry lot, and their cheer only grew with each passing minute.

Ballard, the mastermind behind the whole gathering, was, in his uniquely glamorous and self-destructive manner, doing full justice to his infamous reputation for heavy drinking. His charm had long since been overshadowed by his affinity for excess. Sedley was there too, a man whose delicate, almost feminine beauty belied the wild spirit within. A soul so riotous, it was hard to believe it was housed in such a fragile vessel.

Young Rochester, however, was missing from this shiny assembly. At that very moment, he languished in the Tower as penance for his reckless and utterly unnecessary attempt to abduct Miss Mallet just two nights prior. Still, Sir Harry Stanhope was present, stepping in to fill Rochester's shoes—though perhaps only halfway. Stanhope possessed none of Rochester's wit but doubled down on the debauchery. Then there was Sir Thomas Ogle, Sedley's constant shadow, and two other men whose names history has long since forgotten.

The women were stunning, yet of less noble lineage. Little Anne Seymour, her fair skin glowing under the candlelight, wore a neckline so daring it scandalized even the liberated fashion of the day. Wedged between Stanhope and Ogle, she soon became the object of their intoxicated affections, setting the stage for inevitable jealousy.

Moll Davis, from the King's House, was seated to the Duke's left, her every word and gesture monopolized by Ballard. And then there was Jane Howden, dark, statuesque, with eyes like daggers, lazily casting her net for Sir Charles Sedley, who seemed all too eager to be caught. One other lady, seated to Ogle's left, tried desperately but in vain to divert his attention from Miss Seymour.

The grandeur of their surroundings resonated with their high standing. The room, with its intricately carved wainscoting and towering ceiling supported by elegant, fluted pillars, was illuminated by a hundred candles resting in massive, gilded girandoles. It was a feast fit for their exalted host and the noble chamber in which they reveled.

Wine flowed like a river, and sharp jokes, spiced with a bit of sharpness, flowed right along with it. Laughter swelled, growing louder as the jokes got fewer. Dinner was finished, but they lingered, chatting over their wine, waiting for the late guest who still hadn't shown up. Above that empty seat sat the Duke, a striking figure in a suit of dazzling white satin, sparkling with diamond buttons that looked like tiny water drops. From his gilded throne, he seemed apart, disconnected, his mind clearly on the lady they were all waiting for. It annoyed him how much her absence bothered him, like he was some lovesick teenager waiting for his first date. Unlike the rest of the crowd, he didn't touch the wine much. Time and again, he waved off the velvet-footed servers trying to refill his glass. Occasionally, he'd crack a smile at a particularly witty remark that set the guests laughing. His eyes roamed over the group, taking in the red faces and carefree postures as the party reached its peak. He wanted to calm them down, but as the host, he knew that would be bad manners. His eyes drifted from the chaotic table, loaded with expensive silver and gold plates, sparkling crystal, piles of fragrant fruits, and lavish flowers now being thrown around by his merry guests. From the frigid peak of his own unusual sobriety, they appeared crude and tiresome; their laughter grated on his nerves. His weary gaze shifted to the curtains covering the tall windows, draped almost from floor to ceiling. These bold curtains were wedges of bright blue and green, adorned with golden peacocks standing out against the dark wood paneling. He strained to hear the rumble of wheels in the courtyard outside but was thwarted as another round of raucous laughter drowned out any other sound.

Sedley, his voice slurred with drink, began to belt out a racy song he'd penned himself, all while Miss Howden made a farcical show of trying to hush him. He was still at it when Stanhope jumped up and climbed onto his chair, holding high a delicate shoe he'd stripped from Miss Seymour. He yelled out for wine. Little Anne tried to snatch her footwear back, but Ogle restrained her, pulling her onto his lap where she squirmed, screamed, and giggled all at once.

With a ceremonious air, as if this were the most normal thing in the world, a servant poured wine into the shoe at Stanhope's command. Stanhope, standing above them, eyes sparkling with mischief and the flush of drink, proposed a toast so indecent I won't even try to repeat it. He was midway through his bawdy flourish when both doors behind the Duke swung open, a chamberlain's voice piercing through the raucous clamor.

"Miss Sylvia Shallmont, your grace."

Silence fell, stretched taut in surprise, then the noise swelled back, louder and more jubilant than before. Buckingham leaped up, joined by several others, to properly greet the latecomer. Stanhope, one foot on his chair, the other on the table, gave an exaggerated bow, still holding the slipper he'd just drained.

At the top of the three steps descending into the chaos, Sylvia stood frozen, breathless and abruptly pale, her wide, fearful eyes taking in the scene. She saw little Anne Seymour, whom she knew well, struggling and laughing in the grasp of Sir Thomas Ogle.

She saw Ballard, a face she recognized, flushed and leering, an arm draped around Miss Howden. Howden's dark, lovely head rested unnaturally on his shoulder. Stanhope, perched high, was a sight of absurdity with his wig askew and stumbling, indecent speech. Others were caught in bold, unseemly poses, revealing the licentious spirit dominating this debauchery she had been invited to witness. Finally, she saw the tall, pale figure of the Duke approaching her. His eyes narrowed with a half-smile playing on his lips, and both hands outstretched in welcome. He moved with an almost excessive grace, seemingly immune to the intoxication that gripped his guests at this hellish feast. But this provided her no comfort. Her cheeks, which had flushed scarlet moments earlier, began to pale once more, this time with terror and disgust.

She watched his approach, paralyzed with fascination. Suddenly, like someone who had stared into the abyss of hell and recoiled in horror before being pulled in, she turned and fled. Behind her, silence fell, thick with astonishment, lasting just long enough to count to six. Then, a peal of demonic laughter exploded, propelling her fearfully onward.

She ran down the long, paneled gallery as if in a nightmare, her efforts only yielding a sluggish pace on the polished, slippery floor. She gasped for air, convinced she heard footsteps in pursuit. She darted through the hall, across the vestibule, her light silk mantle trailing behind her, and made it to the open door. The lackeys stared in wonder, but did nothing to stop her.

Too late, the Duke's shout rang out, ordering them to block her way. By then, she was already across the courtyard, running like a hare toward the gateway that opened onto Whitehall.

The hackney coach was lumbering away, the wheels crunching over the cobblestones as it gained speed. Breathing heavily, she caught up to it, shouting for the driver to stop just as he reined in the horses.

"Salisbury Court," she wheezed. "Fast as you can!"

She scrambled inside, slamming the door shut behind her, just as the Duke's lackeys—three hulking figures in livery—caught up, yelling for the carriage to halt. Desperate, she leaned out the opposite window, her voice frantic.

"Go! For God's sake, drive on!"

Had they still been within the courtyard walls, the driver might have succumbed to fear, caving under the pressure. But they had already burst through the gateway and were now on the streets of Whitehall, the coach veering left towards Charing Cross. Here, amidst the chaos of the city, the driver could afford to laugh at the Duke's lackeys, who, wary of causing a scene, hesitated to interfere. The carriage rattled onward, and Miss Shallmont slumped back, finally able to catch her breath and shake off the sinister pall of dread.

Inside the Duke's manor, the mood was far from jovial. Returning with a scowl etching his face, the Duke was met with a chorus of mocking laughter from his rather inebriated guests. Under different circumstances, they might have held their tongues, but emboldened spirits played their part tonight. Attempting to laugh it off, the Duke's efforts only half-heartedly masked his humiliation. He threw himself into his grand chair with the petulance of a thwarted child.

Mr. Ballard, his suave demeanor untouched by the evening's indulgence, reached across Miss Howden, his white-jewelled hand resting lightly on the Duke's arm. Though he had drunk perhaps as much as the rest, the only evidence was a slight flush around his eyes, his gaze clear and unsettlingly sober.

"I did warn you," he said, voice low and smooth like oil, "that she's not one to be easily swayed. You'll need more than impatience to win her over. Consider this a lesson in perseverance."

CHAPTER EIGHT

As midnight approached, the last of the guests had left, save for Ballard. The once lively room was now dimly lit by flickering candles, their wax pooling in groaning sconces. The Duke, a bundle of restless energy, sat across from Ballard, the younger libertine whose smug serenity masked a keen intellect. The servants were dismissed, the doors closed, and an uneasy silence enveloped them. The Duke unburdened himself, his words a mix of bitterness and raw frustration. Patience, Ballard's oft-repeated counsel, eluded him entirely. Especially now, when his cautious moves had only served to alarm the little prude, rendering him worse off than when he started. Ballard's lips curled into a knowing smile.

"You're ridiculously ungrateful. You bungle things up and then pin the blame on me. Had you sought my advice, I'd have warned you: a pack of rowdy fools and drunken sots know nothing of subtlety. Had she arrived on time, while they still had their wits, things might have turned out differently. She could have been drawn into their revelry, the wine blurring her judgment, making their antics seem less offensive. Instead, you subjected her to a revolting spectacle. Hardly what I suggested."

"Regardless," the Duke snapped, his temper flaring, "there's a joke at my expense that needs rectifying. I'm done with patience. Direct action is needed now."

"Direct action?" Ballard arched an eyebrow and let out a musical, mocking laugh. "Is this your idea of patience?"

"To hell with patience..."

"Then she's not meant for you. Hold on, Bucks. I understand precisely what you mean by direct action, and it's foolish. You might be more sober than I am right now, but I assure you, I'm the smarter of the two. Let me educate your sobriety with my intelligence."

"Oh, get to the point already."

"I'm getting there. If you're contemplating kidnapping the girl, let me remind you—it's a crime that'll see you hanged."

The Duke's eyes widened in contemptuous disbelief.

Then he let out a sharp, derisive laugh.

"Law? Seriously, George, what do I have to do with the law?"

"You mean you think you're above it, right?"

"That's typically been my experience."

"Usually. But these times are anything but usual. Take Rochester, for instance. When he kidnapped Miss Mallet on Friday night, he probably thought exactly like you. Yet now, he's rotting in the Tower."

"And you think they're gonna hang him?" Buckingham sneered.

"No. They won't hang him because the whole abduction was an idiotic stunt. He's ready to make amends by marrying Miss Mallet, which is the only thing saving his neck."

"Seriously, George, you must be drunker than I thought. Miss Mallet is a woman of immense importance with powerful friends."

"Miss Shallmont has friends too. Betterton's one of them, and he's got a significant amount of clout. It's not like you're short on enemies eager to stir up trouble for you."

"A mere actress?" Buckingham scoffed, disbelievingly.

"Those 'mere actresses' are adored by the public, and right now, the mood in London is volatile. There's a war brewing, and the threat of plague has people examining their consciences. Preachers are traveling up and down the city, proclaiming all this as God's punishment on a new Sodom. People are listening. They're beginning to blame White-hall for all the sins that have invoked Heaven's wrath. And, Bucks, they don't love you any more than they love me. They don't get us. Truth be told, our names—yours, mine, and several others—are starting to reek in their minds. Give them a reason to target you, and they'll ensure the law is enforced. Don't doubt it for a second. The English might seem easygoing on the surface, but that's led some fools to their downfall by underestimating them."

The place where His Majesty's father lost his head is right within view of these windows.

"And so I tell you, what you're planning, risky at any time, is guar-anteed destruction right now. The throne's spotlight shines merciless-ly on everyone around it. An unknown man might pull it off with less risk than you."

His grace finally dropped his incredulous scorn and descended into dark contemplation. Ballard, lounging in his chair, watched with faint, cynical amusement. Eventually, the Duke stirred and fixed his sharp eyes on his friend.

"Quit sitting there grinning like a damn fool! Give me some advice."

"Why should I, since you never listen?"

"Just tell me. What should I do?"

"Forget the girl. Go after easier prey. You're not exactly young anymore for such a strenuous and exhausting chase."

His grace cursed him soundly for a mocker and swore he wouldn't give up; whatever the cost, he'd pursue it.

"Then you need to start by erasing the bad impression you made tonight. That's not going to be easy; it's actually the hardest part. But there are factors in your favor. For one, you weren't drunk, for once, when you welcomed her. Let's hope she noticed. Visit her on Monday at the theater to offer your most humble apologies for the disgraceful conduct of your guests. If you had known they were capable of such vulgar behavior, you'd have never invited her to such company. You'll be glad she left immediately; that's what you would have advised anyway."

"But I chased after her. My lackeys tried to stop her coach."

"Naturally, so you could apologize and support a departure you should have insisted on, given the circumstances. Damn, Bucks!"

"You lack originality and dream of calling yourself a playwright."

"Do you think she'll believe me?" The Duke's skepticism was clear.

"That all depends on your acting skills, something you're supposedly quite good at. You played the charlatan well enough once before, haven't you forgotten?"

"No, no. But will it work, do you think?"

"For a start, yes. But you have to build on it. You need to show her a different side of yourself. So far, she knows you only by reputation and tonight's experience as a rogue. That alone will make her cautious of you. Let her see you as a hero—a savior of a damsel in distress. Rescue her from some dire threat, and you'll earn her gratitude and maybe even awe at your bravery. Women adore heroes. Be heroic, and who knows what kind of fortune might come your way for it."

"And this dire threat?" the Duke muttered darkly, half-suspecting his friend was mocking him. "Where do I find that?"

"If you wait for it to come around, you might be waiting a long time. You'll need to create it yourself. A bit of scheming, a bit of ingenuity, and you'll have what you need."

"Can you suggest something? Can you be more specific?"

"I think so, with a little contemplation..."

"Then, by God, contemplate away."

Ballard chuckled at the Duke's intensity. He filled his wine glass, admired the way it glowed in the candlelight, and downed it in one go.

"Inspiration is coming. Creativity stirs within me. Now listen." Leaning in, he laid out a scheme with that mischievous wit that was both his triumph and his downfall.

CHAPTER NINE

N ed McCormick didn't waste any time pressing his proposal to Dempsey. He sought him out again three days later at the Paul's Head, on a Sunday, and spent a long while talking with him in the small parlor. This was to the profound discomfort of Mrs. Quinn, who, judging by the gentleman's demeanor and attire, saw him as a person of significant import. She stood by, watching nervously, her wrinkled hands fluttering at the kerchief tucked into her apron, while McCormick tested the waters of Dempsey's resolve.

The Colonel was a touch more pliable today, a little less adamant about serving only established governments. Days had dragged on without any word from Northridge, and Dempsey began to think McCormick might have been right all along. His hopes were sinking, weighed down by the mounting bill at the Paul's Head. Despair was tightening its grip. Still, he didn't fully yield to McCormick's argument; he neither accepted nor rejected the offer, but he did allow McCormick to promise another visit the next day, with an old friend from their Parliament days in tow.

True to his word, McCormick returned on Monday, accompanied by a gentleman named Rathbone, a few years his senior. Dempsey recognized him vaguely, like a face from a long-forgotten dream. They came armed with a solid proposal, claiming to represent someone whose name they still withheld, a name that, when revealed, would erase any remaining doubts.

"For that, Randal, you will trust us, I know," McCormick said, his expression grave. Dempsey nodded, and the cards were laid on the table. The position offered was dazzling, even more so given the precarious state of things. For a man lost in desperation, feeling the gnawing hunger for one last gamble, the stakes couldn't have been higher. The risks were severe, yet the potential rewards were breathtaking. To further entice him, they detailed their preparations, thorough and far-reaching.

"Heaven," said Rathbone, his voice solemn and heavy with conviction, "is on our side. It has sent this plague to awaken men, to make them reflect on the rulers they have chosen."

Dempsey's heart thudded in his chest as he listened, the gravity of their words pulling him deeper into the dark whirlpool of their cause. He could see the shimmering bait just out of reach, feel the enticing thrill of the gamble. It was a lifeline, thin and fragile, yet shining with promise, and its lure was becoming impossible to ignore.

Our contacts unearthed four new cases in the city today: one on Wood Street, one on Fenchurch Street, and two on Crooked Lane. The authorities hoped to keep it hush-hush, but we're making sure word gets out. Right now, our preachers are spreading the news, stirring up terror to drive men onto the path of righteousness.

"When the devil was sick, he'd turn monk," said Dempsey, his tone laced with dark understanding. "I get the picture."

"Then you need to make sure everything's set. The groundwork is laid," McCormick warned. "This is your chance, Randal. Hesitate now, and..."

A knock at the door cut him off. McCormick shot up, propelled by his paranoid conscience. Even Rathbone glanced around, unease written on his face.

"What's got you two so spooked?" the Colonel asked calmly, a cold smile playing on his lips. "It's just our gracious host."

She walked in from the common room, carrying a letter meant for Colonel Dempsey. He accepted it, his brow furrowing in curiosity. Then, noticing the imposing seal, a touch of color flushed his cheeks. He unfolded the paper and read, under the watchful gazes of his friends and their hostess. Their shared tension hung thick in the air. Twice, he perused the letter before speaking. The unexpected had happened, and it had come at the eleventh hour, offering deliverance from a potential abyss. He saw it now, his perspective shifting with his fortunes.

"Luck has favored you sooner than we could have hoped," Northridge had written. "An important military post in the Indies has just become available, as informed by recent correspondence. This role is well-suited to your skills, and overseas, you'll be safe from all inquisitions. Visit me at the Cockpit this afternoon for further details."

With a hurried apology, he excused himself from his companions, then snatched up pen and paper from the sideboard to quickly scribble a response. Mrs.

Quinn had left to deliver that note to the messenger, and as the door clicked shut and silence settled in, the two uneasy conspirators sprang to life. Questions erupted from both of them, their voices tangled in a tense overlap. Instead of answering immediately, Dempsey slid Northridge's letter onto the table. McCormick snatched it up with a fervor, and Rathbone leaned over his shoulder to read it too. When McCormick finally lowered the page, his grave eyes locked onto Dempsey with an intense scrutiny.

"And what was your reply?" he demanded.

"I told them I'd meet with His Grace this afternoon, just as he requested," Dempsey responded.

"To what end?" Rathbone pressed. "You're not seriously considering working for a government that's on its last legs, are you?"

The Colonel shrugged nonchalantly. "Like I've always said to McCormick, I serve governments. I don't create them."

"But just now," McCormick began.

"I wavered, it's true," Dempsey admitted. "But this," he said, raising Northridge's letter as if it were an unseen threat, "this tipped the scales."

They tried to argue with him, but it was as if they were beating against a stone wall. Their words fell flat.

"If your new government finds me useful once it's established, you'll know where to find me. And today should prove that I'm trustworthy."

"But we need you now, in the struggle that's coming," McCormick urged. "We're ready to reward you handsomely for your help."

Dempsey remained unmoved, like an old oak in a storm. Northridge's letter had reached him just in time—a moment too soon for his wavering resolve. As they parted, Dempsey assured them their secret was safe with him and that he'd forget everything they'd spilled. It wasn't much of a comfort; after all, they hadn't shared any critical details worth betraying. Still, the assurance hung awkwardly in the air as they left, resentment etched into their steps.

McCormick, however, returned alone shortly after.

"Randal," he said quietly, the urgency in his voice slicing through the tension, "maybe, when you think it over, you'll see the mistake in tying yourself to a doomed government and a king already cursed by fate. The greatness we offer in the future might seem better than the meager offering Northridge dangles in front of you now."

If you have any sense, you will. If that's the case, you know where to find me. Seek me there and count on my welcome as much as my friendship."

They shook hands and went their separate ways. With a sigh and a smile, Dempsey turned to load his pipe. He didn't think he'd see McCormick again. That afternoon, he met with Northridge, who laid out the details of the job on offer. It was a position of significance, the pay was good, and as long as Dempsey did his job well—and the Duke had no reason to doubt he would—there would be even better opportunities on the horizon.

"To wipe out the past, you need a term of solid service, wherever it may be. Later, when I recommend you for something else, maybe here at home, and people ask about your history, all I need to do is point to your substantial service in the Indies. No one will ask further questions. It's a temporary exile, but you can trust me to make sure it lasts only as long as necessary."

Dempsey didn't need much convincing. The position, after all, was more than he could have hoped for. He expressed his deep gratitude openly.

"In that case, come see me again tomorrow morning. Your commission will be ready by then."

The Colonel left, feeling jubilant. At long last, after countless frowns, Fortune granted him a smile. And it came at the perfect moment, just as he was on the brink of despair, about to throw his lot in with a group of insane radicals dreaming of yet another revolution.

So, he returned to Paul's Head with his spirits soaring and called for a bottle of the finest Canary wine. Mrs. Quinn read the signs expertly.

"Things went well at Whitehall, I take it?" she said, half-question, half- statement.

Dempsey lounged in an armchair, his boots kicked off, his legs stretched on a stool in front of him, and a pipe hanging from his lips. His head tilted back, he looked almost serene.

"Yeah, they've done well. Better than I deserved," he said, grinning up at the ceiling.

"Never say that, Colonel. That's impossible," she said, smiling as she handed him a brimming goblet. He sat up, took it, and smiled back at her.

"You're probably right. But I've gone without my just rewards for so long, I've forgotten what they even look like."

"Others haven't," she replied, daring to ask what kind of prosperity he meant. He paused, sipping a quarter of the wine, then set the goblet down on the table beside him before addressing her. As he spoke, her expression darkened. The regret in her eyes told him he had found a friend in Mrs. Quinn.

"When are you leaving?" she asked, suddenly breathless.

"In a week's time."

She looked at him, seemingly saddened, her complexion losing some of its color.

"The Indies!" she exclaimed slowly. "Dear God, among savages and heathens! You must be out of your mind to consider it."

"Beggars can't be choosers, ma'am. I go where the work is. Besides, it's not as bad as you think."

"But why go at all?" she argued, her voice rising. "I've already told you, a man like you should be settling down, finding a wife."

She knew it was time to make her move. Now or never. She launched her first, cautious attempt.

"Just look at you," she continued before he could respond. "Look at the state of you." She pointed accusingly at the gaping hole in the heel of his right sock. "You ought to be looking for a woman to take care of you, instead of dreaming about soldiering in foreign lands."

"Solid advice," he laughed. "There's just one problem."

"Marry a wife, keep a wife. If I stay in England, I won't even have enough to keep myself. Looks like it's going to be the Indies for me after all."

She stepped forward, leaning against the table, fixing him with an intense stare.

"You're forgetting something. There are plenty of wealthy women out there, and many men have married for a joint fortune when they couldn't have married otherwise."

"You've mentioned that before." He chuckled. "You think I should be on the prowl for an heiress. You think I have what it takes to pull that off?"

"I do," she replied, catching him off guard. "You're a proper man with a name and status to offer. There are lots of wealthy women from humble beginnings who'd be glad to have you, just as you'd benefit from what they bring to the table."

"You're thorough, I'll give you that. Alright, Mrs. Quinn, if your matchmaking skills are as solid as your advice, find me this rich and willing woman, and I might just reconsider the Indies. But hurry—I've only got a week."

His challenge was light-hearted, never expecting she'd take him up on it. But when she broke eye contact, visibly uneasy, his laughter grew louder.

"Not as easy as giving advice, is it?" he teased her. She composed herself, meeting his gaze head-on.

"Oh, yes, it is," she said confidently. "If you were serious, I could find you a woman, attractive enough and about your age, with thirty thousand pounds and some property to boot."

That sobered him. He stared at her, pipe paused between his fingers.

"And she'd marry a rogue like me? What's wrong with her?"

"Nothing's wrong with her. If you were serious, I'd introduce you."

"Damn! You're making me serious. Thirty thousand pounds is serious enough."

"I could live like a lord on that," he said.

"Then why don't you?" She really baffled him with her calm assumption that it was his call to make.

"Because there's no such woman."

"And if there was?"

"But there isn't."

"I'm telling you, there is."

"Where is she, then?"

Mrs. Quinn moved away from the table and circled to his side.

"She is... right here."

"Here?" he echoed, incredulous. She stepped closer, nearly beside him now.

"Here, in this room," she insisted, softly. He looked up at her, still not getting it. Then, as he caught sight of the shy smile that tried to mask her nerves, the truth hit him like a ton of bricks. The clay stem of his pipe snapped in his hand, and he scrambled to pick up the pieces, thankful for a distraction. He needed time to think, to figure out how to navigate this unexpected twist. When he rose, his face was flushed—whether from embarrassment or the act of bending over, he couldn't say. He felt a laugh bubbling up inside but knew it would be entirely inappropriate. Standing there, his shoulder turned toward her, he spoke awkwardly, clearly flustered.

"I... I had no idea... you meant..." He faltered, but his obvious discomfort seemed to give her confidence. She edged closer again.

"And now that you know, Colonel?" she whispered.

"I... I don't know what to say."

His brain slowly kicked into gear, understanding now why a man of his shabby appearance and obvious need had been granted unlimited credit in this house.

"Then say nothing at all, Colonel dear," she purred. "Just promise me you'll forget all about sailing to the Indies."

"But... but I've already given my word." He clung to it desperately, a flimsy lifeline. It was an unfortunate choice, though, as it implied that his honor was the only thing holding him back.

His eyes widened as she stepped even closer, so close she could feel his warmth mingling with hers. He stood half-turned, almost hesitant, but she pressed further, resting her hand on his shoulder, her voice a mix of coaxing and urgency.

"But this promise was made before... before you knew," she urged. "His grace will understand. He won't hold you to it. Just explain it to him."

"I... I can't. I just can't," he replied, his voice barely above a whisper.

"Then let me."

"You?" He turned to look at her, noticing the steely determination beneath her pale exterior. "Yes, me," she asserted. "If your promise is the only thing keeping you, I'll go to Whitehall myself. George Monk will see me, and if he doesn't, his Duchess will. I knew her back when I was just a girl, and she was a seamstress struggling for every penny.

Nan Clarges will never turn away an old friend. Just give the word and I'll handle it."

His face seemed to age before her eyes, weighed down by whatever dark thoughts the confession dredged up. He glanced away, speaking more softly than before.

"That's not all, Mrs. Quinn," he said. "The truth is... I'm not the kind of man who can make a woman happy."

To her, this seemed like mere modesty, and she brushed it off with a quick wave. "I'm willing to take that risk."

"But... but... you see, I've lived as a wanderer for so long that I don't think I could ever settle down. Besides, ma'am, what do I have to offer?"

"If I'm content with the arrangement, why dwell on that?"

"I have to," he insisted. "The truth is, your feelings touch me deeply. I didn't think I could inspire such affection, or even regard, in any woman. But despite how much that means to me, it doesn't change my mind. I'm not cut out for marriage."

"But..."

He raised his hand commandingly, cutting her off. He had finally found the rationale he needed, and he planned to stick to it.

"There's no use arguing, ma'am. My decision is made. My reasons stand, and so does the fact."

I'm touched; I'm really touched, and grateful. But that's how it is."

His unyielding tone turned her pale with humiliation. To have offered herself and to be rejected! To have this lowlife dismiss her, finding her so undesirable that not even her thirty thousand pounds could make her appealing! It was a bitter pill, summoning bitterness from the deepest pits of her soul. As she glared at him with her intense blue eyes, her face grew blotchy. Suddenly, a wave of hatred surged through her. Only his death, she felt, could extinguish this gnawing hatred. She felt the urge to lash out at him, but found no words to do so. If only she could accuse him of leading her on, playing with her emotions, charming her only to deliver this crushing insult, it might relieve some of the bile rising within her. But she had nothing substantial to charge him with, nothing that could be put into words. So, she stared at him silently, her ample chest heaving, her eyes morphing into almost a sinister glare while he stood there awkwardly, his gaze averted, staring out the open window, making no effort to add anything to what he had already said. At last, with a long, drawn breath, she moved.

"I see," she said quietly. "I'm sorry to have..."

"Please!" he interrupted, raising his hand again to stop her, an overwhelming pity stirring in him. She walked to the door, her movements a bit heavy. She opened it and then paused under the lintel. Over her shoulder, she spoke to him again.

"Since things are like this, perhaps you'll find it convenient to secure another lodging by tomorrow."

He nodded slightly in agreement.

"Naturally..." he began, but the door closed behind her with a bang and he was left alone.

"Jesus," he exhaled, sinking back into his chair. He wiped a weary hand across his forehead, finding it damp.

Chapter Ten

Colonel Dempsey hummed a soft tune as he dressed meticulously, preparing for his significant appointment at the Cockpit. When he finished, he was a far cry from the shabby adventurer of the previous day, now looking downright dapper.

Earlier that morning, he'd emptied his purse onto the bed, counting his modest fortune. It totaled thirty-five pounds and some shillings. Northridge had promised that, alongside his commission, he'd receive an order from the Treasury that very morning for thirty pounds to cover his equipment and other expenses. Dempsey knew he had to present himself well for his patron; he felt it was his duty. Showing up at Whitehall in rags would disgrace the Duke of Northridge, and there might be introductions. He couldn't have the Duke embarrassed by the sight of him.

After an early breakfast, where he was surprisingly attended by Tim the drawer instead of Mrs. Quinn, Dempsey set out. He made his way to Paternoster Row, indulging in his passion for fine clothing—a trait common among adventurers with a penchant for living beyond their means. Considering the military role he was about to take on, he bought a splendid red camlet coat laced with gold, along with matching breeches, stockings, and a cravat. He also picked up a pair of fine Spanish leather boots, a black silk sash, a new gold-broidered baldric, and a black beaver hat with a trailing red plume.

By the time he was done, three quarters of his small fortune had vanished; he had but eight pounds left. Yet, this didn't faze him. In a couple of hours, he'd have an order from the Treasury in his pocket. He'd merely anticipated events, fortunate to still be able to act with such confidence despite his limited means.

Returning to Paul's Head with a bundle, he stood in front of the mirror and surveyed his reflection. The freshly shaven face that stared back boasted thick, gold-brown hair artfully curled and a clump of its curls caught in a ribbon on the left. A long, pear-shaped ruby glowed in his ear, and a frothy cascade of lace embraced his throat. His fine red coat fit perfectly on his broad shoulders, and he couldn't help but grin at the transformation. Just yesterday, he had been a ragged scarecrow. Now, he looked not a day over thirty.

Descending to the common room decked out in his finery caused quite a stir. The sight of him in his new Spanish boots made it unthinkable for him to tread the filthy streets. Thus, Tim was hastily ordered to fetch a hackney-coach to take the Colonel to Whitehall. It was still an hour before noon. The Colonel believed it was the earliest acceptable time for him to make his entrance. Yet, another man had beaten him to the punch. The Duke of Buckingham and his companion, Sir Harry Stanhope, had already paid an early visit to the Duke of Northridge at the Cockpit, a full hour before Colonel Dempsey was even ready to leave his lodgings.

A gentleman of the Duke's stature was never kept waiting. He was immediately shown to the wainscoted room overlooking the park, where His Grace of Northridge conducted his affairs. Despite the vast divide between the two dukes—the extravagant libertine and the stern soldier—a cordial relationship existed between them. Monk, the Duke of Northridge, while correct and circumspect, bore neither bigotry nor prejudice. Beneath his stern exterior, he possessed a lion's bravery but also the meekness of a lamb. His courteous aloofness, while it didn't win him many devoted friends, earned him even fewer enemies.

As a man gives, so he receives; and Monk, being pretty stingy with both his love and his hate, rarely stirred up either feeling in others. He was always careful not to make enemies but never went out of his way to make friends.

"I'd like your permission to introduce my good friend Sir Harry Stanhope, a young soldier deserving your support," he requested.

Northridge had heard all about Sir Harry, known as one of the most degenerate young rakes around the Court, and, observing him now, the Duke figured the man's look matched his reputation. This was the first time he'd heard him called a soldier, which intrigued him. But he didn't let that show. He gave a cold nod in response to the deep bow that Sir Harry offered.

"There's no need to ask for my favor for any friend of yours," he replied with icy politeness. "A seat, your grace. Sir Harry!" He gestured to the smaller, less significant of the two chairs facing his writing desk. Once they were seated, Northridge leaned forward, placing his elbows on the table. "What service might I provide?"

"Sir Harry," said Buckingham, leaning back in his armchair and nonchalantly crossing one elegantly stockinged leg over the other, "wants, for his own reasons, to see the world."

Northridge wasn't naive about what those reasons were. It was widely known that Harry Stanhope had not only gambled away the inheritance he got three years ago, but he was also drowning in debt. Unless someone bailed him out soon, his creditors would make his life a living hell. He wouldn't be the first charming rogue of the Court to get acquainted with a debtor's prison.

But any hint of that thought, flashing through the Commander-in-Chief's mind, stayed hidden behind his dark, stoic face and vacant eyes.

"But Sir Harry," Buckingham resumed after the briefest pause, "is commendably motivated by the wish to make his absence from England of value to His Majesty."

"In short," Northridge interrupted brusquely, unable to mask his disdain, "Sir Harry wants a posting overseas."

Buckingham dabbed his lips with a lace handkerchief. "That, in short," he admitted, "is the situation. Sir Harry, I trust, will earn your grace's favor."

Northridge looked at Sir Harry and found that he did anything but. Northridge, impartial as he was, felt a deep disdain for the preening fop aspiring to escape his creditors.

"And the nature of this appointment?" he asked in a flat tone.

"A military role would best fit Sir Harry's preferences and abilities. He has a bit of military experience, having held a commission in the Guards for a time."

"In the Guards!" Northridge thought, "Good God, what an endorsement!" But his face betrayed nothing. His calculating eyes fixed coldly on the young rake, who smiled ingratiatingly and, though unaware of it, only deepened Northridge's disgust. After a pause, he spoke, "Very well. I'll keep your grace's request for Sir Harry in mind, and when a suitable position becomes available..."

"But one is available now," Buckingham interjected lazily.

"Is it?" Northridge's dark eyebrows rose, wrinkling his heavy forehead. "I wasn't aware."

"There's a command in Bombay left vacant by poor Macartney's death. I heard about it last night at Court. Perhaps you've forgotten. It seems a perfect fit for Sir Harry here."

Northridge frowned and pondered, a habit of his slow deliberation. Then he gently shook his head and knitted his heavy brows.

"I have to consider, your Grace, whether Sir Harry is really fit for the job, and to be completely honest, I must say I don't think he is."

Buckingham was stunned. He glared at Northridge with cold disdain. "What are you trying to say?" Northridge sighed deeply and began to spell it out.

"For a job as demanding as this, we need someone with seasoned experience and strong character. Sir Harry, with all due respect, has many fine qualities, but given his age, he simply hasn't accumulated the necessary experience to handle the heavy responsibilities awaiting him. And that's not the only problem, your Grace. I've already picked my man—a man who fits the bill perfectly—and he has accepted the commission. The position is no longer available."

"But the commission was signed just last night by His Majesty—signed in blank, which I am well aware of."

"True. But I'm still committed. I'm expecting the gentleman to arrive any minute now, the one who already has the job."

Buckingham made no effort to hide his anger. "May I ask his name?" he demanded. Northridge hesitated, instinctively protecting Dempsey. If Buckingham knew, he might do anything to push him out, and Dempsey's past—his very name—left him vulnerable. "His name wouldn't be familiar to you, your Grace. He's a relatively unknown soldier, but one whose abilities I am well aware of. I'm confident there's no better man for the role. However, something else suitable will surely come up in a few days..."

Buckingham cut him off, his tone dripping with arrogance.

"This isn't about finding something else, your Grace. It's about this. I already have His Majesty's approval. It was at his suggestion that I came here."

"It is lucky, you know, that the person you chose for command isn't well-known. He'll have to step aside, and you can offer him the next available post. If you need more detailed orders, I can get the King's commands in writing for you."

Northridge felt trapped. He sat there, stern and unmoving, his face a mask of stone. But inside, his mind churned with rage. It was always the same. The roles that needed sharp minds and steady hands, the ones that could best serve England, were constantly being handed to the worthless parasites swarming around Charles's debauched Court. His anger was further stoked by the helplessness of his situation. If it were any other man with Dempsey's soldierly skills, one whose background allowed his name to be openly revealed, he'd storm across to the palace and argue the case with the King himself. He knew how to win that argument against Buckingham's shameless career-hunting.

But he couldn't do it this time. Confronting the King would likely ruin Dempsey and bring severe consequences upon himself. "Odds-fish!" the King would snap. "Do you dare tell me that you favor the son of a regicide over the friend of my friend?" What could he possibly say to that? He lowered his eyes to the commission on the table, the blank space where Randal Dempsey's name should go mocking him in its emptiness. He was beaten, and for Dempsey's sake as much as his own, he needed to accept it without further protest.

With a smooth and deliberate motion, he picked up the pen, dipped it in ink, and drew the document closer.

"Since you have His Majesty's sanction, there's no further room for debate."

The pen scratched and spluttered across the parchment as he inscribed the name, Sir Harry Stanhope, with a bitter grimace. He might as well have written Nell Gwynn's name, for all the good it did. He sprinkled the thick writing with pounce and handed it over without a word. But his eyes were dark and heavy. Buckingham stood up, a smile playing on his lips, and Sir Harry sprang up beside him, mirroring that smile. For the first and last time during that brief encounter, Sir Harry spoke.

"At your service," he declared with a bow and a grin. "I'll strive to perform my duties well and dispel any doubts you may have about my youth."

"And youth," Buckingham chuckled, shooting a reassuring glance at Northridge, "is a flaw that time always fixes."

Northridge got to his feet slowly, and the others bowed before leaving his presence. He sank back into his chair, cradled his head in his hands, and softly cursed. Dempsey arrived an hour later, looking radiant with expectation, a bright, commanding figure in his splendid red coat. Yet all that exuberance was crushed by the news—Fortune's fool, once again. He took it well outwardly, but the iron was deeply lodged in his soul. For once, it was Northridge who showed excitement, railing vehemently against the corrupt Court and the damage it was causing.

"That office needed a man, but they forced me to give it to a dandy, a fop in breeches, a strutting peacock."

Dempsey thought back to McCormick's condemnations of the government. The truth sunk in, the realization that McCormick and his associates were perhaps right. The people might indeed be ready to rise and sweep this Augean stable clean. Northridge was offering him a sliver of hope.

No doubt, another opportunity would come along soon.

"Just to be picked up by some sleazy pimp trying to dodge creditors," Dempsey muttered, his voice laced with bitterness that he could no longer conceal. Northridge looked at him with sorrow. "This hits you hard, Randal, I understand."

The Colonel managed a strained laugh. "Been taking hard hits all my life."

"I know." Northridge moved to the window and back, his shoulders hunched, weighed down by worry. He finally stopped in front of the Colonel. "Keep me posted on where you're staying, and expect to hear from me soon. I'll do everything I can to help."

A flicker of hope ignited in the Colonel's eyes, barely keeping the despair at bay. "You really think something will come up?"

Northridge hesitated, the sadness in his face deepening. "To be honest, Randal, I barely dare to hope. Opportunities for someone in your situation are rare, as you know. But the unexpected can happen sooner than we think. If it does, I won't forget you. Count on that."

Dempsey thanked him and stood up to leave, every inch of him radiating despair. Northridge watched him, concern creasing his brow. As Dempsey reached the door, Northridge called out again.

"Randal, wait a moment."

The Colonel paused and turned, watching as Northridge slowly approached, deep in thought.

"You're not in immediate need of money, are you?" Northridge finally asked. Dempsey's reluctant laugh and gesture admitted that he was. Northridge considered him for a moment longer before slowly pulling out a purse from his pocket. It looked light, even from a distance.

"If a loan would help you until then..."

"No, no!" Dempsey cried, his pride warring against accepting what felt like charity. Still, his refusal lacked conviction. Northridge sensed it but didn't push the offer.

He tightened the purse strings once more, letting out a breath that seemed to have been caged forever. The look on his face was almost one of relief, as though some heavy, invisible weight had been lifted.

CHAPTER ELEVEN

Colonel Dempsey trudged back to the city on foot. The hackney-carriage he had once triumphantly entered to head to the Cockpit was no longer an option; nor could he afford the luxury of taking a boat now that the tangibility of despair had come knocking at his door. Yet, despair wasn't the only guest; it had brought an unruly companion—desperation. An alternative existed, a last-ditch plummet into the abyss McCormick had long tried to drag him into. Thoughts of the rebellion stirred in his forlorn mind as he dragged his feet through the stifling May heat that had gripped London like a vice.

Temptation whispered in his ear now, nourished not just by the dread of starvation but by a simmering rage against an uncaring and unjust government that tossed loyal soldiers like him into the streets while pampering the worthless sycophants of a debauched prince. Vice, he mused bitterly, seemed to be the only way to secure a place in this England ruled by the restored Stuarts. McCormick and Rathbone were right. At least their actions had a veneer of righteousness, blessed by the urgent need to save their country from the moral rot seeping into its bones. This moral disease, he believed, was more devastating and deadly than the plague the republicans hoped would wake the nation to its dire state.

He measured the cost of failure, but with a sneer. His life would be forfeit. That was the wager he was placing. Yet, with that life being the only chip he had left in the game, why hold back? What was this life worth if not to gamble on this final roll of the dice? Fortune favors the bold. Perhaps he had just never been bold enough. Lost in these thoughts, he found himself at St.

Clement Danes was jolted awake by a grating voice, stern and commanding.

"Stay back, sir!"

Startled, he whipped his head to the right, where the voice had originated. Before him stood a gaunt man wielding a pike, barring entry to a door secured with a heavy padlock. The door bore a blood-red cross, a foot long, and above it, scrawled in the same ominous red, were the words: LORD HAVE MERCY UPON US. A chill slithered down his spine, like the touch of something vile and loathsome. With haste, Clement moved to the middle of the rough, unpaved street. He paused, casting a wary glance at the barred windows of the infected house. It was the first one he'd encountered since he last passed this way a week ago, when the plague was already gnawing at the fringes of the neighborhood. Back then, it was mostly confined to Butcher's Row on the north side of the church, and the warren of squalid streets that branched out from there. But to find it now, glaringly present on the main thoroughfare between the City and Whitehall, was a stark, unpleasant reminder of its terrifying spread. His pace quickened instinctively as he continued down the road, each step stirring his thoughts into a chaotic frenzy. The revolutionaries would surely find a way to exploit this dreaded pestilence.

His fevered mind, warped and tormented by the city's creeping doom, twisted further towards a bleak conclusion. This plague, he thought, wasn't just a random scourge; it was a divine reckoning, punishment for a city steeped in sin and corruption. And surely, heaven must side with those striving for purifying change. By the time he ascended Ludgate Hill, approaching the looming silhouette of St. Paul's, his decision was cemented. That very evening, he would seek out McCormick and pledge himself to the republican cause.

Arriving at Paul's Yard, Clement found a considerable crowd gathered before the western doors of the Cathedral. The throng was a motley mix: merchants and shopkeepers, ragged apprentices, horseboys, scavengers, rogues slinking out from the labyrinthine alleys behind the Old 'Change, alongside idlers and sharpers from Paul's Walk. Amidst them were a sprinkling of women, town gentry, and soldiers, all drawn into the Cathedral's magnetic pull.

On the steps of the grand portico stood the man who had drawn them all in—a dark, vulture-like figure named Jack Presbyter, preaching the city's doom with a voice that seemed to echo through the ages. His sermon was like a haunting refrain:

"You have defiled your sanctuaries with your countless sins, with the iniquity of your dealings."

His words echoed from between the Corinthian pillars that loomed behind him, a stark reminder of a time when milliners' shops had once populated that very spot during the Commonwealth. You could almost see it in the eyes of some onlookers; perhaps a misplaced irony, or maybe just the infectious, mischievous spirit of a group of young apprentices nearby. Whatever the cause, mocking laughter erupted, a cacophony that would have drowned a lesser man. But not Jack Presbyter. He stood firm, his eyes blazing with fervor.

"Repent, you mockers!" His voice cut through their laughter like a blade. "Remember where you stand! Forty days from now, London will be destroyed! Pestilence sieges this city of the godless! It prowls like a ravenous lion, waiting to pounce. Forty days, and..."

The tirade halved, an egg hurled by a butcher's boy splattered against his face. He reeled, the sticky mess of yolk and white sliding down his beard, staining the rusty black of his coat as it oozed downward.

"Mockers! Scoffers!" he shrieked, whipping his arms through the air in wild condemnation, resembling nothing so much as a wind-blown scarecrow. "Your doom approaches. Your..."

The crowd's laughter erupted anew, a thunderclap of derision punctuated by a hail of projectiles. One particularly audacious missile—a living, clawing cat—latched onto his chest, spitting and hissing in terror. Overwhelmed, the prophet turned tail and fled up the steps, disappearing between the pillars into the dim sanctuary of St. Paul's itself, all the while pursued by a torrent of jeers and insults. But as abruptly as the laughter had swelled, it died back to an eerie sputter, leaving the crowd in an unsettled silence.

A deadly silence fell. Then, like a dam breaking, the crowd scattered, shrieking as their horror swallowed the laughter that had filled the air moments earlier. Colonel Dempsey stood alone, bewildered, unable to fathom what had driven the crowd to such panic. Stepping forward onto the empty space before the cathedral steps, he saw a man writhing on the cobbled ground. The man was in his prime, dressed smartly, likely a tradesman doing well for himself. His round hat lay close by, his head jerking side to side, accompanied by faint moans. His eyes, or what little remained visible, were rolled back, revealing only the whites.

Dempsey moved closer, thinking he was merely witnessing a man taken ill, when a voice from the fleeing crowd shouted out a warning.

"Watch out, sir! He might have the plague!"

The Colonel froze, the sheer terror of that word halting him mid-step. Then he spotted a stout, elderly man with a heavy wig, dressed plainly but meticulously in black. The man's round face was marked by a pair of horn-rimmed spectacles that gave him a disturbingly owl-like appearance. He strode forward to the afflicted man without hesitation. Standing over the sufferer for a moment, he then signaled to two burly men equipped with staffs.

From his pocket, the stout man produced a kerchief and sprinkled something from a vial onto it. Holding the cloth to his nose with one hand, he knelt beside the victim and began to unfasten the man's doublet with the other. Watching this, Dempsey felt a pang of shame for his own fear and cowardice. Summoning his courage, he advanced to join the small group. The doctor glanced up as the Colonel approached.

But Dempsey's attention was riveted on the patient, whose chest the doctor had just exposed. One of the guards was pointing out a purplish, swollen patch at the base of the man's throat. His eyes were wide, his expression deadly serious, and his voice came out in a hushed, startled whisper.

"Look! The marks!" he said to his comrade. The doctor then turned to address Dempsey.

"I advise you not to come any closer, sir."

"Is it... the plague?" Dempsey asked quietly. The doctor nodded, pointing to the offending patch. "The signs are unmistakable," he said. "Please, sir, you must leave." And with that, he once more pressed a handkerchief to his mouth and nose, turning his back on the Colonel.

Dempsey retreated as instructed, moving slowly, his mind heavy with the sight of the plague claiming its first victim before his eyes. As he neared the edge of the gathered crowd, who kept their distance but remained fixated on the scene, he noticed that people recoiled from him as if he carried the disease himself.

The impact of witnessing a solitary event is far more profound than hearing about a thousand similar ones. Up until now, the people of London had treated the plague lightly. Barely ten minutes ago, they had been mocking and pelting a preacher warning them about Heaven's wrath, dismissing his calls for repentance. Then, like a thunderbolt from a clear sky, the affliction struck one of their own, freezing their derision and filling their hearts with dread.

Dempsey continued on, contemplating that this incident in St. Paul's Yard had done more to convert people to the Commonwealth cause than any number of advocates could have managed. It was a potent sign. And if he had any lingering doubts about aligning himself with McCormick, this sealed it.

But first, there was the desperate need to quench the monumental thirst brought on by his long trek through the sweltering heat. After that, he'd head to Cheapside and McCormick to offer his sword to the revolutionaries. By doing so, he could settle his debts at the Paul's Head and finally part ways with the infatuated Mrs. Quinn. Staying with her any longer was out of the question—he couldn't afford it.

As he walked into the common room, she turned from a group she was chatting with to follow him with her eyes, her lips a tight line. He moved on to his modest parlor at the back. Moments later, she followed him. He tossed off his hat and began to loosen his doublet in an attempt to cool down, greeting her casually as if there hadn't been a near-tragic argument between them just yesterday. His lighthearted

and seemingly tactful demeanor annoyed her to no end. She stiffened
with indignation.

"What do you want, Colonel?" she asked coldly.

"A mug of ale if you would be so kind," he replied. "I'm as dry as a
desert. Damn this heat!" He threw himself down on the window seat,
seeking any breeze he could find. She walked off without a word and
returned with a tankard, placing it on the table in front of him. He
eagerly lifted it to his lips, feeling the cool liquid soothe his parched
throat, a brief respite in a world teeming with troubles. Taking a moment to savor the drink, he silently thanked Heaven for small mercies
like a good ale.

She watched him, her frown deepening. As he paused, finally satisfied, she spoke up.

"You've made your plans to leave my house today as agreed last
night?" Her tone was half question, half assertion.

He nodded, lips pursed slightly. "I'll be moving to the Bird in Hand
across the Yard this afternoon," he said.

"The Bird in Hand?" Her voice dripped with disdain, an eyebrow
arched in contempt for that shabby establishment. "It suits your fine
coat perfectly."

"Ah, but that's not my concern, as long as you leave, I'm satisfied."

Her words carried an ominous weight, cutting through the tension
in the air. She stepped forward, leaning heavily on the table. The shift
in her demeanor was stark; gone was the gentle caregiver, replaced
by a woman who now stood as his adversary. "This is a respectable
establishment," she said, her voice firm. "And I intend to keep it that
way. No traitors, no criminals will find shelter here."

He was about to drink again, but her declaration halted him, the
tankard frozen midway to his lips.

"Traitor? Criminal?" he repeated slowly, disbelief etched in every syllable. "Are you serious, woman? Are you calling me a traitor? Me?"

"Yes, you," she replied, her lips pressed into a tight line. He stared at her, frowning, the room falling into a charged silence. Then, with a dismissive laugh, he shrugged it off.

"You're mad," he declared, and downed the ale in one gulp.

"No, I'm not mad, neither am I a fool, you rebel," she snapped back. "A person is judged by the company they keep. Birds of a feather, as they say. How can you be anything but a traitor when you fraternize with traitors? I've seen it with my own eyes, could swear to it in a court if I needed to. But I don't wish you harm. Leave my house today, or I might reconsider."

He slammed the tankard onto the table and stood up, eyes blazing.

"Damn it, woman! What in the hell are you talking about?" he shouted, his anger stoked by a flicker of fear. "Which traitors have I been associating with?"

"Which traitors?" she sneered, her voice dripping with disdain. "What about your friend Danvers, currently hunted by the men from Bow Street?"

Relief washed over him as the name registered. "Danvers?" he echoed incredulously. "My friend Danvers? I know no such man."

"I've never heard of him before," he stammered.

"Oh, really?" Her voice dripped with sarcasm now. "And maybe the names McCormick and Rathbone don't ring a bell either? They were here with you just yesterday, and I'd swear to it. What were they doing with you? What's your connection to them? The Justices will want those answers. How did you wind up so buddy-buddy with two traitors who got nabbed this morning, along with a dozen others, for plotting to bring back the Commonwealth? Oh, and that scoundrelly scheme to kill the King, seize the Tower, and burn the City."

It felt like a physical blow to the head. "Arrested," he repeated, jaw slack, eyes wide. "McCormick and Rathbone arrested, you say? You're mad!" But deep down, he knew she wasn't. How else could she know about their conspiracy?

"Am I?" She cackled, her laugh drenched in malice. "Step outside in Paul's Yard and ask the first person you see about the arrests in Cheapside just before noon, and the hunt going on right now for Danvers, their leader, and the others involved. I don't want them coming here. I don't want my house mentioned as a meeting place for traitors, and you've turned it into just that, taking advantage of a woman without a man to protect her. And all the while deceiving me with your smooth talk. If it weren't for that, I'd inform the Justices myself right now. Be grateful I care about my house's good name. That's the only thing keeping my mouth shut. But you must leave today or I might change my mind."

She snatched up the empty tankard and headed for the door before he could gather his numb thoughts enough to respond.

On the threshold, she paused.

"I'll bring you your bill in a bit," she said. "Once that's settled, you can pack up and leave." She slammed the door behind her. The bill! It was minor compared to the looming threat of prison and execution. It didn't matter that he was essentially innocent of any involvement in the reckless republican plot that had been uncovered. If he was turned in for associating with McCormick and Rathbone, there would be no mercy for the son of Randal Dempsey, the Regicide. His lineage and background would be the ultimate evidence against him. That, he understood all too well. And yet, the bill, while a relatively minor issue, was more immediate, and thus occupied his mind more at the moment. He knew it would be steep, and he knew his remaining funds were nowhere near enough to cover it. Yet unless he paid it, Mrs.

Quinn would show him no mercy; and this new twist of fate, throwing him into association with McCormick just before the conspirator's arrest, put him at Mrs. Quinn's mercy to a degree that was unbearable to think about.

Of course, he thought bitterly, this kind of thing always happened to him. Then he set his frustrated mind to figuring out a way to pay his debt. Like many in his situation, he had to sell whatever belongings he had. Cursing his overconfidence from earlier that morning, he got to work.

So, before long, there he was, back in the old worn-out clothes he thought he'd never wear again, walking out of the Paul's Head with a bundle of fine clothes he had hoped to keep forever. He trudged back to the shops in Paternoster Row, where he had so recently and joyfully bought them. It was here he learned the stark difference in how a buyer is treated compared to a seller.

He realized that the true worth of a suit was in its pristine condition. As soon as it lost that newness, the value plummeted. He was a soldier who knew the art of warfare, dealing now with merchants who excelled in the ruthless tactics of trade. The crux of their success lay in their sharp ability to gauge others' needs and exploit them without mercy. All he could muster for his gear, which not long ago had cost close to thirty pounds, was a measly ten. Begrudgingly, with no other choice, he sold. The negotiation was heated; his anger flared, even reaching the edge of violence. But the merchant remained unruffled. Insults meant nothing as long as the profit margin was good.

Colonel Dempsey trudged back to the Paul's Head Inn, where Mrs. Quinn waited with his tab. The sight of it nearly made him ill. It was the crowning misfortune in a day already laden with bad luck. Slowly, he scanned the list, trying to mask his horror, aware of Mrs. Quinn's steely blue eyes fixed on him, her lips drawn into a disapproving line.

The sheer amount of Canary wine and ale he had consumed over the past weeks left him stunned. Briefly, his mind wandered, attributing his costly drinking habits to his long stint in the Netherlands where heavy drinking was standard. But his attention snapped back to the pressing issue: the total was over twenty pounds. An enormous sum. He had anticipated a hefty bill, but this was beyond even his worst expectations. He toyed with the notion that perhaps Mrs. Quinn had factored in the affronts to her dignity. The thought crept in—what if the only way out was to marry her, assuming she would still have him? Aside from that, he had no idea how he would settle the debt.

His haggard eyes, despite his best effort, couldn't hide his fear from those terrifying figures. He met the vengeful glare of the woman who, once unable to marry him, had become his relentless enemy. Her stare unnerved him more than all the worries combined. He lowered his gaze, clearing his throat.

"This is quite a hefty bill," he managed to say.

"It is," she replied. "You've indulged deeply and enjoyed the best hospitality. I hope you'll find such luxuries at the Bird in Hand."

"Mrs. Quinn, let me be honest. My affairs are in disarray through no fault of my own. His Grace of Northridge, upon whom I heavily relied, has failed me. Right now, I'm a hard-pressed man, nearly out of resources."

"That didn't bother you while you devoured and drank the best my establishment had to offer. Your tale is nothing new; many pitiful rogues have spun the same yarn..."

"Mrs. Quinn!" he thundered, but she continued, unshaken, reveling in the chance to wound the pride of the man who had badly bruised hers.

"... and there's a way to deal with rogues. You might think that because I'm a woman, I'm soft and tender; and so perhaps I am with those who deserve it. But I know your kind, Colonel Dempsey, if that's who you really are. You're no stranger to a house like mine, but I've never been bested by any down-and-out rascal, and you won't be the first. I'll say no more, though I could say much. But I'll simply say this: if you give me trouble, I'll call the constable, and then maybe you'll have more than just this bill to worry about. You know what I mean. You know exactly what I could say if I chose to."

"My advice to you," Mrs. Quinn said icily, "is to pay your bill without all the whining. It won't melt my heart, and it sure won't change that piece of wood there into something that listens."

His face burned with shame as he stood before her, struggling to keep himself under control. He could explode into violence if cornered, but his lazy nature rarely let him get to that point. Even now, with rage brewing inside, he knew that letting it loose would only backfire and push him further into disaster.

"Mrs. Quinn," he replied as calmly as he could muster, "I've sold all my belongings to settle my debt with you. Still, the debt outweighs my means."

"Sold your belongings, have you?" Her laugh was harsh, almost like a cough. "Sold the fancy clothes you bought to show off at Whitehall, more like. But you're not completely broke yet. Look at that jewel dangling from your ear. It alone would cover your bill twice over."

He flinched and reached up to touch the earring. A ruby. A token from a mysterious royalist boy he had saved fifteen years ago, a souvenir from the bloody aftermath of the Battle of Worcester. The superstitions he'd spun around that jewel had kept him from ever considering it as something he could sell. Now, even facing this dire situation, the thought of parting with it made him recoil. Yet maybe this was exactly why he had held onto it for all these years of struggling fate, guarding it against every misfortune—as if it were his last lifeline. His head drooped.

"I... I forgot," he murmured.

"Forgot?" Her voice was sharp, cutting right through him. She clearly thought he was lying. "Well, you're reminded now."

"Thank you for the reminder. It... it will be sold immediately. Your bill will be settled today. I'm... I'm sorry, that, that..."

"Oh, don't worry about it."

With those words, he threw himself into the task of tracking down a jeweler who had mastered the dark art of turning precious stones into pure, gleaming gold.

CHAPTER TWELVE

M iss Sylvia Shallmont lived in a charming apartment in Salisbury Court, a change in her circumstances brought about by her newfound fame and fortune, thanks in no small part to Betterton, who happened to reside right across the street. It was from the doorway of Betterton's house that she first glimpsed the gaunt, predatory face of Bates.

This happened on the very same morning that Colonel Dempsey faced disappointment at the hands of Northridge and later tribulations care of Mrs. Quinn. Miss Shallmont needed some dress materials which she had been told could be found at a particular mercer's shop in Cheapside. Setting out on this errand in the early afternoon, she entered the waiting sedan-chair at her door. As the chairmen lifted her into motion, she glanced out the unglazed window on her left, towards Betterton's house, and saw that sly, malevolent face peering from the shadows as if to spy on her.

The sight of Bates gave her an instinctive chill, making her retreat quickly into the depths of the chair. A moment later, she was laughing

at her own paranoia and soon brushed off the unsettling glimpse of
the watcher from her mind.

The journey to her destination—the Silver Angel in Cheapside—took a full half-hour, for the chairmen moved at a slow pace.
It would have been unkind to rush them in the sweltering heat, and
unkindness was not in Miss Shallmont's nature. Besides, she was in
no particular hurry. Hence, she allowed herself to be carried leisurely
through Paul's Yard, where a preacher of doom was still admonishing
a crowd that, as you might recall, would eventually mock him.

When her chair finally came to a rest at the door of the Silver Angel,
she stepped out and entered the shop, prepared for a task that no
woman ever rushes.

It may be that Mr. Bates, slinking after that chair with three tough
bullies following at a cautious distance, and another three even farther
back, knew a thing or two about femininity, concluding that it might
take Miss Shallmont about an hour to emerge again. His dark, beady
eyes observed everything, his wicked mind always calculating. He'd
noticed the little crowd by Paul's steps, heard the preacher's message,
and his cunning brain saw an opportunity for the nasty little drama he
was designing on behalf of the Duke of Buckingham. He just needed
to get the Duke reasonably close to the scene. If he could manage that,
everything would proceed as smoothly as a well-rehearsed play.

Mr. Bates slipped like a shadow into a porch, pulled out a pencil
and some paper, and laboriously scribbled a few lines. He folded the
note and handed it, along with a crown, to one of the bullies who had
appeared at his signal.

"Get this to His Grace immediately," he ordered. "Take a coach and
hurry. Now!"

The man vanished, and Bates, leaning back into the shadows, casually filled a pipe and settled into his watch. He was a small, wiry

fellow with leathery, clean-shaven cheeks and long, wispy black hair that draped around his face and scrawny neck like seaweed. His attire, a rusty black suit that had seen better days, gave him an almost clerk-like appearance, enhanced by his singular, fanatical face and a round, high-crowned hat. It lent him an air of religious zealotry.

Miss Shallmont was in no rush. An hour and a half ticked by before she finally emerged, the mercer trailing behind, weighed down with parcels that were soon packed into the chair along with her.

The chairmen hoisted the sedan, while the shopkeeper almost bent in half with fawning gratitude towards the renowned actress, and they moved westward along the well-worn path. It seemed as if Providence itself favored the Duke that morning, aiding the cunning Bates in orchestrating the day's events. Just half an hour earlier, a man struck down by the plague had been cleared away from the very steps of St. Paul's Cathedral. As Miss Shallmont's chair approached the scene, they edged through a crowd steeped in fear, huddled in anxious clusters to debate what had occurred. She detected a shiver of dread in the air. The grave, haunted faces of those in conversation, punctuated by occasional loud laments, caught her attention and set her mind abuzz with wary curiosity.

Suddenly, rising above the murmurs of the crowd, a harsh, raspy voice cut through the air from somewhere uncomfortably close to her chair:

"There goes one of those who have summoned the wrath of the Lord upon this cursed city!"

She heard the curse repeated, each iteration striking her ears with a little more force and malice. The groups she passed fell silent, those who had their backs to her spun around, their eyes locking onto her with a piercing, unsettling intensity. It dawned on her, with chilling clarity, that the ominous voice was targeting her. Despite her usually spirited demeanor, under the weight of that sea of hostile eyes, she shrank deeper into the chair, pulling one of the leather curtains across to better conceal herself.

Once again, the voice rose, shrill and fierce, piercing through the bustling market square.

"There sits an actress draped in her silks and velvets, while the God-fearing folks suffer in rags, and Heaven's fury lashes us with disease because of the sin she brings among us!"

Her chair rocked violently, her bearers struggling to keep it steady. A few ragged men, always on the prowl for a chance to cause trouble, had joined the ranting fanatic and were now closing in on Miss Shallmont's sedan chair. Fear gripped her as tightly as a vice. It didn't take much imagination—something she had in abundance—to foresee what a mob could do when driven by blind rage. She forced herself to remain composed, stifling the panicked rise of her breath and the desperate urge to scream. But her burly carriers, steadfast and solid like old oaks, who respected her deeply, marched steadily forward through the chaos. To their credit, they kept their tempers and maintained an air of calm. They found it hard to believe that the crowd would turn on their beloved actress just because of this deranged black-clad preacher frothing at the mouth behind them.

Still, the group of troublemakers swelled, their muttered threats merging with the madman's cries, growing more ominous with each step.

"It's Sylvia Shallmont of Duke's Playhouse," shrieked the preacher. "A daughter of Belial, a shameless harlot. It is her kind that brings the Lord's wrath upon us. It's because of her and her ilk that we suffer, and will continue to suffer, until this city is purged of their wickedness."

He was right beside the chair now, brandishing a short club, and Miss Shallmont's terrified eyes caught a glimpse of his twisted, malevolent face.

To her shock, she recognized the face immediately—it was the same man who had glared at her from the shadows of Betterton's house in Salisbury Square just two hours ago.

"You've seen one of your own struck down by the plague right before your eyes," he was raving. "And more will fall, to pay for the sin of harlotry that festers in this city."

Despite the fear gripping her slender frame, Miss Shallmont's sharp mind remained clear. This madman, according to his tirade, seemed to believe he was divinely appointed to deliver her a righteous judgment, inflamed by some recent event in Paul's Yard. His words hinted at a divine punishment for the city's transgressions. But her insight told her otherwise. He had been lurking in Salisbury Court, waiting for her to leave, trailing her with a deliberate, sinister intent.

Now, the rough men who had joined him were jostling the chairmen with growing aggression. The chair rocked violently, flinging Miss Shallmont precariously from side to side. Even the bystanders, those she had almost hoped might come to her aid, were closing in, adding to the chaos. Some of the women in the crowd hurled insults, their faces twisted with disdain.

Boxed in by the snarling mob, the chair was forced to a jarring halt right in front of the Paul's Head Inn. On the steps, Colonel Dempsey stood observing the commotion. He had been on his way out, intent on selling a precious jewel, when the uproar caught his attention. He paused, frowning as he took in the scene.

The spectacle revolted him. The woman they tormented might indeed be guilty of whatever sins the frenzied fanatic accused her of, but she was still a woman, vulnerable and alone.

In the depths of Dempsey's soul, there was no vice more repugnant to him than virtue taken to extremes. Over the heads of the mob, he caught a glimpse of the wildly rocking chair finally being set down. From his vantage point, he couldn't make out the occupant's face clearly, but he didn't need to. The sheer terror she emanated, and the cruelty of her tormentors, was palpable.

Colonel Dempsey mused that he might find some satisfaction—and perform a righteous act—by slicing the ears off the black-clad zealot inciting the crowd. But just as he resolved to this course and prepared to act, unexpected help surged forth, swift and resolute. Its origin was elusive, almost magical. A tall, elegant man, his golden wig crowned with long, white ostrich feathers, seemed to materialize out of thin air, his arrival startling in its suddenness.

His attire spoke volumes: a high-born gentleman from Whitehall, clad in a rich sapphire velvet coat and knee-length breeches, lavishly adorned with gold lace. His waist and chest were embellished with an opulence of linen and lace, and the broad hat on his head was secured with a brooch encrusted with jewels. Dazzling gems sparkled on his sleeves and on the priceless necktie he wore. With a swift motion, he drew his sword, the steel gleaming menacingly under the dim light. His voice, commanding and imperious, cut through the din like a blade.

He pushed his way through the throng with an ease that bordered on the supernatural, his presence compelling and unyielding, until he reached the chair. In that moment, he was an avenging specter, a figure both beautiful and terrible, whose purpose was as clear and focused as the sword in his hand.

Astride his horse, a figure came next, clad in a stylish ensemble that screamed both wealth and authority. Four burly men followed close behind, brandishing whips they clearly had no hesitation in using. Their lashes landed with gusto on the heads and shoulders of the black-cladded zealot and his ragtag team, who were the immediate threat against the woman in the chair. Like a vengeful archangel descending from the heavens, this dazzling yet commanding savior scattered the vile attackers. The gleaming edge of his sword cut swift arcs through the air, carving out a growing circle of safety around the chair, his voice thundering through the chaos:

"You mangy curs! Filthy scum! Back off! Move away from the lady! One more step, and I'll send you straight to hell!"

Intimidated by his fierce resolve, the once-brave assailants scampered beyond the deadly reach of his sword. His men, relentless in their duty, pursued them with sharp, cracking whips, driving them further until they melted into the surrounding crowd of spectators, who themselves retreated before the unyielding advance of these determined grooms. The man, dressed in a vivid blue coat, turned to the bearers of the chair.

"Lift it," he instructed, cool and commanding. Seeing their attackers pushed back, and eager to escape the volatile scene under the protection of this apparent savior, the chairmen hurried to comply. The crowd had already identified him - whispers of "His Grace of Buckingham" spread rapidly, spoken with a mixture of awe and reverence. He stepped forward confidently, waving away the throng as if they were mere pests.

"Clear the way!" he ordered, with the imperious tone of a king addressing servants. He no longer needed to wield his sword, now sheathed under his left arm; his sheer presence and authoritative voice were enough. A path opened within the dense audience, allowing him to stride forward with unshakable confidence, the chairmen urgently following with their precious burden.

The goons gathered behind the chair, closing in tight like a pack of wolves readying for the kill. But it turned out to be unnecessary. All efforts to frustrate or harass the chair had vanished into thin air. The crowd, having found the climax of their grim entertainment, began splintering off, returning to their humdrum lives. The zealot who had stirred the chaos and his thuggish accomplices had disappeared as if swallowed by the ground itself.

Among the few lingering onlookers was Dempsey, drawn mostly because Miss Shallmont was being escorted in the same direction he was heading. He stepped off the inn's porch, trailing behind them at an unhurried pace. They kept a steady course until they hit Paternoster Row, where the sparse traffic gave way to quieter surroundings. Here, the Duke finally called a halt, and with a gesture, the men carefully set the chair down.

His grace stepped up to the window, doffing his broad, feathered hat in a dramatic bow, the golden curls of his periwig nearly touching as they fell forward. Inside the chair, Miss Shallmont, though still pale, had regained her composure. She eyed the Duke with an expression that could only be described as speculative.

"My dear child," he exclaimed, placing a hand theatrically over his heart, a stunned look crossing his handsome features. "I swear, you've taught me the true meaning of fear today. Never in my life have I been so frightened until now. What recklessness, Sylvia, to show yourself in the City when people's minds are so frayed by war and plague that they look for scapegoats anywhere. I may not be a pious man, but I feel devout at this moment. From the depths of my soul, I thank the heavens for the miracle that placed me here to save you from this peril!"

Miss Shallmont leaned forward, her light silk hood falling back to reveal the radiant glow of her beauty.

She wore a faint smile that twisted her delicate lips, adding a certain hardness and disdain to her otherwise gentle eyes. Those eyes, a wistful blend of blue and green, naturally spoke of softness.

"It was quite the stroke of luck, Your Grace," she said, her voice nearly flat.

"Indeed, very fortunate!" he agreed eagerly, mopping his brow with a fine handkerchief, his hat clutched in the other hand.

"Your Grace was remarkably close at hand!"

Her tone now dripped with sarcasm, laden with hidden meaning. She finally understood whose bidding that fanatic had been at, spying on her comings and goings, then launching an assault—all to set the stage for this gallant rescue. With a calculated grin, the actress in her woke up, eager to play the scene. She repeated the phrase with a sly edge, "Your Grace was remarkably close at hand!"

"I'm grateful for it, and so should you be, child," he replied quickly, brushing off her mockery though he felt its sting. But Miss Shallmont showed no inclination to join in his pious gratitude.

"Does Your Grace often find himself east of Temple Bar?" Her next question was a mocking challenge.

"And you?" he shot back, perhaps lacking a better rejoinder.

"So rarely that the coincidence defies even the most imaginative plots you or Mr. Dryden could concoct for your plays."

"Life is full of such coincidences," the Duke mused, feigning an innocence that bordered on the insipid. "Coincidence is what spices up the blandness of existence."

"Is that so? Then it was to spice up life that you rescued me—and to ensure you had the chance for such a heroic act, you must have orchestrated the danger."

"Me? Caused the danger?" He was stunned, at first not comprehending. "I caused the danger? Child!" His exclamation carried a mix

of hurt and indignation, and the latter was genuine. Her contemptuous tone cut through him like a lash.

He realized she saw him as a fool, and the Duke of Buckingham
disliked being seen as ridiculous, perhaps even more than most. "How
could you think that of me?"

"Think that of you?" She chuckled. "Oh, come on! I knew it the
moment you dramatically took the stage right on cue, playing the hero.
Very gallant. But, sir, I'm not so easily tricked. I can't believe I let those
other idiots— the first murderer and his cronies— scare me. It was
poorly done. Yet, it bowled over the common folks in Paul's Yard, and
they'll praise your great performance for a whole day, at least. But did
you really expect to impress me too? I'm part of this play, after all."

It was said, and rightly so, that he was the most brazen man in
England, this handsome, talented, foolish son. Her teasing now threw
him off balance, and it took all his strength to quell the anger it stirred
in him. Yet, quelling it he did, lest he make an even sorrier spectacle of
himself.

"I swear... I swear you're being monstrously unfair," he finally managed to stutter. "You've always thought the worst of me. It's all because
of that cursed dinner party and the behavior of those drunkards. But
I've told you it wasn't my fault. I only found solace in your quick exit
from a scene that I would never have wanted to offend you with. Yet
even though I've sworn it, I doubt you believe me."

"Do you really wonder?" she asked coolly. He looked at her, his eyes
dark and full of malice, brooding.

Then he let a bit of his rage slip out, but directed it at a mere excuse.

"I wish to Heaven I had left you to those scoundrels!"

She burst into laughter. "I wonder how the comedy would have
unfolded then, if you had missed your cue. Maybe my 'persecutors'
would have had to rescue me themselves just to avoid your wrath. That

would have been quite the show. Oh, but enough!" She set aside her laughter. "Thank you for the entertainment, but since it turned out to be a waste, I hope you won't trouble yourself with another spectacle. If you can feel shame for anything, let it be for the dullness of your scenarios."

She turned from him with a nearly contemptuous abruptness and addressed the chair-bearer standing beside her.

"Take up, Nathaniel. Let's go, quickly, or I'll be late."

She was obeyed and left without a second glance at the Duke of Bucks. He stood there, hat in hand, pale with anger, biting his lip. She had stripped away his mask, exposing him to mockery and revealing him for the fool he was. His lackeys in the background struggled to keep their faces straight, while a few passersby paused to gawk at the splendid, bareheaded figure—a courtly sight rarely witnessed in the city's streets. Imagining their gazes to be more penetrating than they were, he believed them all to be gleeful witnesses to his embarrassment. With a swift stomp of his heel and a clenching of teeth, he slapped his hat back on and turned to leave, headed for his waiting coach.

But then, a firm grip caught his right arm, and a voice, quivering with wonder and something else, reached his ears.

"Sir!"

"Hey!"

The Duke spun around, locking eyes with the piercing gaze of Colonel Dempsey. Dempsey's clean-shaven face and hawkish features brimming with curiosity had drawn him nearer and nearer, like a moth to a flame, while the Duke was immersed in conversation. Surprised, the Duke sized him up, head to toe. Seeing another witness to his embarrassment, his temper surged, searching for a target.

"What is this?" he barked. "Do you dare lay a hand on me, you scoundrel?"

The Colonel, unfazed by the Duke's sharp and arrogant tone, met the blazing eyes without flinching. He replied calmly, "I touched you once before, I believe, and you accepted it with more grace. That time, I was serving you."

"Ha! So now you touch me to remind me of that, do you?" the Duke snapped back, his voice dripping with contempt. Dempsey's composure shattered momentarily; a flush of anger crept beneath his tanned skin, and he returned the Duke's scorn with a hardened stare. Without a word, he pivoted to leave. The oddness, the deliberate offense in such an action, irked the Duke, someone accustomed to unfaltering reverence. Spurred by sudden rage, he grabbed Dempsey's arm, stopping him in his tracks.

"Wait!"

They stood face to face once again, but now arrogance cloaked Dempsey. The Duke's expression was a tumult of astonishment and indignation.

"I think," the Duke began, his voice trembling with suppressed anger, "you lack some respect."

"At least you're right about that," the Colonel replied, his tone unwavering. The Duke's amazement deepened.

"Do you know who I am?" he asked after a heavy pause.

"I figured it out just a few minutes ago."

"But you said you once did me a service."

"That was many years ago," Dempsey said. "And I didn't know your name back then."

"Your grace has probably forgotten," the Colonel said, his voice dripping with a disdain that commanded attention.

The Duke was intrigued. "Will you not assist my memory?" he asked almost gently.

The Colonel responded with a grim chuckle, then shook off the Duke's hand. He lifted his own, pushed back his light brown curls, and revealed his left ear adorned with a long ruby earring. Buckingham stared, then leaned in closer, his breath catching.

"How did you come by that jewel?" he asked, his eyes searching the Colonel's face.

"It was given to me after Worcester by a fool whose life I thought worth saving," the Colonel responded, bitterness lacing his voice.

To his surprise, the Duke didn't react with anger. Instead, he seemed overcome by curiosity.

"So! It was you!" His eyes continued to roam over the Colonel's lean features. "Yes," he added, almost with a sigh. "The man I remember had the same nose and height. But otherwise, you don't resemble the Cromwellian who helped me that night. You didn't have these curls then; your hair was cut short to a godly length. But you're the man. How strange to meet you again like this! How profoundly strange!"

The Duke seemed lost in thought. "They cannot be mistaken!" he muttered, still observing the Colonel, his eyes distant, as if he were seeing something far beyond the present. "I have been expecting you," he said, and repeated enigmatically, "They cannot be mistaken."

Now it was the Colonel's turn to be bewildered. "Your grace has been expecting me?"

"For many years. It was foretold that we would meet again and that our lives would be intertwined for a time."

"Foretold?" Dempsey repeated in disbelief.

Suddenly, he thought about the superstitions that had made him cling to that jewel through every twist and turn of fate. "How was it foretold? By whom?" he asked. The question seemed to jolt the Duke from his deep reverie.

"Listen," the Duke said, "we can't stand here talking all night. We didn't come all this way, after all these years, to leave everything unresolved." His demeanor snapped back to its usual arrogance. "If you have business, it'll have to wait until I say so. Now come with me."

The Duke grabbed the Colonel by the arm and barked orders in French to his waiting servants, commanding two of them to follow. Dempsey, unresisting and awash with curiosity, felt as if he were walking in a dream, a man swept along the relentless current of fate, unable to do anything but float along with the tide of Destiny.

Chapter Thirteen

In an upstairs room at an inn on the corner of Paternoster Row, they sat alone: the Duke of Buckingham and the man who had saved his life. There was no denying the magnitude of the debt, as they both were keenly aware. That fateful night, long years past, when his grace lay weak and wounded on the blood-soaked battlefield, he'd become prey to a pair of human jackals—scavengers of the living and the dead. The young Duke had valiantly tried to fend off their looting, but as one pinned him down, the other raised a knife to finish him off.

Then, out of the encroaching darkness, young Dempsey appeared, led there by a stroke of pure chance. His heavy cut-and-thrust blade cleaved the skull of the knave wielding the knife and sent the other fleeing into the night. After that, half-carrying, half-dragging the beautiful, broken boy he'd saved, the young Cromwellian officer brought him to the safety of a royalist yeoman's cottage. They both remembered this vividly, and now they lingered on those memories, letting the past breathe its cold breath in the warm room.

A table stood between them with a quart of Burgundy that the Duke had summoned to toast his guest.

"In my heart," Dempsey said, "I always believed we'd meet again someday. That's why I've held onto this jewel. If I'd known your name, I'd have sought you out. Instead, I kept faith that Fate would cross our paths."

"Not Fate. Destiny," corrected his grace with a quiet, unshakable belief.

"Destiny, if you will," Dempsey conceded. "Still, it's very strange, this jewel."

I've held on to it all these years, as I mentioned; I clung to it through countless tough times when selling it would have offered relief. I held onto it for the day we'd meet again, so it could serve as my proof. What I didn't mention is that the strangest thing is that today, right when we met, I was on my way to sell the jewel, forced by utter desperation. The Duke nodded thoughtfully. "Destiny. It was meant to be. The meeting was foretold. Didn't I say so?"

Dempsey asked again, as he had before, "Foretold by whom?"

This time the Duke answered directly.

"By whom? By the stars. The only true prophets, and their messages are clear to those who can read them. I suppose you've never sought that knowledge?"

Dempsey stared at him for a moment before shaking his head with a disdainful smile.

"I'm a soldier, sir," he said.

"Why, so am I, when needed. But that doesn't stop me from reading the heavens, writing verse, creating laws up north, being a courtier here, and many other roles. A man plays many parts in his time. If you only play one, you might as well play none. To live, my friend, you need to sip from many wells."

He expanded on this, speaking smoothly, wittily, with an inescapable charm that was now entrancing our adventurer just as it had years ago in that brief but life-changing encounter.

"Just now when you stumbled upon me," he concluded, "I was playing the hero, the lover, the author, and the actor all at once—and doing such a poor job that I've never found myself in a more frustrating role."

I swear, if you didn't owe me anything before, you certainly do now. You've managed to pull my mind away, even if just for a little while, from the torment of that tempting little minx who keeps me in agony. Maybe you noticed how brazen she was with me." He let out a chuckle, although there was a sharp edge to it. "But I screwed up the act, like she said. Deserved to be laughed out of the theater, and that's exactly what happened. One of these days, she'll pay for every bit of trouble she caused me, with interest. She will... Oh, to hell with her! It's you I want to talk about. What are you doing now, after being such a staunch supporter of the Commonwealth?"

"No one's man right now. I've seen plenty of action since then, both here and abroad, but it hasn't brought me much, as you can see."

"Indeed." Buckingham scrutinized him. "You don't look like you're rolling in riches."

"Desperate's the word, and you wouldn't be exaggerating."

"Really?" The Duke raised an eyebrow. "It's that bad? I'm genuinely sorry to hear that." His face softened into a look of polite sympathy. "But perhaps I could help. I do owe you a favor. I'd be glad to repay it. What's your name, sir? I don't believe you've mentioned it."

"Dempsey. Randal Dempsey. I was a cavalry colonel in the Stadtholder's service."

The Duke's brow furrowed in thought. The name sparked a faint memory. For a moment, it danced just out of reach, but then it clicked.

"Randal Dempsey?" he repeated slowly, almost unsure. "That was the name of a regicide who... But you can't be him. You'd be at least thirty years too young."

"He was my father," the Colonel said.

"Oh!" The Duke looked at him blankly. "No wonder you can't find work here in England."

"My friend, I truly want to repay you for the great service you did for me, but it's not going to be easy."

The glimmer of hope in the Colonel's eyes extinguished, replaced by a deep shadow.

"I had a feeling this might be the case..." he started, with sorrow dripping from his voice. The Duke cut him off, leaning forward to place a reassuring hand on his arm.

"I said difficult, Colonel, not impossible. There's nothing I find impossible if I truly desire it, and believe me, right now there's nothing I desire more than to see you prosper again. But for me to help you, Colonel Dempsey, I need to know more about your journey. How does a former officer of the Commonwealth Army and recent servant to the Stadtholder find himself risking his life in the London of Old Rowley, this King's memory for vengeance stretching longer than eternity?"

Colonel Dempsey began to speak, leaving out only the part about how McCormick and Rathbone had lured him into the disastrous Danvers conspiracy. With raw honesty, he confessed the missteps he'd taken, driven by misguided impulses. He recounted the streak of bad luck that had snatched away every prize just as it was within his grasp, right up to the command in Bombay that Northridge had almost handed him. The Duke, with an air of casual sympathy, mixed condolences with humor, as if to promise a better future. Yet, when the conversation reached the topic of the Bombay command, a note of sorrow crept into the Duke's laughter.

"And to think, I was the one who took that from you," he exclaimed. "See how strangely Destiny works! This only increases my debt to you. Now I have even more to make up for. I promise, I'll find a way to get you on the path to success. But we need to tread carefully, you understand that. Trust me to move with certainty, even if it's slow."

This time, Dempsey's face lit up, flushing with pure joy.

Fortune had played him for a fool many times, but she hadn't completely shattered his faith in humanity. So, miraculously, at the eleventh hour, salvation arrived. And it came through that precious ruby he'd clung to with stubborn intuition. The Duke pulled out a green silk purse, its mesh revealing the warm glow of gold coins inside.

"Meanwhile, my friend, as an earnest of my good intent..."

"Not that, Your Grace." For the second time that day, Dempsey refused a proffered purse, his foolish pride putting up its defenses. Throughout his tumultuous career, he'd acquired money in all sorts of dubious ways, but never as a gift from someone whose respect he wished to uphold. "I'm not in immediate need. I... I can make do for now."

But the Duke of Buckingham was cut from a different cloth than the Duke of Northridge. Lavish and generous where Northridge was stingy, he wasn't one to take no for an answer. He smiled a little at Dempsey's protests and moved forward with a smooth, compelling insistence, oozing charm.

"I admire your refusal, but..." He continued to extend the purse. "See, this isn't a gift I'm offering. It's an advance, a modest loan, which you'll repay soon enough when I make it easy for you. Come now, sir, there's more between us that can't be settled with gold alone. Your refusal would offend me."

And Dempsey, truth be told, was relieved to have his self-respect shielded this way.

"As a loan, then, since you insist so graciously..."

"Why, what else did you think I had in mind?" The Duke dropped the heavy purse into Dempsey's hand, which was finally open to receiving it, and stood. "You'll hear from me again soon, Colonel. Let me know where you're staying."

Dempsey paused for a moment, considering.

He was leaving Paul's Head, and he had made it clear he planned to move to the Bird in Hand, a modest inn where the rates were almost laughable. But he had a taste for fine food and drink, just as he had a penchant for fine clothing, and he would only stay in such a miserable place if he had absolutely no other choice. Now, with this unexpected windfall, his pockets heavy with gold and the promise of more on the way, that bleak necessity vanished. He remembered, and quickly decided on, another inn known for its excellent fare.

"You'll find me at The Harp on Wood Street," he declared with a confident smile.

"Expect to hear from me very soon."

They left the tavern together, and the Duke headed for his coach, which had been brought around for him. His French servants moved in step beside it, while Colonel Dempsey, his spirits soaring, strutted toward Paul's Yard, fingering the now-famed jewel in his ear. There was no longer any need to sell it, although keeping it wasn't a necessity either, for it had finally, after many long years, served its destined purpose. In high spirits, he swaggered into Paul's Head, ready to confront a disastrous encounter with Mrs. Quinn. It was this damnable jewel that triggered the calamity. The mere sight of it enraged her, leading her to rash and unfounded assumptions.

"You haven't sold it!" she screamed as he walked into the back parlor where she was busy with something or other. She pointed at the earring, which gleamed like a single, infernal ember beneath the tangle of his brown hair. "You've changed your mind. You plan to come sniveling back here, trying to save that trinket at my expense." And then, as if the devil himself was whispering in her ear, an unfortunate thought took root, blooming into a fierce and sudden jealousy.

Before he could reply, before he could shake off the shock of her sudden fury, she was already shouting again. "I get it!" she sneered, her eyes full of malice. "A love token, huh? From some well-fed Flemish housewife you probably conned just like you tried to con me. That's why you refuse to part with it—not even to pay for the roof over your head, the food you've stuffed yourself with, and the wine you've downed, you worthless scoundrel. But consider this your final warning. Since you won't heed it, you'll—"

"Shut your mouth, woman," he roared, suddenly silencing her with the sheer force of his rage. He stepped towards her, causing her to stumble back in alarm, her defiance flickering but still present. Then, just as abruptly, he stopped, reined himself in, and laughed. Reaching into his pocket, he pulled out a heavy, ornate purse. He undid the gold rings binding it and let the gleam of broad, yellow coins spill into view.

"What's the total of your bill?" he asked with a sneer, the remnants of his anger boiling in his words. "Name it, take your money, and leave me in peace."

But her focus had shifted. Stunned by the sight of the purse and the wealth it contained, she could only gape. Her eyes darted between the bulging purse and his face. Unable to fathom the source of his sudden fortune, she leaped to the worst possible conclusion, as minds like hers so often do.

The suspicion etched deep furrows into her piercing blue eyes, tightened into a steely resolve, and twisted her wide mouth into an unpleasant sneer.

"And how did you come by this gold?" she asked, her voice a sinister hush.

"Is that any of your business, ma'am?"

"I thought you were above stealing," she replied, dripping with disdain. "But it seems I was wrong about you in more ways than one."

"You brazen hussy!" he roared, his fury turning her complexion pale.

"You filthy vagrant, is that how you speak to an honest woman?"

"Honest, you thieving wench! Do you pride yourself on honesty? Your deceitful accounts say otherwise. Give me the total so I can pay your swindling amount and leave your wretched tavern behind."

That, as you might guess, was only the beginning of a scene too wild for me to recount in full detail. Some parts are downright unmentionable. Her voice shot up like a fishwife's, grabbing the attention of the few patrons scattered in the common room and bringing Tim, the bartender, to the door in alarm. Despite his anger, Colonel Dempsey started to feel a creeping anxiety. His conscience was far from clear, and appearances could easily turn against him.

"You treacherous, shameless wretch," she screamed. "Do you think you can barge in here, roaring at me, after turning my reputable inn into a den of treason? I'll teach you some manners, you gallows-bound scoundrel!" She then spotted Tim's terrified face peeking through the door. "Tim, fetch the constable," she bellowed. "This gentleman needs a new lodging at Newgate, which suits his kind better. Fetch the constable, boy. Run!"

Tim scurried off. So did the Colonel, suddenly realizing that staying any longer would lead to nothing good.

He dumped half the contents of the duke's purse into his hand and, like a twisted parody of Jupiter showering Danaë, he rained the coins down on her without a hint of love, only malice.

"Shut your screeching mouth with that," he snarled. "Take it, you witch, and damn you to hell."

He stormed out, rage crackling around him, barely a step behind Tim. The half- dozen men in the common room scattered out of his way, not one daring to challenge him. Bursting into the street, he vanished, leaving behind a few stray belongings as grim reminders of his turbulent visit. The hostess, drained and furious, collapsed in tears, whispering curses into the empty space he'd left behind.

CHAPTER FOURTEEN

F or three agonizing weeks, Colonel Dempsey clung to The Harp on Wood Street, waiting in vain for the promised message from His Grace of Buckingham. Each passing day gnawed at his patience and resources, an unseen hand tightening around his dwindling coffers. He had never been one for frugality; extravagance was in his blood. He lodged in comfort, dined on the finest, paraded in one of the two dashing suits he had procured from second-hand clothiers in Birchin Lane, deeming it smarter to avoid the high-end shops of Paternoster Row. And then there was his everlasting vice: gambling. He indulged, recklessly throwing dice with the devil, until finally, he found his pockets nearly empty and his optimism eroding under the unending silence of the Duke who had once filled him with such hope.

But the Duke's elusive message wasn't the only shadow over Dempsey's days. Mrs. Quinn's scorched-earth fury still loomed, propelling a relentless manhunt that he had so far evaded only by sheer luck and secrecy. She had no clue of his current hideout, a fortunate twist of fate that kept him one step ahead of the law. Dempsey knew she'd sent bloodhounds to the Bird in Hand, where he'd falsely claimed he was headed. It would be foolish to assume the search was over. Any moment now, they might track him down and haul him away. The fact he remained a free man this long was likely due to more pressing chaos that choked the streets of London.

London was a cauldron of nerves these days. On the third of the month, the city rewound in shock as the distant thunder of cannon fire echoed through its streets, rumbling incessantly to announce that Dutch and English fleets were locked in combat, perilously close. The battle raged near Harwich, a brutal dance of death and strategy that left the Dutch fleet limping back toward the Texel with heavy losses.

Dempsey knew it wasn't just the war at sea causing this unease. There were darker, more sinister currents beneath the surface, fears and whispers that not even the crash of waves and fury of cannons could quiet. And caught in this uneasy balance, he waited, each day a blend of dread and false hope.

Of course, there were the usual tall tales from both the English and the Dutch, each claiming total victory and lighting bonfires in celebration. But our story isn't about Holland. In London, from June 8th—when news first broke about the complete routing of the Dutch and the destruction of half their fleet—up to the 20th, named as a day of thanksgiving for that great victory, the city was ablaze with celebrations. These revelries hit their peak at Whitehall on the 16th, welcoming back the Duke of York, who returned from sea as Mr. Pepys noted, all fat, lusty, and ruddy from soaking in the sun.

And maybe it was for the best—or perhaps not—that there were such festivities to distract the people from the looming horror spreading among them. The plague, slow but relentless, was an enemy more insidious and deadly than the Dutch ever could be. The wild celebrations on the 20th were like a last hurrah before reality came crashing down. People suddenly awoke to their dire situation, the sense of dread possibly beginning in Whitehall, which was emptying out at a disturbing pace. The Court fled to the cleaner air of Salisbury, and on the 21st and 22nd, a constant stream of coaches and wagons rolled westward past Charing Cross, packed with folks fleeing the infected city for the safety of the countryside.

That mass exodus filled the City with a sense of doom, the inhabitants feeling like sailors left aboard a sinking ship. Panic began to spread, fueled by the measures taken by the Lord Mayor to combat the terrifying disease. Sir John Lawrence was forced to issue strict regulations, appoint examiners and searchers, and enforce the quarantine of infected houses—actions so severe they shattered any lingering illusions of safety within the City walls.

Horses were the hottest commodity in London, with their rental prices skyrocketing. At every exit from the city—from Ludgate to Aldgate, across London Bridge and beyond—the roads were clogged with a mass exodus of horsemen, pedestrians, coaches, and carts. It was as if London was suffocating under an invisible weight, paralyzed by the shrinking population. The suburbs fared no better; rumors spread like wildfire, whispering of men dropping dead like flies with the approach of winter. Doom preachers multiplied, and instead of being met with jeers or pelts of rotten food, they were listened to with silent dread. The once-rowdy apprentices of London were so subdued that they even let a lunatic run naked through the streets near Paul's, a burning cresset of coals on his head, shrieking that the Lord would cleanse the city with fire for its sins.

Colonel Dempsey, however, was too wrapped up in his own troubles to care much for the city's collective hysteria. When he finally caught wind of the evacuation from Whitehall, worry set in like a stone in his gut. His last hope, the Duke of Buckingham, might leave just like everyone else. Desperation fueled his decision to send a letter to the Duke, reminding him of his existence. Two grueling days passed with no response, his anxiety metastasizing into bleak despair.

One evening, returning after dark from a grim errand of selling a precious jewel—its final purpose a tragic mockery of fate—he found a new layer of despondency. He had practically given it away, the buyer smugly telling him that nobody was in the mood for adornments these days.

As he stepped back into the inn, Banks, the landlord, ambled over, pulling Dempsey aside, away from the few patrons lingering in the common room.

"There've been two men asking about you, sir."

Dempsey tensed, his mind jumping instantly to the Duke of Buckingham. Banks, recognizing the flash of hope, shook his head with a solemn expression. Banks was a stocky, dark-skinned man, with kindness etched into his soft features. This crestfallen guest had clearly stirred his sympathy. He leaned in, lowering his voice, though there was hardly any need.

"They were Bow Street messengers," he whispered. "They didn't say it outright, but I know them. They asked a load of questions. How long you've been here, where you came from, what you're up to. They told me not to mention this to you. But..." The landlord shrugged his broad shoulders and sneered in contempt of the order. His dark eyes bore into the Colonel, noting the sudden seriousness on Dempsey's face. Dempsey wasn't concerned with guesses about why justice had sent its minions. His association with McCormick and Rathbone must have come to light, perhaps during McCormick's trial, where the poor man had been convicted and sentenced to be hanged and quartered. Dempsey had no doubt that if he fell into the law's clutches, his own conviction would soon follow, despite his innocence.

"I thought, sir," the landlord continued, "that I'd warn you. So if you've done something to put yourself on the wrong side of the law, you wouldn't wait around for them to catch you. I don't want to see you come to any harm."

Dempsey gathered himself. "Mr. Banks," he said, "you're a good friend, and I appreciate it. I haven't done anything wrong, I assure you. But appearances can be damning. The unfortunate Mr. McCormick was an old friend of mine…"

The landlord sighed heavily. "Aye, sir, I figured as much from what those men let slip."

That's why I'm taking the risk of telling you. For God's sake, sir, get out while you can."

The Colonel blinked, momentarily startled. Fortune, for once, had graced him with a slim smile. The landlord of The Harp, it turned out, was secretly supportive of the republicans. Heeding the man's urgent advice, the Colonel settled his tab—nearly draining the profits from the sold jewel—and, without bothering to gather his belongings, he hastened to leave the suddenly perilous quarters. None too soon. Just as he stepped into the dim, fog-choked street, two shadowy figures materialized, blocking his path. A lantern was abruptly uncovered and thrust into his face.

"Halt, sir, in the King's name!" a gruff voice commanded. Whether they held weapons or not, he didn't pause to find out. In a swift, brutal move, he knocked the lantern out of one man's hand and delivered a blow that sent him sprawling. The second man's arms encircled him, attempting to wrestle him to the ground. But Dempsey, with a sharp jab of his elbow, knocked the wind from his would-be captor. As the man's grip loosened, the Colonel flung him violently against the wall. Without a second glance to assess the damage, Dempsey bolted down the dark alley, fleeing like a hunted hare as shouts and the rapid stomp of footsteps echoed behind him.

The chase didn't last long. Soon, the Colonel found himself able to slow to a more dignified pace, though fear followed him, relentless and gnawing, driving him deeper into the labyrinthine heart of the city. That night, he hunkered down in a tavern near Aldgate, his mind a storm of grim contemplation about the dire straits he found himself in.

Before dawn, he had made up his mind. There was only one sane choice left for him, and that was to leave England behind. This land had offered him nothing but heartache and disappointment. He cursed the misplaced patriotism that had dragged him back home, declaring that love of country was nothing but an illusion, its devotees nothing but fools. He would leave immediately and never return to this wretched birthplace again. With the Dutch ships back in Texel and the seas open once more, it wouldn't be hard; not even his lack of money should stand in his way. He'd sign on as a deckhand on some ship headed for France.

With this plan, he set out early the next morning for Wapping. There were plenty of ships, and they all needed crew, but no captain would take him on until he had a health certificate. The plague had made such measures necessary. No one could travel abroad or even into the country without proof that they were clean. Every town and village now refused entry to anyone from London unless they had a certificate confirming their health. It was a frustrating hurdle. But what else could he do?

So, the Colonel trudged wearily to the Guildhall, taking the lonely, shadowy streets of the city, where he saw more than one door marked with a cross and guarded by a watchman who warned everyone to keep their distance. The few people he passed were all too eager to keep to the middle of the street, avoiding not just the infected houses but also anyone they might encounter.

Many of those Dempsey saw out and about were officials whose jobs the plague had made necessary—examiners, searchers, keepers, and surgeons, each distinguishable by the red wand they carried, as required by law. All of them were shunned as if they were the ones carrying the disease.

The Colonel grasped the gravity of the plague, its tendrils reaching out and claiming victims by the thousands. When he finally arrived at the Guildhall, the scene before him was bedlam—a writhing mass of coaches, sedan-chairs, and desperate souls on foot, all fighting to get their hands on the elusive Lord Mayor's certificate of health, their ticket out of the doomed city.

The whole day he spent there, trapped in that sweltering throng, stomach gnawing with hunger, throat parched and dry. Hawkers pushed through the crowd, but they weren't selling anything remotely useful. Gone was the cheerful cry of "Sweet oranges!" Instead, they peddled trinkets of false hope: "Infallible Preservative Against Infection," "The Royal Antidote," "Sovereign Cordial Against the Corruption of the Air."

Money could have bought him a faster route, slipping a bribe to one of the ushers, but he couldn't spare the coin. So he waited, as powerless as anyone else, grappling with the fact that arriving late meant he'd likely wait till the bitter end, or perhaps not even get his turn at all.

As the sun dipped and shadows stretched, the prudent among the crowd hunkered down, ready to brave the night to be first in line come morning. But the Colonel, empty-handed and increasingly irritable, gave up toward dusk. He shuffled off, stomach still growling, throat still dry, morosely believing the day wasted.

And then, fortune twisted in his favor, albeit subtly. In a dim, half-empty eating-house off Cheapside, he sought some respite, having gone without food or water since dawn. There, the ambient murmur of conversation drifted to his ears. Two men at a nearby table were deep in discussion, their voices carrying just enough to catch his attention.

They spoke of an arrest made earlier that day, their words floating through the haze of dinner chatter and ale stains. One phrase cut through the noise, seizing Colonel Dempsey's focus like a vice.

"But how was he taken?"

The question dangled in the air, heavy with possibilities.

"How'd they find out?" one of them asked.

"At the Guildhall, when he tried to get a health certificate to leave town. I'm telling you, it's no joke trying to get out of London these days; criminals are learning that the hard way. They'll nab Danvers eventually. They're watching for him, and others too."

Colonel Dempsey pushed his plate away, his appetite dead. He felt the walls closing in. It took those eavesdropped words to bring it home. Running equaled getting caught. Sure, he could try getting a health certificate under a fake name, but that was a gamble. There'd be questions about his background, checks to make sure he was free of infection. Any lies or fake identity would be exposed. It was a damned-if-you-do, damned-if-you-don't situation. If he stayed, they'd eventually catch him; the law was after him more fiercely than ever since he'd roughed up those officers the night before. If he ran, he'd walk himself right into their hands.

Brooding over his limited choices, he decided to seek help from Northridge. With that in mind, he set out. But by the time he reached Charing Cross, doubt gnawed at him. He recalled Northridge's cautious, self-serving nature. What if Northridge refused to risk his own neck over Dempsey's innocence, especially given the serious accusations? Dempsey doubted Northridge would go that far, but you never know; after all, the Duke had already distanced himself from old friends. Yet, fear of rejection made him hesitate.

Finally, he resolved to make one last attempt to sway the Duke of Buckingham. Following that impulse, he turned into the courtyard of Wallingford House.

CHAPTER FIFTEEN

The Duke of Buckingham hadn't joined the Court in its hurried retreat to Salisbury. His duties called him to York, but duty and caution were voices he chose to ignore. Instead, he remained anchored in London, ensnared by his infatuation with Miss Shallmont—a passion that fared poorly. His attempts to play the gallant savior had only made him look foolish in her eyes. This obsession with Miss Shallmont caused him to neglect Dempsey's letter. The letter arrived just as he learned that Sir John Lawrence had decreed all theaters and public venues to close on the upcoming Saturday—a dire but necessary step in the Lord Mayor's war against the plague. With the Court absent, no one was left to oppose the order, assuming anyone would have dared to in the first place.

The theater closures meant the players would leave Town, thus ending the Duke's opportunities to woo Miss Shallmont. Faced with this, he had to either surrender or act swiftly. A straightforward course of action had always been available, one he would have taken long ago if he hadn't heeded Mr. Ballard's warnings so weakly. Ironically, the theater closures now made this course less risky—a minor concern for the Duke, who flouted all laws except those dictated by his own desires.

Finally, he resolved to act and summoned the cunning Bates, the Chaffinch of Wallingford House. The Duke issued commands, shrouded in complexity, that Master Bates struggled to fully grasp regarding a particular house.

It was the Monday of the week when the theaters were set to close by Saturday. That was the very day Dempsey made his hasty exit from The Harp. By Tuesday morning, the ever-reliable Bates reported to his master that he had located just the kind of place his grace had been seeking, though Bates had no idea why his grace wanted it so urgently.

It was a spacious, well-appointed house on Knight Ryder Street, recently left vacant by a tenant who had fled to the countryside out of fear of the plague. The owner, a merchant from Fenchurch Street, was eager to lease it at a reasonable rate, aware of the difficulty in finding tenants in the city these days. Bates, with his usual discretion, conducted his inquiries without revealing he was acting on behalf of his grace.

The Duke burst into laughter at Bates's veiled assurance and the implications of his assumed discretion. "You've become a rather competent scoundrel in my service."

Bates bowed with a hint of mockery. "I'm pleased to meet your grace's approval," he replied dryly. There was a streak of insolent humor in him that the Duke tolerated, perhaps because he knew no one else could be so unerringly familiar with the shadows of his conscience.

"You're a reliable rogue. The house will do perfectly, though I would've preferred a less crowded neighborhood."

"If things keep progressing as they are, your grace won't have to worry about that. Soon, the City will be the most deserted place in

England. Already, more than half the houses in Knight Ryder Street are empty. I trust your grace isn't planning to live there."

"Not... not exactly," the Duke muttered, deep in thought. "There's no plague in the street yet, I hope?"

"Not yet. But fear is spreading, just like everywhere else in the City."

The merchant in Fenchurch Street didn't bother hiding his belief that I was out of my mind for looking for a house in London at such a time.

"Ridiculous," his grace waved off the matter of fear dismissively. "These citizens scare themselves into believing the plague is everywhere. It's actually quite timely. It'll keep people too preoccupied to snoop around Knight Ryder Street. Tomorrow, Bates, you'll find this merchant and make sure to secure the house—under your name, not mine. Got it? Don't mention me. And to avoid any questions, pay him six months' rent upfront."

Bates nodded. "Understood, your grace."

His grace leaned back in his grand chair, eyeing his servant through narrowed, calculating eyes, a sly smile playing on his lips.

"Of course, you've probably figured out why I need this house."

"I wouldn't presume to guess your grace's intentions."

"Which means you can't. That's an admission of your own dullness. You remember that little charade we pulled off a month ago for Miss Shallmont?"

"How could I forget? My bones still ache from the beating I took. Your grace's damned French lackeys are too good at their roles."

"The lady didn't think so. At least, she wasn't convinced. We need to up our game."

"Yes, your grace." There was a hint of uncertainty in Bates' voice.

"This time, we'll add a more serious touch to our performance. We're going to kidnap her. That's why I need this house."

"Kidnap her?" Bates' expression suddenly turned grave.

"That's exactly what I need from you, Bates."

"Me?" Bates gasped, his face paling, his mouth agape like a wolf caught off guard. "Me, your grace?" It was clear the idea terrified him.

"Of course. What's there to be so shocked about?"

"But your grace, this... this is... very serious."

"Bah!" said his grace.

"It... it's a hanging offense."

"Oh, stop being foolish. A hanging offense?"

"When I'm behind you?"

"Exactly. They wouldn't dare hang you, Your Grace. But they'll want someone to blame if things go south, and they'll gladly use your pawns to quell the mob's cries for justice."

"Have you lost your mind?"

"No, Your Grace, I'm quite sharp. And if I might venture to offer some advice..."

"That would indeed be a presumption, you impudent rogue!" The Duke's voice lashed out, his brow furrowing deeply. "I think you forget your place."

"I beg Your Grace's pardon." But that didn't silence him. "Your Grace might not realize the level of panic in the city over this plague. Everywhere people claim it's a punishment for the sins of the Court. That's the rumor those sanctimonious Nonconformist preachers have spread. And if you follow through with this plan of yours..."

"My God!" thundered Buckingham, unmistakable irritation etched into his voice. "It seems you intend to advise me despite my objections."

Bates went quiet but stood firm, his defiance unwavering. Calming slightly, Buckingham continued, "Listen, Bates. While the plague may plague us, it also serves us well. Kidnapping Miss Shallmont from the theatre would ignite a pursuit that could lead to unwanted discoveries and result in dire consequences. But the Lord Mayor has ordered all theatres closed on Saturday. So, it will be Saturday night when we move, when Miss Shallmont's absence will cause little stir. The fear of the plague keeps people preoccupied enough."

"And afterwards, Your Grace?"

"Afterwards?"

"When the lady brings a complaint."

A sly grin spread across Buckingham's face, brimming with worldly cunning. "Do ladies ever truly complain about such matters afterward? Besides, who would believe her if she claimed she was taken to my house against her will? She's an actress, not a princess."

"I still hold some sway in this country, you know," the Duke insisted, his voice a touch too loud to mask the desperation beneath.

But Bates, with a solemn shake of his head, countered, "I don't think you have enough pull to save me if things go south. And they will, trust me on that, your grace. Just too many troublemakers lying in wait, looking for a way to turn things to their favor."

"Who's going to point the finger at you?" the Duke snapped, irritation obvious.

"The lady herself, if I kidnap her for you," Bates replied. "Besides, didn't you say the house should be taken in my name? That would be enough to seal my fate. I've served you loyally, and God knows I'm not squeamish about it. But this... no, your grace. I can't do it."

A mix of amazement and disdain flashed across Buckingham's face. He felt like roaring with fury, but at the same time he nearly laughed at the absurdity of Bates being the stumbling block in his plans. His fingers drummed on the table as he pondered his next move. Then, he decided to play his highest card.

"How long have you been in my service, Bates?"

"Five years this month, your grace."

"And are you tired of it?"

"You know I'm not. I've served you faithfully in all things..."

"But now you think you can cherry-pick the tasks you'll do for me. Bates, I think you've been in my service too long."

"Your grace!"

"I might be wrong. But I'll need proof before I believe it. Luckily for you, it's within your power to provide that proof. I suggest you do so."

His gaze was icy, and Bates, trembling, couldn't hold it. The little man fidgeted with his neckcloth, his bony hand briefly touching his throat as if he were already imagining the noose tightening around it.

"Your grace," Bates implored, his voice cracked with fear, "there is no task I won't perform to show my loyalty."

"Command me to do anything, Your Grace—anything but this."

"Your protestations touch me, Bates," the Duke replied icily, his tone dripping with condescension. "Unfortunately, this is the only service I require of you at the moment."

Bates plunged into despair, his face a portrait of anguish.

"I can't, Your Grace! I can't!" He cried out, desperation cracking his voice. "It's a hanging matter, as you well know."

"For me, Bates, in the eyes of the strict law, perhaps it is," the Duke replied with chilling indifference.

"And since Your Grace is beyond the reach of the noose, it's me who would swing in your place."

"You repeat yourself. It's a tiresome habit," the Duke remarked, his voice cold and dismissive. "Yet I'm willing to offer a hundred pounds or so as a douceur..."

"It's not about money, Your Grace. I wouldn't do it for a thousand."

"Then there's nothing more to discuss." Despite the fiery anger simmering just below his calm exterior, Buckingham remained outwardly composed. "You have leave to go, Bates. I shalln't require your services further. Apply to Mr. Grove; he'll settle what moneys are due."

A flick of his white, bejeweled hand signaled Bates' dismissal. The smaller man hesitated for a moment, torn by his reluctance to accept this ending. But fear—cold, relentless fear—won over. The consequences were too daunting, too certain. Had it been anything less than a hanging matter, he might have braved it. But this... this was beyond him. Realizing that further pleading would be futile against the Duke's unyielding arrogance, Bates bowed in silence and departed, his heart heavy with discomfiture.

He left behind a discontented Duke. Buckingham's plan had faltered, and he had no replacement for Bates. Later that day, Mr. Ballard visited, only to find the Duke pacing in his opulent library, still in his bedgown, as restless as a beast trapped in a gilded cage.

Ballard was well aware of the allure binding the Duke to the city. Having just finalized his own exit plan, he made one last earnest attempt to knock some sense into his friend, urging him to trade London's stifling air for the health- giving embrace of the countryside. Buckingham's laughter was hollow, devoid of humor.

"You're overreacting, George. This plague thrives in filth and preys on the filthy. Look at the cases reported – they're all in the dingiest houses on the dingiest streets. The plague is quite discerning; it doesn't dare touch those of us with a touch of class."

"Even so, I'm not taking chances," Ballard replied, pulling out a handkerchief imbued with the strong scent of camphor and vinegar that quickly filled the room. "I firmly believe that getting out of here is the best medicine. Besides, what's left for us in this fevered hellhole?

The Court has fled, and the city feels like an antechamber to hell. For heaven's sake, let's find some fresh, cool countryside air."

"Bah! You're such a rustic. More like Dryden with his pastoral fantasies. Go on, then, tend to your sheep. We won't miss you in this forsaken town."

Ballard settled into a chair, scrutinizing his friend with a furrowed brow.

"All this fuss for a prude who wouldn't know kindness if it bit her? Damn it, Bucks, I barely recognize you!"

The Duke let out a weary sigh. "Sometimes I don't recognize myself either. God, George, I think I'm losing my mind!" He paced to the window, staring into the bleakness beyond.

"Well, at least you won't have far to go," Ballard replied, his tone devoid of sympathy. "How a man of your age and experience can risk himself for a chase that—"

The Duke spun around, cutting him off sharply.

"A chase! That's the cursed word. A chase that drives me mad because I can never catch up."

"Not a bad line for you," Ballard observed.

Ballard shook his head, his eyes narrowing. "But remember, 'they fly that wound, and they pursue that die.'"

Buckingham rambled on, his voice suddenly taking on an edge of desperation. "I have a hunter's instinct, I suppose. The prey that slips through my fingers is the one I must, at any cost, conquer. Can't you see that?"

"No, thank God! I still have my sanity. Come to the countryside, man, and find yours. It's waiting there for you, among the buttercups."

"Pshaw!" Buckingham turned away with an agitated shrug.

"So that's your answer?"

"It is. Don't let me keep you."

Ballard stood up and placed a hand on Buckingham's arm.

"If you stay here, especially now, you must have some solid plan. What is it?"

"What was in my mind before you came to muddle it, George. To end this where I should have started." And he muttered a few lines, twisting them to fit his mood:

"If she won't love me willingly, I'll make her, The devil take her!"

Ballard sighed, a mix of despair and disgust churning inside him.

"You're not just mad, Bucks," he said. "You're crass. I warned you once about the dangers of this obsession. I won't bother repeating myself. But I can't help but be amazed that you find satisfaction in…"

"Marvel all you want," Buckingham cut him off sharply. "Maybe I am a marvel, after all. I'm a man tormented, consumed, burnt to the core by my feelings for this woman who's laughed at me, dismissed me, made a fool of me. If I could believe in her virtue, I'd walk away, accept her stubborn rejection. But virtue in an actress? It's as likely as snow in hell."

She indulges in a twisted thrill, tormenting a man who's clearly wasting away from his love for her." He paused, as if gathering the storm within him, his face blanching with the intense emotional cocktail of love and hatred that so often brews from thwarted desire. "I could rip that woman apart with my bare hands, and revel in it. God help me, I could! Or just as easily, I could throw myself on the rack for the sake of her twisted pleasure! Her tricks have driven me to this miserable state."

He stormed off, throwing himself into a chair with petulant force, burying his blond head in his finely adorned hands. After that eruption, Mr. Ballard concluded that nothing could be done with such a man except to abandon him to his fate. He said as much, with disarming honesty, and took his leave. His grace made no effort to stop him, sitting alone in that dim, book-filled room, a fool ensnared by wisdom and learning. Brooding over the matter, his frustration only mounted with Bates's desertion, leaving him without an accomplice to carry out his designs.

His stewing was disrupted by the entrance of a footman, announcing that a Colonel Dempsey was demanding an audience. Exasperated, Buckingham nearly dismissed the interruption out of hand.

"Tell him…" He paused, recalling the urgent letter from three days prior. An idea sparked, igniting a shift in his demeanor. "Wait!" He licked his lips, eyes narrowing as his mind worked rapidly. The gloom lifted, replaced by the glint of calculation. Abruptly, he stood. "Bring him in," he commanded.

Dempsey walked in, his posture still upright and disciplined, his clothes holding up decently, but his face told a different story. The long, exhausting day spent dodging through Wapping and Guildhall left him looking haunted.

"I hope you can forgive my persistence," he started, his voice shaky. "But what was urgent when I wrote to you has now become desperate."

Buckingham studied him, eyes piercing from beneath heavy brows, but didn't say a word. He waved off the waiting footman and motioned to a chair. Dempsey collapsed into it, every muscle relieved. The Duke stayed standing, arms crossed, fingers tapping a thoughtful rhythm against his robe's belt.

"I got your letter," Buckingham said, his voice slow and calm. "You might've thought my silence meant I'd forgotten you. Not so. But you must realize—helping you isn't exactly easy."

"Less so now," Dempsey replied, grimacing.

"Oh?" There was a spark in the Duke's eyes, as if he was anticipating this. Dempsey didn't hold back the details.

"And so," Dempsey concluded, "now I'm not just on the edge of starvation, but also facing the noose."

The Duke hadn't flinched during Dempsey's tale. Now he seemed to finally process it, turning away in a slow, contemplative walk.

"What a reckless move," he finally said, "for a man in your situation to get involved, however slightly, with those miserable Fifth-Monarchy men. You've practically tied a noose around your own neck."

"But there was no harm in our connection. McCormick was an old comrade. You've been a soldier, you understand. He did try to tempt me with his plans, I admit that now—it can't hurt him anymore."

But those proposals? I refused them outright."

The Duke smirked slightly. "Do you think the Justices will believe you when you tell them that?"

"Given that I'm Randal Dempsey and we have a government eager to hang my father's son over any excuse, no, I don't. That's why my situation is so dire. I'm a man living under the shadow of the gallows."

"Shh, shh," the Duke chided softly. "Let's not use such language, Colonel. Your tone reeks of disloyalty. And you're being unreasonable. If you were truly loyal, there was a clear duty you wouldn't have neglected. As soon as this proposal landed at your feet, no matter your friendship with McCormick, you should have gone straight to the Justices and reported this plot."

"Your grace suggests something you wouldn't have done yourself. But even if I had taken that action, how could I have made them believe me? I knew nothing concrete about the plot. I had no evidence. It would have been my word against McCormick's, and my name alone would have discredited me. My attempt might have been seen as a brazen move to curry favor with those in power. They might even have twisted it against me in some convoluted legal fashion. So I kept quiet."

"Your word is enough for me," the Duke said kindly. "And God knows I see your predicament, how you've been dragged into this peril. Our first priority is to get you out of it. You need to do what should have been done long ago. Go to the Justices and tell them the story just as you told me."

"But your grace, you just said they won't believe me."

The Duke paused, a small, sly smile creeping onto his face.

"They won't believe you without evidence."

"If someone of prominence and power vouched for your integrity, they'd hardly dare question it. That would settle everything, no more chance of any accusations," said the Duke, his voice a mix of authority and reassurance.

Dempsey's eyes widened with a surge of cautious hope. "Your grace... are you saying you'd do that for me?"

The Duke's smile grew warmer, almost paternal. "Of course, my friend. If I plan to employ you, as I intend, this is a necessary first step."

"Your grace!" Dempsey leaped to his feet, overwhelmed. "How can I ever thank you?"

The Duke motioned for him to sit back down. "I'll show you soon enough, my friend. But understand, there are conditions—tasks you must undertake."

"Anything, your grace. Just name it."

The Duke paused, a hint of satisfaction in his gaze. "You mentioned in your letter that you're ready for any work, any service."

"Yes, I did. And I stand by it."

"Good." The Duke exhaled, a sound of relief trailing his words. He paced towards the book-lined walls, as if seeking wisdom from their spines before turning back to face Dempsey. "We're both desperate, though for different reasons. Each of us has what the other needs."

"If only I could believe that!"

"You should. The rest is up to you." He paused briefly, adding with a touch of irony, "I'm not sure how much of your honesty and scruples have survived your hardships."

"Not enough for you to worry about," Dempsey replied, a hint of bitterness in his words.

"That's reassuring. But be warned, the task might be... distasteful."

"I doubt it. Frankly, I'm not picky these days. But if it does bother me, I'll let you know."

"Fair enough." The Duke nodded, then, perhaps sensing his own reluctance to share his true intentions, his tone suddenly grew steely.

It was almost as if he were a grand lord addressing his servant. "That's why I'm warning you. If you've got something to say, spit it out without any unnecessary theatrics or bravado. You don't need to play the part of a brash hero or a blustering rogue. Just say 'No,' and spare me the melodrama."

Dempsey stared at the man, speechless for a moment, stunned by his audacity. Then he let out a short, bitter laugh.

"Shocking though it may be, I'm not sure I've got any virtue left to be outraged."

"All the better," snapped the Duke. He pulled up a chair and sat down opposite Dempsey, leaning in close. "Over the years, you must've played a lot of roles, Colonel Dempsey?"

"Yeah, a good many."

"Ever played Sir Pandarus of Troy?"

The Duke studied Dempsey's face intently, searching for any flicker of recognition. But the Colonel's education had its gaps.

"Never heard of him. What sort of role is that?"

The Duke sidestepped the question, steering the conversation in another direction.

"Do you know Sylvia Shallmont?"

Dempsey's eyebrows shot up in surprise. It took him a beat to respond.

"Sylvia Shallmont?" he repeated, thinking hard. "Oh, right. She's the one you saved from that mess in Paul's Yard the day we met. Yeah, I remember the name now. An actress from the Duke's House, if I recall correctly. But what's she got to do with us?"

"She's got everything to do with us, unless the stars have it wrong. And they don't. The stars are unwavering and true, even in a world filled with lies and fickleness. It's written in them, as I told you before, that you and I were destined to meet again, tied together in some fateful matter with her."

"My friend, that woman is Sylvia Shallmont," he declared, finally dropping all pretense. His usually composed voice now trembled with raw emotion.

"Look at me, Colonel. I'm a man who wields immense power, shaping destinies for better or worse. Yet there are precious few things I can't command, and Sylvia Shallmont is one of them. She toys with me, flaunting a veneer of innocence, driving me mad. That's why I need your help."

He stopped, watching the Colonel carefully. The man's eyes widened, and a faint blush crept onto his weathered cheeks. When he finally spoke, his voice was icy and calm.

"You haven't said enough, Your Grace."

"Imbecile! What more needs to be said? Can't you see I'm desperate to end this torment? I need to break through the façade of respectability this capricious woman puts up."

"Trust me, I get it," Dempsey chuckled dryly. "What I don't get is where I fit into this sordid scheme. Be clear with me."

"Clear? I want you to abduct her for me," the Duke replied with a sudden, chilling simplicity.

They stared at each other in tense silence, the Colonel's face stoic and unreadable. The Duke searched his expression, trying to gauge his response. Eventually, a sardonic smile crept over the Colonel's lips, and he spoke with a tone laced in mild mockery.

"Surely, with your vast experience, you're more equipped for this than I am."

The Duke, oblivious to the sarcasm, nodded eagerly. "My experience will guide you."

"I see," said Dempsey, understanding the gravity of his words.

"I'll give you the specifics," the Duke continued, leaning closer. "There's a well-furnished house on Knight Ryder Street that you need to secure in your name."

And with that, the Duke laid out his devious plan, his voice thick with anticipation and the desperate need for conquest, as the candlelight flickered ominously around them.

Having received the orders, he was to set everything up to bring the girl to the designated place on the evening of next Saturday, right after the last show at the Duke's House.

"Take as many men as you need," the Duke said, "it should be simple to ambush and capture her as she's being carried home. We'll go into the details if you're willing to accept this task."

The Colonel's face burned red. He felt a surge of bile rising, a molten wave of fury. Finally, his anger took over, and he stood up to confront the handsome wastrel who dared propose such a scheme in cold blood.

"My God!" he growled. "Do you let your vices lead you like a blind man follows his dog?"

The Duke retreated a step, startled by the sudden menace in Dempsey's voice and bearing. Almost immediately, he cloaked himself in arrogance.

"I warned you, sir, I won't tolerate theatrics. No one plays the hero with me. You asked for a way to serve me. I've shown you how."

"Service?" Dempsey echoed, his voice almost strangled by his rage. "Is this a job for a gentleman?"

"Perhaps not. But a man with the hangman's noose hanging over his head shouldn't be too picky."

The color drained from the Colonel's face; a familiar dread haunted his eyes. The Duke, seeing him suddenly struck by that grim reminder, burst into cruel laughter.

"It seems you need to understand, Colonel Dempsey, that there's no music without tension. You balk at a minor task even when I'm offering to make your fortune in return. Yes, that's what I'm offering. You need my help as much as I need yours. Serve me as I ask, and I assure you, I won't forget it."

"But this... this... is something for thugs, for scavengers," Dempsey stammered.

The Duke shrugged. "Damn it, why split hairs?" Then his tone shifted again. "The choice is yours. Fortune presents you with an offer: gold on one hand; a noose on the other."

"I'm not pushing you either way," the Duke said, his voice as sharp as a well-honed blade.

Dempsey stood there, torn between fear and some vestige of honor that clung to his tattered soul. In his mind's eye, he already felt the coarse rope around his neck, imagining his wasted life finding its grim conclusion in the gallows of Tyburn. Fear urged him to comply, to save his wretched skin. But old ideas of honor, gossamer-thin though they were, still whispered to him, reminding him of the ambitions that once burned so brightly within his heart.

His mind summoned an image of Nancy Russell, as beautiful and pure as he'd last seen her, framed by her window, her eyes filled with the kind of light that could drive the darkness from any man. The thought of that face twisted in horror at the sight of him, a man reduced to a loathsome task, gnawed at his resolve. He'd ventured out into the cruel world with dreams of conquering it for her, and many times her image had saved him from the temptations that crawled like worms through his mind.

"I'll find my own path," he said, his voice heavy with the weight of choices. He turned, almost ready to leave.

"Do you know where that path leads?" The Duke's voice was a chilling whisper.

"I don't give a damn," Dempsey replied.

"As you wish."

Dempsey bowed his head in silence, defeat etched in every line of his face. He trudged toward the door, each step a loud echo of his dying hope. Just as he reached for the handle, the Duke's voice stopped him cold.

"Dempsey, you're a fool."

"I've known that for a long time. I was a fool when I saved your life, and you pay me like one," Dempsey snarled, bitterness creeping into his tone.

"You're paying yourself. And you're doing it with the currency of a fool's pride."

Dempsey halted, his feet rooted to the spot, hesitation warring within him. The Duke, sensing the fragile state of his resolve, moved closer. Desperation glimmered in the Duke's eyes—a desperation as keen as the edge of a knife. Dempsey's unexpected presence had been a divine stroke of luck, and finding another man to serve his purpose seemed an impossible task.

In a rare display of camaraderie, the Duke laid a hand on Dempsey's shoulder.

Dempsey, almost shrinking under that touch, couldn't have imagined that this Duke, eager to turn him into a pawn, was himself but a blind instrument of Fate, carving a path to her mysterious ends. As the Duke spoke with persuasive charm, dangling promises like glittering bait and weaving threats of grim consequences, the Colonel's tormented mind churned. Were his hands truly so clean, his life so faultless, that he couldn't stomach this villainy even if it meant they'd stretch his neck and gut him rather than comply? And what, after all, did this villainy comprise? A baggage from the theater, a mere plaything of an actress, who had toyed with the Duke, seeking to squeeze more profits from him. The Duke, weary of her schemes, wanted to end the game abruptly. That was how the Duke painted the picture. And why should Dempsey doubt its accuracy? The girl was an actress, and therefore, naturally wanton. The puritanical disdain for the theatre and its denizens, a relic from his Commonwealth days, left him no question there. If she were a lady of quality, a woman of virtue, things would be different. Then, indeed, to partake in such an act would be unthinkable wickedness, something he'd rather face death over. But here, where was the vileness, truly? What was the real offense? Against himself, against his soldier's dignity. The task asked of him was befitting a hired thug. It was ignoble. But was hanging any less ignoble? Should he let them wrap a noose around his neck and tarnish his name out of compassion for a theater baggage he didn't even know? The Duke's logic cut deep; he was right. Dempsey was a fool. All his life, he had been a fool, scrupulous in trifles, negligent in greater matters.

And now, driven by the most insignificant reason, he was ready to stake his life. Suddenly, he turned and looked the Duke directly in the eye.

"Your grace," he rasped, "I am your man."

Chapter Sixteen

His Grace behaved with a blend of generosity and cunning that showcased the sharp mind of a man who might have been truly great if not for his indulgences. Early the next morning, he appeared with Dempsey before the Justices, confidently stating he could personally vouch for the truth of Colonel Dempsey's interactions with the discredited McCormick. His Grace went further, declaring his willingness to stand surety for this man he now considered a friend. That was all it took. The sycophantic court, ever so eager to impress this notable gentleman who enjoyed the king's close friendship, readily accepted Buckingham's testimony. They even went so far as to express regret that baseless and malicious accusations had led them to disturb Colonel Dempsey's peace and inconvenience His Grace.

Without Buckingham's protection, the Colonel's dubious past would have surely spelled disaster. Yet, the matter was not even touched upon. It wasn't unreasonable. Had Colonel Dempsey's suspected offense been anything less than treason, the Duke might not have carried such authority. But it was unthinkable that His Grace of Buckingham, loyal to the core, whose life testified to his devotion to the House of Stuart and who was a known intimate of His Majesty, would vouch for anyone under a shadow of disloyalty.

Thus, Dempsey was delivered from his gravest peril. The relief on his face was palpable as he learned that, owing to his father's reputation, serving in England with distinction was unlikely. However, Buckingham would provide him with letters of introduction to several high-ranking friends in France, where a capable soldier with the right endorsements would find ample opportunities.

Colonel Dempsey knew that if he seized this chance, his future would be secure, and his days of hardship would be over. He understood this perfectly, and the thought smothered any lingering guilt about the dubious task at hand. He convinced himself that he would be a fool to let any sentimental nonsense rob him of the biggest opportunity of his life.

In his decision to ship Dempsey out of England once the job was done, Buckingham showed his shrewdness. He went a step further by assigning four of his French henchmen to assist the Colonel. Buckingham planned to send them all back to France with Dempsey as soon as their task was completed. This way, if any legal trouble arose, he would have eliminated the only witnesses. The only testimony left would be that of Miss Shallmont, and in Buckingham's eyes, the chance of her not accepting the situation was slim. Even if she did cause a stir, he wasn't worried about handling the accusations of an actress. He could easily counter those claims.

After facing the Justices, Colonel Dempsey headed straight to Fenchurch Street to finalize the lease for a house on Knight Ryder Street. He secured the property under his own name for a year. The merchant, who couldn't hide his surprise, thought Dempsey was insane to want to live in an infected city that everyone else was scrambling to leave.

The Colonel didn't need a reminder, but life had a way of offering one anyway. He was forced to walk, not just because hackney-coaches had become scarce, but because using them was an invitation for trouble now. So many had been ridden by the infected. Doors marked with the red cross and watched over by grim-faced sentries were becoming as common as street lamps, and the few souls who still braved the avenues moved with the weariness of despair or the haunted alertness of prey.

The air was thick with the cloying scents of medicines and camphor, a wretched olfactory cocktail that clung to every man he passed. It might've crossed his mind again—how Buckingham, driven by his blinding passion like a blind man led by his dog, shoved himself headlong into the City at such a perilous time. The Colonel likely took some grim satisfaction in knowing that, soon enough, he'd be kicking the poisonous dust of London from his boots.

With business wrapped up with the merchant, the Colonel marched on to take possession of the house. There, he stationed two of the four French lackeys that the Duke had lent him. They were to be his enforcers. After that, it was just a matter of waiting until Saturday. The Duke had given solid reasons for the delay, so the Colonel bided his time.

But nights were long, and so, on the following evenings, he haunted Lincoln's Inn, keeping a shadowy vigil over Miss Shallmont's exit from the theatre. From a safe distance, he observed her patterns. Both evenings, she emerged at the exact same time, just after seven, sliding into her waiting sedan chair, which then spirited her away.

On Friday evening, Dempsey showed up again at six, taking his post early. An eternity passed before her usual chair appeared, carried by the same two men. Dempsey sauntered forward, ready to strike up a conversation.

Despite the sweltering heat, he deliberately cloaked himself in a scuffed leather jerkin, masking the decent coat underneath. Gone was the feather from his hat, along with any trinkets or finery, replaced by a plain leather baldric. His old boots added to the carefully crafted look of a down-on-his-luck drifter, one who could befriend anyone at a moment's notice. He shuffled towards the chairmen, puffing on a clay pipe, exuding the aura of a man with all the time in the world. The chairmen, perched on either side of the chair's shafts for balance, welcomed the diversion his appearance hinted at. They craved an end to their boredom, and he did not disappoint.

He chatted about the plague, the war, and the Court's favoritism that handed out commands to inept fops, while seasoned soldiers like him wasted away in London's disease-ridden streets. The more he talked, the more ridiculous he seemed, making them laugh and mock him covertly, relishing the amusement at his expense. His inflated sense of self-importance made him oblivious to their mockery.

Eventually, he offered to treat them to drinks, and they eagerly accepted, hoping to squeeze every bit of enjoyment—and expense—out of his offer. They suggested heading to The Grange, a pricier spot, but he had his own reasons for preferring the modest alehouse at the corner of Portugal Row. So, he led his newly minted friends and guests to his chosen haunt.

When they finally parted ways, driven by the need to return to their post by seven, it was with many loud proclamations of friendship from Dempsey. He swore he would visit them again soon, a vow both genuine and steeped in the theatrics of the evening.

They were his kind of people, he assured them. They laughed and agreed, and as they made their way back to the theater, they chuckled about how they tricked that silly pigeon and praised themselves for their wit and cleverness. Their laughter might have faltered if they'd seen the cunning smile curling the lips of that supposedly foolish man as he walked away from their cheerful encounter.

The following evening, a Saturday, found him there again at the same hour, greeted by Miss Shallmont's chairmen with a blend of mockery and welcome that bordered on insolence.

"Good evening, Sir John," called one, and "Good evening, my lord," chimed the other. The Colonel, his steps unsteady and his swagger exaggerated, as though mildly intoxicated, planted his feet wide apart and looked at the two men with an owlish gaze.

"I am not Sir John, nor am I your lord," he corrected them, drawing more laughter. "Though, mind you," he added, more seriously, "I might be both if I had my just deserts. There are many a Whitehall pimp who bears the title of lord with far less claim to it than I do. Yes, far less."

"Any fool can see that by looking at you," said Timothy.

"Any fool," echoed Nathaniel, his tone laced with sarcasm. The Colonel chose to interpret their words in a way that flattered him.

"You're good fellows," he praised them. "Very good fellows." Then, abruptly, he asked, "How about a cup of sack?"

Their eyes lit up. Ale would have been more than welcome, but sack—that was a nobleman's drink, a rare luxury for them. They exchanged glances.

"What do you say, Timothy?"

"A little drink never hurt anyone, Nat," replied the other.

"Indeed, it won't," Nat agreed. "And there's plenty of time tonight. Her ladyship will be busy packing for a while."

The two men took the Colonel between them, and with arms linked, the three of them set off toward the small alehouse at the corner of Portugal Row.

The Colonel was more talkative than ever, spilling his secrets with a grin that made his eyes twinkle like a cat's in the dark. He'd bumped into an old buddy, some war comrade who'd recently struck it rich, and had managed to squeeze a hefty loan out of him. He confessed with a chuckle that it would be quite a stretch before he would be completely sober again. And oh, how he admired them both—fine fellows, he said, lively company during these unbearably dull days in town, as boring as a monastery, swearing he wouldn't part from them without a fight. They staggered into the alehouse, led by the Colonel's steady hand to a quiet corner far from windows and the prying eyes of daylight. He banged the table with the hilt of his sword and bellowed for the landlady, his voice slurred but insistent.

"Three pints of Canary, laced with a stiff shot of brandy."

The landlady, silenced by his loud demand, quickly sprung into action. The Colonel pulled up a rickety stool, planting himself firmly in front of his companions who sat there, licking their lips in eager anticipation.

"It's not every day you meet an old soldier not only lucky, but willing to share his luck. Bring the wine, lady! And make it your best."

"Well said, old warhound!" Nat chimed in, and they both dissolved into boisterous laughter. When the wine arrived, their delight knew no bounds. They gulped it down hungrily, smacking their lips and rolling their eyes in delight, even laying off their usual mockery of the one who'd supplied such a treasure. When he suggested another round, they became almost somber; when he ordered a third, they nearly had a mood shift to real respect. The Colonel sat back, swaying just a bit on his unsteady stool, eyes vacant and distant.

"Why... why're you staring at me like that?" he challenged, voice suddenly taut with a hint of menace. They glanced up from their refilled but untouched glasses. His demeanor had changed, with a hardness to it now. "Maybe you think I can't... pay for all this booze?"

A cold fear crept up their spines.

He seemed to catch it in their eyes.

"Why, you bunch of scoundrels, do you dare... doubt... a gentleman? Do you think a gentleman asks for wine and can't pay? Here's something to put your filthy minds at ease."

He yanked a hand out of his pocket and violently thrust it forward under their noses, his fingers unfurling. Gold coins tumbled out, a handful of them clattering across the grimy table and the even grimier floor. In an instant, the two of them dived after the coins, crawling on hands and knees around the table legs, scavenging for the scattered money. When they finally emerged, each laid two coins before the Colonel with exaggerated courtesy.

"Sir, you should be more careful with your gold," said Timothy.

"You might've lost a piece or two," added Nat.

"In some circles, I might," replied the Colonel, his expression sagely. "But I know honest men when I see them; I know how to choose my friends. Trust a fortune hunter for that." He picked up the coins with clumsy, fumbling fingers. "I thank you," he said, slipping them back into his pocket. Timothy winked at Nat, who hid his grin in his tankard to keep the Colonel from seeing it. The pair was enjoying a very pleasant—and profitable—night with this wandering, thirsty braggart.

They drank noisily. Timothy smacked his lips with each swig, frowning slightly as he savored the taste.

"I don't think it's as good as the last one," he complained. The Colonel took a careful sip from his own tankard.

"I've had better," he bragged. "But it's good enough, and just the same as the last. Just the same."

"Maybe it's just my imagination," said Timothy, nodding at his companion. The Colonel then launched into a loud, boastful monologue. The landlady, who was starting to dislike the look of them, came closer. The Colonel beckoned her even nearer and pressed a gold coin into her hand.

"That should cover the bill," he said, grandly.

She stared in astonishment at the extravagance, curtsied, and withdrew, musing on how deceiving appearances could be. The Colonel resumed his monologue, and whether it was from the numbing dullness of his prattle or the strength of the drinks, Timothy's eyelids began to droop with exhaustion. Nat wasn't far behind. Giving in to the heavy, drowsy feeling that engulfed him, Timothy crossed his arms on the table and rested his head on them.

Seeing this, his companion grew uneasy and leaned over to shake him awake.

"Timothy! We've got to get her ladyship home."

"Damn her ladyship," Timothy muttered, already half-asleep. Nat, his vision blurred, glanced helplessly at the Colonel, struggling to form words.

"Too much... drink," he slurred. "Not used... to wine."

He made a half-hearted attempt to stand, failed miserably, and surrendered entirely. He mimicked Timothy, creating a makeshift pillow of his arms on the table, and lowered his head. Within moments, both men were dead to the world. Colonel Dempsey pushed back his stool quietly and stood, contemplating whether he should retrieve the gold coins he knew those scoundrels had stolen from him. Ultimately, he decided against it, deeming it an unnecessary cruelty.

He staggered out of the corner, and the hostess, hearing him move, approached. Taking her arm with one hand, he incredulously pressed another gold piece into her palm with the other. He closed one eye, aiming for a conspiratorial look, and pointed at the two slumbering men.

"Good fellows... friends of mine," he told her. "Very drunk. Not used... to wine. Let them sleep it off."

She grinned, clinging to the additional gold piece. "Indeed, sir, they can sleep as much as they like. You've paid for their stay."

Dempsey scrutinized her thoughtfully. "Good woman. You're a good woman."

He paused, his gaze softening further. "Handsome woman! Let them sleep in peace."

"God bless you," he muttered, his eyes flickering with something dark.

She anticipated a kiss, but he left her disappointed. Letting go of her arm, he staggered away, spun around, and stumbled out onto the street. A little distance down, he halted, swaying slightly as he glanced back to ensure no one was watching. Satisfied, his step transformed—from unsteady to purposeful. He tossed something aside, and the faint tinkle of shattering glass could be heard as the vial landed. It had held the potent narcotic he'd laced into the wine, each drop meant to take his guests down while they clawed at the money he'd spilled.

"Animals," he spat with utter disdain, purging them from his thoughts. The bells of St. Clement's Danes chimed seven as he passed the back door of the theater, where an empty chair awaited Miss Shallmont. Further down the narrow, dimly lit street, two men loitered. From a distance, they could've been mistaken for the very chairmen who snored in the nearby alehouse, their plain liveries and broad-brimmed hats eerily similar. Concealing their faces in shadows, their angles mirrored those of Miss Shallmont's usual bearers. Sauntering with apparent ease, Colonel Dempsey approached them. The street was eerily deserted.

"Is everything set?" he asked, his voice low and measured.

"The theater emptied about ten minutes ago," one of the men replied in clipped, broken English.

"Get into position. You know the story if anyone asks."

They nodded, moving leisurely before adopting their stances beside the theater wall, blending into the backdrop as Miss Shallmont's bearers. The excuse, if questioned, was that Timothy had fallen ill, suspected to be stricken by the plague. Nat, staying with him, had asked these two to stand in for them. Dempsey slipped into a shadowed alcove, positioning himself to surveil the unfolding scene, and settled into his patient vigil.

The vigil stretched on, longer than anyone really wanted. Timothy had rightly noted to his companion that Miss Shallmont wouldn't be in any rush to leave. Being the last night at the Duke's Theatre, she'd have packing to do, and no doubt a string of long goodbyes with the other actors. Several of them had already trickled out of that small door and walked off into the night, but still, there was no sign of Miss Shallmont. Evening shadows were creeping down the street, cloaking everything in a haunting twilight. Colonel Dempsey felt a mixture of impatience and satisfaction. The later she came out, the better; the deed he had in mind thrived in the murk of dusk, maybe even the pitch-black of night.

So he waited, his breath matching the rhythm of Buckingham's two French lackeys, who were still posing as porters. They had a distinct advantage, having seen Miss Shallmont up close twice before—once at Wallingford House and again during her staged rescue in Paul's Yard.

Finally, at around half-past eight, when the streetlights cast long, eerie shadows and the shapes of people and buildings blurred into one another, she appeared. Miss Shallmont stepped into view, flanked by Mr. Betterton and the theatre's doorkeeper. She stopped to give the doorkeeper some final instructions about her luggage before Mr. Betterton, ever the gentleman, led her to the waiting sedan chair.

The disguised porters snapped to attention at her arrival. One moved behind the chair, lifting its hinged roof to cloak himself in shadow. The other tried to blend into the body of the chair from the front. Miss Shallmont wrapped her cloak tightly around herself and stepped into the sedan. Betterton bowed deeply, kissing her hand in a final, overly dramatic farewell. As he stepped back, one of the porters closed the sedan's apron while the other lowered the roof. They positioned themselves, lifted the chair, and started down the street. Inside, Miss Shallmont waved daintily through the window at Mr. Betterton, her delicate hand a ghostly silhouette in the dim light.

Betterton, who stood bowing, his head exposed to the chilling evening air, had a presence that demanded attention.

CHAPTER SEVENTEEN

The carriage swung past the eerie wooden structure of Temple Bar and down Fleet Street, the summer evening casting long, dark shadows along the cobblestones. This being the usual route, nothing seemed out of the ordinary for the passenger within. But as the bearers were about to veer right into the narrow alley that led to Salisbury Court, a man burst from the inky darkness to block their path. It was Dempsey, who had hurried to get there ahead of them.

"Stop!" he called out, advancing quickly. "You can't pass through here. There's a riot because a house infected with the plague was broken into, and the disease is spreading everywhere. This way is closed."

The bearers halted abruptly. "Which way, then?" the one at the front demanded.

"Where are you headed?" Dempsey asked.

"To Salisbury Court."

"Well, that's where I'm going, too. You'll have to go around by Fleet Ditch, same as me. Follow me." With that, he briskly led the way down Fleet Street. The carriage bearers adjusted their direction and continued. Miss Shallmont had leaned forward as they stopped to catch snippets of the conversation. She hadn't noticed any quarantined houses in the alley earlier in the afternoon. However, given how rapidly the plague was spreading through the city, she didn't doubt the warning. She felt a wave of relief knowing that the theater's closure meant she could retreat to the countryside, far from the choking grip of the pestilence. Resting back with a weary sigh, she resigned herself to the bearers' silent march.

But as they neared the Fleet Ditch, instead of turning right, the bearers plodded straight ahead, following the tall, cloaked figure who had taken the lead. It wasn't until they were halfway across the rickety bridge that Miss Shallmont realized something was amiss. She leaned forward, her voice sharp with tension, "You're going the wrong way!"

They might as well have been statues for all the notice they took of her cries. Unperturbed, they plodded forward, stone-faced and unyielding. Desperation seeped into her voice as she yelled louder, more insistent. Still, they gave no indication they heard her. The bridge was behind them now, and they veered right, towards the river. Miss Shallmont began to rationalize, thinking maybe they knew a shortcut she didn't, something practical driving their actions. She found it odd they ignored her commands but decided to let them proceed, hoping their guide had a purpose. But as they turned left towards Baynard's Castle, her confusion doubled back on itself, spiraling into something akin to panic.

"Stop!" she shouted. "You're going the wrong way. Put the chair down right now! Put it down!"

Her words vanished into the night, ignored. Not only did they ignore her, but their pace quickened, stumbles and all, over the rough cobblestones that seemed to materialize from the darkness itself. Unease blossomed into full-blown fear.

"Nathaniel!" she screamed, leaning forward, desperation clawing at her voice as she tried to grasp a shoulder just beyond her reach. "Nathaniel!"

Panic sharpened her senses. Was this really Nathaniel, or some stranger leading her into God knows what? There was something disturbingly resolute about the way the man plodded on, impervious to her pleas. The tall figure leading them, now barely more than a silhouette, slowed, allowing the chair to catch up. She fought to rise, to push open the chair's roof, to yank the apron free in front of her. Both resisted her efforts, revealing themselves to be locked in place. The realization struck her like a physical blow—this was no oversight. Her fear erupted into frantic screams, piercing the silent street, bouncing off the narrow stone walls.

The leading man stopped, turned slowly, a dark curse slipping from his lips. With an authoritative bark, he commanded the bearers to set the chair down.

But just as he delivered the command, the sudden flare of a torch pierced the shadows at the corner of Paul's Chains. In its flickering yellow glow, the silhouettes of three or four figures appeared, moving with haste. The light and figures hesitated for a moment, drawn by the girl's frantic cries. Then, in an instant, they surged forward, speed increasing, with the clatter of their footfalls echoing through the night.

"Move on! Move on!" Dempsey barked at the chairmen, pushing forward himself. The chair followed, carrying Miss Shallmont, who was now screaming for help, her fists pounding madly on the roof and apron. She had also seen those would-be saviors sprinting towards them, and in the torchlight, she might have caught the menacing gleam of swords drawn for her rescue.

It was a trio of young noblemen, their way lit by a torch-bearing boy as they headed homeward. They were impulsive and ready for a skirmish, their blades drawn to defend a lady in distress. But Dempsey had anticipated this very scenario—his mind always calculating, always prepared for every possible twist.

The leader of the gallants was upon him quickly, his sword aimed at Dempsey's chest, shouting with melodramatic flair:

"Stand, villain!"

"Stand yourself, idiot," Dempsey retorted with an icy indifference, showing no intention of drawing his own blade. "Back off, all of you, if you value your lives! We're taking this poor woman home. She's got the plague."

Their advance halted abruptly—the fear of this unseen, deadly enemy causing them to retreat, jostling one another in their sudden terror. Brave enough against flesh and steel, they were instantly paralyzed by the mere mention of the plague.

Miss Shallmont, her ears catching the Colonel's warning and seeing its chilling effect on her would-be rescuers, leaned forward, her eyes wide with desperation, fearing the trap was closing around her.

"He's lying! He's lying!" she screamed in terror. "It's not true! I don't have the plague! I don't! I swear it! Don't listen to him, please!"

"Don't listen to him! Save me from these monsters. Please, for the love of God... don't leave me here, or I'm a lost woman!"

The men stood there, torn by her desperate pleas but uncertain of where the truth lay. Dempsey stepped forward, his voice somber.

"She's out of her mind, poor thing. She's my wife, gentlemen, and she thinks I'm her enemy. This dreadful disease has taken hold of her." By now, all of London knew that the plague often led to madness and wild delusions as it tightened its grip. "And to be honest, I fear I might be infected too. I beg you, don't hold us up. Let us get home before my strength gives out."

Behind him, Miss Shallmont continued to shriek her frantic denials and pleaded for someone to save her. Even if the men had doubts, they were too terrified to push it further. In her hysteria, her words seemed to confirm Dempsey's story that she had lost her mind. They hesitated a moment longer, caught between doubt and dread. Then, one of them finally gave in to his growing fear.

"Run! Get away!" he shouted, and with a lurch, he bolted down the street. His terror spread like wildfire. The rest followed in a panic, the link-boy trailing behind, his torch casting eerie shadows.

Miss Shallmont fell back with a moan, her energy spent and her hope gone. But when one of the chairmen, following the Colonel's command, pulled open the apron, she sprang up and tried to escape. The other chairman grabbed her slender body, holding her tight while his partner wrapped a long scarf around her head—the same scarf Dempsey had tossed to them.

Once they'd tied her hands behind her with a handkerchief, they shoved her back into the chair and locked her in. She was utterly helpless now, half-choked by the scarf that muffled her screams and blinded her to where she was being taken. The only thing she knew was that the chair was moving—onward, then a sharp left, and up the steep climb of Paul's Chains. Finally, a right turn into Knight Ryder Street signaled the end of the journey.

The chair halted before a substantial house on the north side, nestled between Paul's Chains and Sermon Lane. Hands seized her, yanking her from the chair as she tried to resist, making herself dead weight in a last-ditch effort. Strong arms hoisted her onto a man's shoulder, and she was carried into the house.

Dempsey brought her inside, the chair—now stripped of its poles—soon followed. In the spacious hall where two silent figures stood at attention—Buckingham's other two French lackeys—the

Colonel made a right turn into a dimly lit square room. The room was somber, furnished with dark wood from floor to ceiling. At its center, a table with heavy corkscrew legs was set for supper, gleaming with crystal and silver under the glow of a large candelabrum.

The long window overlooking the street was shut tight, its shutters barred. Beneath it stood a daybed of cane and carved oak, adorned with velvet cushions in a dull wine color. Dempsey carried her to this daybed. He knelt to untie the handkerchief binding her wrists, his actions almost tender—he knew the restraints must have been painful by now.

Under the broad brim of his hat, his face glistened with sweat from the exertion, his lips pressed into a thin line.

Up until now, he'd been laser-focused on executing his plan, barely considering its sinister implications. But as he leaned over the figure—so graceful, so delicate, its faint, sweet perfume enveloping him in a haze of her dainty femininity—he was hit with a wave of disgust so intense, it almost made him physically sick. He turned away, closing the door behind him, tossing aside his hat and cloak, mopping the sweat from his brow that ran down his face like grease dripping from a roasted bird. As he crossed the room, she managed to struggle to her feet. Her hands now free, she frantically tore at the scarf until it slipped from her face, falling in loose folds around her neck and shoulders, accentuating the low cut of her stylish bodice. Upright and defiant, she glared at him, her words lashing out angrily.

"Sir," she demanded, "you will let me go at once, or you shall pay dearly for this wickedness."

He closed the door and turned to face her, trying to mask his anxious demeanor with a forced smile.

"Unless you let me leave immediately, you shall…"

Her voice trailed off abruptly. She leaned forward, her eyes wide with astonishment, her lips parted as if grappling to catch her breath. It seemed amazement had momentarily overpowered her anger and fear. When she finally spoke, her voice was hoarse and tense:

"Who are you? What... what is your name?"

He stared back at her, halting mid-motion as he wiped his brow. He wondered what she saw in him that had so profoundly unsettled her. She stood partially in shadow, while the clustered candles on the table cast a harsh light on his face.

He was still mulling over his response, debating what name to give, when she jolted him, saving him from the need to fabricate anything further.

"You're Randal Dempsey!" she exclaimed in a crazed, strained tone. He took an instinctive step forward, utterly shaken, breathless, some unexpected, horrific emotion ripping at his heart, his eyes wild, his jaw slack, his entire face ashen as a corpse.

"Randal Dempsey!" she repeated in that same agonized voice. "You! Of all people, to do this!"

Her eyes, once just wide with disbelief, began to fill with a growing horror. She mercifully covered her face with her hands. For a moment, he mimicked her action. He, too, buried his face impulsively. The years fell away; the room, set for that infamous dinner, dissolved, replaced in his mind by a blooming cherry orchard, and in that orchard a girl on a swing, teasing yet adorable, singing a song that had once driven him, young, clean, and honorable, to rush to her side. He saw himself as a lad of twenty, setting out into the world with a lady's glove in his hat—a glove he still cherished—determined to conquer the world for her sake, no less, to lay it at her feet. And he saw her—this Sylvia Shallmont of the Duke's Theatre—as she had been in those long-dead days when her name was Nancy Russell. The years had altered her so completely that she was utterly unrecognizable. Where could he find the little girl he had once loved so desperately in this stunning woman? How could he have ever imagined that his sweet Nancy Russell would transform into the magnificent Sylvia Shallmont, whose name had become synonymous with gallantry, extravagance, and excess, whose fame and infamy rivaled that of Moll Davies or Eleanor Gwynn?

He staggered backward, his eyes wide and fixed on the scene before him. His shoulders hit the closed door with a thud, but he barely registered the impact. The horror of it all, the sheer, unrelenting terror, crashed over him in waves, leaving him a shell of a man, unmoored and adrift in a sea of despair.

"God!" he cried out, the word tearing itself from his throat in a broken wail. "My Nan! My little Nan!"

CHAPTER EIGHTEEN

At any other time and in any other place, this meeting would have filled him with a different kind of horror. His soul would have been ravaged by pain and anger to find Nancy Russell, whom he had always imagined to be as unattainable and pure as the stars, dragged down into this abysmal state. To him, she had always been a saintly beacon, guiding him through the murk of vile temptations with her pure, white light. But now, with his own infamous predicament overshadowing everything else, he could think of nothing but his own disgrace. He staggered forward and collapsed to his knees in front of her.

"Nan! Nan!" he gasped, his voice strangled with emotion, "I didn't know. I never dreamed..."

His words confirmed her worst fears, explaining his presence in a way she had been desperately trying to reject despite the overwhelming evidence. She stood before him, a woman of average height with an almost ethereal grace, yet there was something proud, regal, and aloof about her that didn't waver even in this terrible moment of peril and shattering disillusionment. She was dressed entirely in white, save for the blue scarf still draped around her neck and bosom. Her shimmering ivory satin gown was no whiter than her long, oval face. Around her eyes—those long-shaped eyes that could be by turns provocative, mocking, and tender—dark shadows of suffering were gathering, while in their blue-green depths there was only stark horror.

She put a delicate hand to her forehead, brushing aside the modern tendrils of her chestnut hair. Twice she tried to speak, but her stiff lips failed her.

"You didn't know!" Her voice, once a siren call to multitudes, was now harsh and rasping, cutting like a blade into the heart of the kneeling, frantic man. "So, I thought as much. You did this at someone else's bidding. You're so fallen that you play the hired thug now. And you are Randal Dempsey!"

A groan escaped him, and with a wild gesture of despair, he dragged himself closer to her feet on his knees.

"Nan, Nan, don't judge until you've heard, until…"

But she cut him off. His abject manner was an eloquent admission of the worst.

"Heard? Have you not told me everything? You didn't know. You didn't know it was me you were abducting. Do you think I can't guess who the mastermind is behind this? And you didn't know it was I, someone who once loved you when you were clean and honest…."

"Nan! Nan! Oh God!"

"But I never loved you as much as I loathe you now, for what you've become, you who were supposed to conquer the world for me. You didn't know it was me you were paid to kidnap! And you're so shameless, so devoid of honor, that you dare to use ignorance as your excuse. Well, now you know, and I hope the knowledge punishes you. I hope any lingering sense of shame burns your miserable soul to ashes.

Get up," she commanded, her contempt cold and absolute. "Do you think groveling there will fix any of what you've done?"

He sprang to his feet instantly. But it wasn't, as she believed, in obedience to her command. It was a sudden realization—the urgent need for immediate action.

All the agony that threatened to tear his soul apart needed to be locked away. Anything he had to say to maybe ease that agony would have to wait.

"What I've done, I can undo," he said. Forcing himself to stay calm in the face of urgent necessity, his tone suddenly grew firm. "Are we just going to stand here talking while every passing second puts you in more danger? Let's go! Just as I brought you here, defying everything, I'll get you out of here again—right now, while there's still time."

She pulled back when he reached out, his hand poised as if to grab her and drag her away. Her eyes flashed with a sudden fury, and anger curled her lips.

"You're going to carry me away! You! And I'm supposed to trust you?"

Her contempt hit him like a whip, but he didn't flinch, too focused on the urgency of the situation.

"Would you rather stay here and trust Buckingham?" he retorted, his voice fierce. "I'm telling you, come with me," he insisted, his overwhelming concern for her making him oddly commanding.

"With you? No! Never with you! Never!"

He slapped his hands together in a fit of impatience.

"Don't you realize there's no time to lose? If you stay here, you're doomed. Go alone if you must, go back home right now. But since you'll be on foot, and they might come after you soon, let me at least follow you, do whatever I can to keep you safe. Just trust me on this... for your own sake, trust me... In God's name!"

"Trust you?" she echoed, almost laughing. "You? After this?"

"Yes, even after this. Because of this. I might be as vile as you think I am; I probably am. But I've never been vile to you. Maybe saying I didn't know it was you I was acting against doesn't make it right, but it should show you I'm ready to defend you now that I do know."

"You have to believe me! How can you doubt me about something this important? If I didn't mean well, why would I urge you to leave? Come on!"

He grabbed her wrist more firmly this time, ignoring her half-hearted struggle to pull free. He tried to lead her across the room, and for a moment, she resisted.

"For God's sake!" he begged. "Buckingham could show up any second!"

This time, the urgency in his voice broke through the fog of her earlier hesitation. Between the looming dangers, there was no real choice. She looked into his face, twisted with fear and anxiety.

"Can I trust you on this? If I trust you... will you get me home safely? Do you swear it?"

"On my life!" he choked out, desperation clear in his voice. Her resistance melted away, replaced by an urgency that paralleled his own.

"Quick, then! Quick!" she gasped.

He exhaled a sigh of relief, grabbed his hat and cloak from the chair, and pulled her toward the door. Just as they reached it, the door swung open, revealing the towering, elegant figure of the Duke of Buckingham. His blonde curls nearly brushed the top of the doorway, and a feverish anticipation glowed on his handsome face. In his right hand, he held his feathered hat; his left hand rested lightly on the hilt of a slender dress rapier.

The two recoiled, and Dempsey let go of her wrist, sensing he might need both hands for what was coming. The Duke was clad in a dazzling black and white satin outfit, glittering like a dark magpie, with jewels sparkling in the lace at his throat and a blue garter sash across his chest.

For a moment, Buckingham stood frozen, gaze narrowing as he took in the scene—Miss Shallmont's pale, startled beauty and the tense, stern figure of her companion.

He stepped forward cautiously, leaving the door behind him wide open. He bowed deeply to the lady without a word; his eyes met hers for a brief moment before he straightened and addressed the Colonel.

"Everything seems to be in order," he said, gesturing towards the table and the sideboard. Dempsey turned slightly, following his own gesture, as if pondering the supper set-up, using the moment to assess the situation. Outside, just past the open door, Buckingham's four French lackeys were waiting. At a single nod from their master, they'd slit his throat as easily as they'd carve up the glazed capon on the sideboard. He'd faced tighter spots in his adventurous life, but never before had his concern for a woman's safety weighed on him like this, gnawing at his nerves and clouding his judgment. He silently thanked whatever higher power had kept him from immediately challenging Buckingham when he first appeared. Acting on that impulse would have likely resulted in his quick demise. And once he was gone, Nan would be at the Duke's mercy. Suddenly, his own survival seemed crucial. He had to tread carefully. The Duke's impatient voice cut through his thoughts:

"Well, you fool? Are you going to stand there all night?"

Dempsey turned.

"Everything is here, at your grace's disposal," he said calmly.

"Then get out."

Dempsey bowed submissively. He dared not look at Nan, but he heard her sudden intake of breath. Without seeing, he could picture her wide-eyed horror, the scornful gaze she must have directed at him for this apparent display of cowardice. He walked to the door, aware of the Duke's eyes on him, filled with suspicion as if trying to decode the hidden tension in the air. Gripping the edge of the open door, Dempsey half-turned again.

He was still buying himself time to figure out his next move.

"Will you need me for anything else tonight, Your Grace?"

The Duke pondered for a moment. Beyond him, Dempsey caught a glimpse of Nan, wide-eyed and as pale as a ghost, leaning against the table. She pressed her right hand to her chest, trying to calm her racing heart.

"No," the Duke finally said, slowly. "But you should stay close with François and the others."

"Very well," Dempsey replied, and turned to leave. He noticed the key was on the outside of the door. He bent over and took it out of the lock. "Perhaps Your Grace would prefer the key on the inside," he said with a nasty smirk. The Duke, shrugging his indifference, allowed it. Dempsey transferred the key, shut the door quickly, and quietly turned the key in the lock, pocketing it before the Duke could recover from the oddity of his action.

"What's this?" the Duke demanded sharply, stepping toward Dempsey. From Nan came a faint, barely audible cry, a sob signaling the resurgence of hope from the depths of despair.

Dempsey, his back to the door, now wore a grim, determined look. He tossed aside the hat and cloak he had been holding.

"It means, Your Grace, I want a private word with you, safe from the nosy interruptions of your lackeys."

The Duke straightened, looking stern and a bit intrigued by the unfolding events, but fully in control. Fear, as I mentioned, was a foreign concept to him. Had he managed to master himself in other aspects of his life, he could have been the greatest man in England.

He didn't shout, didn't ask pointless questions that might undermine the dignity he believed he had to uphold.

"Go on, sir," he said icily. "Let's hear your excuse for this insolence so we can end it."

"That's easy to explain." Dempsey's tone was equally calm. "This lady, your grace, is an old friend of mine. I didn't realize it until after I brought her here. When I found out, I wanted to take her away, and I was about to do that when you walked in. Now, I need you to promise on your honor that you'll let us leave peacefully and won't interfere, either personally or through your servants."

Buckingham stood still, considering Dempsey from where he stood between him and the girl, his shoulder turned to her. Apart from a slight reddening around his eyes and cheekbones, he showed no emotion. He even smiled, though it was anything but warm.

"How straightforward," he said with a short laugh. "Such endearing simplicity. And how touching the scenario is, how romantic. An old friend, you say. And of course, because of that, the world is supposed to stop." His voice turned steely. "And if I refuse to give my word, what then, Colonel Dempsey?"

"That would be very bad for you, your grace," Dempsey replied.

"Are you threatening me?" Buckingham sounded almost incredulous.

"If you like."

The Duke's demeanor shifted violently. He ripped off his mask of arrogant indifference.

"By God!" he snapped, his voice like a rasp. "That's enough of your insolence, man."

"Unlock that door right now and leave, or I'll call my men to beat you to a pulp," Buckingham demanded.

"It's to save your grace from such extreme measures that I locked the door in the first place," Dempsey replied, his voice smooth and calm. "Before you summon your lackeys, take a good look at the door. It's solid, and the lock is secure. You might call them, but before they even get near, there's a strong chance you'll already be burning in hell."

Buckingham laughed but wasn't one to waste time on empty threats. In a flash, he whipped his rapier from its scabbard and lunged across the room, closing the distance with the precision and swiftness of a seasoned fighter. His movement was designed to catch Dempsey off guard, a fatal strike meant to end the confrontation immediately.

But Dempsey was no novice. He had faced death too many times to be caught so easily. He had seen the calculating glint in the Duke's eyes, recognized the predatory focus. With reflexes honed by countless life-or-death encounters, Dempsey drew his own sword and parried, blocking the Duke's cunning thrust.

Nan's scream pierced the tension-filled air as the two blades clashed. The sound echoed momentarily, giving way to the swift clanging of steel. Dempsey's parry transitioned smoothly into a counterattack aimed at Buckingham's face, forcing the Duke to retreat just as quickly as he had advanced to avoid the deadly riposte.

Both men stood, eyes locked, each knowing the next move could be their last.

Standing tall once more, his grace stepped back, his breathing quickening slightly, and for a moment, the two men stood in silence, their swords lowered, sizing each other up with their eyes. Then Dempsey spoke.

"Your grace, this is a game rigged against you," he said seriously. "You'd be wise to take my earlier suggestion."

Buckingham let out a sneering laugh, completely misunderstanding Dempsey's intent.

"You blustering captain, you pathetic blowhard, think you can scare me with swords and threats? It's you against whom the odds are stacked. Unlock that door and get out, or I'll slice you into ribbons."

"Oh, really? And who's the blustering captain now? Who's the blowhard? Who's the very butcher of fine silk?" Dempsey fired back, anger sharpening his tone. He might have said more, but the Duke cut him off.

"Enough talk!" he snapped. "The key, you rogue, or I'll run you through where you stand."

Dempsey grinned. "I never thought when I saved your life that night at Worcester that I'd be the one to end it."

"Think you can sway me with that memory, do you?" said the Duke, lunging forward.

"Not at all. I'll move you another way, you lovesick fool," Dempsey snarled back. Then their blades clashed once more, locked in deadly combat.

CHAPTER NINETEEN

I doubt any two men ever faced off with more confidence than Dempsey and the Duke of Buckingham. Neither entertained a shadow of doubt about the outcome. Each saw the other as a fool barreling toward certain doom. Dempsey, seasoned in the brutal crucible of real combat, was rusty but still formidable. It hadn't crossed his mind that a man more at home in courtly intrigue would be much of a challenge. On the flip side, the Duke of Buckingham, though not one to boast about it, was likely the finest swordsman in England. His years of adversity and the thrill of desolate escapades had honed a natural talent with the blade. An effortlessly cool presence in danger, with a strong, agile frame and a long reach, the Duke had the edge when other factors matched evenly. To him, this was just an inconvenient delay, something to be brushed aside hastily.

The Duke attacked with vigorous disdain, his contempt making him careless. It was fortunate for him that in those initial moments, Dempsey realized the gravity of killing the Duke could unravel a series of dire consequences. Buckingham's eager lackeys were lurking nearby, ready to engage. After dispatching their master, Dempsey would have to fight his way past them before he could escape with Nancy. His strategy had to be to disarm or incapacitate the Duke and, holding him at his mercy, extract a promise of safe passage, something the Duke wasn't willing to give willingly right now.

In the opening seconds of their clash, Dempsey ignored the gaps in the Duke's defense caused by overconfidence, focusing instead on rendering the Duke's sword arm useless.

Two attempts, sharp and quick, slashed over the Duke's guard on a riposte. Each strike flashed in Buckingham's mind, revealing both the intention and the skill of the swordsman he faced. The Duke, with a calm grace, deflected them effortlessly, causing Dempsey to rethink his strategy. In those first teeming seconds, both men realized the folly of underestimating their adversary. Their mutual respect grew like wildfire, igniting a shift towards a more measured, cautious duel.

From the shadows of a tall armchair, Nancy Russell watched, her face a mask of terror. She had collapsed into the chair, her body trembling, breath coming in shallow, hitching gasps that left her on the verge of hyperventilation. Her pulse thundered in her ears, a frantic drumbeat of fear as she watched the deadly dance unfold before her. The Duke's broad back blocked some of her view, but she had an unflinching line of sight to Dempsey. His face was calm, muscles set in hard lines, and his piercing grey eyes locked unblinkingly on his opponent. There was something almost feral in his crouched, elastic stance, the way his sword moved with fluid precision, a testament to both his skill and the power coiled in his wrist. For a moment, the sheer confidence radiating from him seeped into her bones, dispelling some of the frigid terror freezing her mind.

And then, in a heartbeat, everything shifted. Buckingham exploded to his left in a near leap, lunging with a savage precision aimed at Dempsey's flank. But, like a dancer in mid-pirouette, Dempsey pivot-

ed with fluid grace, rotating to face his attacker head-on. His feet slid
across the ground with a deadly elegance, and he met the incoming
thrust with a poised readiness, eyes locked in a lethal communion with
the Duke's.

Because of the way things had gone, she could now see both of
them in profile. Only now, when it was too late, did she realize the
chance she had missed to fight back. She could have, should have done
something while the Duke had his unprotected back to her. If she had
been anything other than the numbed, dazed, witless creature she felt
she was, she would have grabbed a knife from the table and plunged it
between his shoulder blades. Maybe it was a sense of that danger, the
fighter's instinctive dread of an unguarded back, that had driven the
Duke to move as he had. He repeated the maneuver again and again,
making Dempsey spin to face the constantly changing attacks, until
finally, the Duke had maneuvered himself so the door was behind him,
with Dempsey and the girl in front.

The sounds of combat filled the locked room—the scuffling of feet,
the clashing of blades—and had drawn the attention of the men in the
hallway outside. There came vigorous knocking on the door, accompanied by voices. The noise was a welcome relief to Buckingham, as he
hadn't anticipated that his opponent would be so hard to deal with.
Despite his fearlessness, he was starting to realize this duel was no walk
in the park. This rascal Dempsey was unusually strong.

"Help me! François, Antoine! Help!" Buckingham yelled.

"Monseigneur!" François's voice wailed from the other side of the
heavy oak door, thick with panic.

"Break down the door!" Buckingham shouted back. Heavy blows
rained on the door in response, followed by silence and the shuffling
of feet, indicating the men were leaning their weight into it. But the
stout timbers resisted these crude attempts. Their footsteps retreated,

and a tense silence settled, clear in meaning to both combatants. The grooms had gone to fetch tools to break down the door.

The Colonel realized with a sinking heart that his hopes of disarming the Duke were fading fast, the task proving nearly impossible. He steeled himself, knowing he had only one choice left: to kill Buckingham before the grooms could break through the door, or everything would be lost. He knew that Buckingham's men or the law would likely claim him afterward, but at least Nancy would be saved from her tormentor. Brimming with fierce determination, he switched his approach. No longer focused on wearing the Duke down, he launched a relentless, aggressive attack.

His maneuvers became a blur of lightning-fast moves, his blade striking with deadly precision, forcing the Duke to retreat. Soon, Buckingham was stepping back, wary of positioning himself against the door, fearful of being trapped there by the Colonel's relentless blade. It was a flicker of fear, a fleeting but telling sign that even Buckingham craved an escape route, a glimpse of space behind him to retreat if needed.

Until now, Dempsey had fought with a calculated, almost methodical precision, just enough to achieve his goal. But now, with that goal shifting, and realizing that brute speed and strength weren't enough to breach the Duke's iron-clad defense, he drew from deeper reservoirs of cunning. There was a trick, a lethal move he had learned from an Italian master years ago—a vagabond soldier who had drifted into mercenary service with the Dutch, much like Dempsey himself. It was time to use it.

Side-stepping to his left, Dempsey lunged with a controlled fierceness, his blade arching towards the Duke's throat in a high tierce. The move wasn't meant to strike true, but to force Buckingham into a desperate parry. A feint, a deadly twist, setting the stage for the final, fatal strike.

Without meeting the opposing blade as it shifted to the threatened line, Dempsey dropped his point and his body simultaneously, until he was supported, at the maximum stretch, by his left hand on the ground. With a swift movement, he whirled his point upward under the Duke's guard. As Dempsey had calculated, the Duke was carried just a bit too far around in the speed required, leaving his left flank dangerously exposed. The Duke saw the blade coming straight for his heart. He was barely in time to swipe it aside with his left hand, and even then, it ripped through the sleeve of his doublet and slashed his flesh just above the elbow. But for that wound, it might very well have been the end for Dempsey.

This trick of his was high-risk—either it succeeded or it left him utterly vulnerable. That moment of vulnerability was there, but it vanished as quickly as it appeared, just before the Duke could capitalize on it. The Duke's recovery and downward-driven riposte were swift, but missed by mere milliseconds. Dempsey was no longer there to be skewered.

They stood, eyes locked, grim smiles creeping across their faces, pausing for a heartbeat after their mutual brush with death. Then, a succession of heavy blows pounded against the door, and Dempsey launched at the Duke with renewed ferocity. From the sound of the pounding blows, it seemed the grooms had found an axe and were intent on breaking through the lock. Dempsey realized there was no time to lose. The Duke, on the other hand, understood that his hope lay in stalling, letting Dempsey's frenzied attacks exhaust themselves against his defense.

Twice more, despite his bleeding wound, the Duke used his left hand—blood dripping freely—to parry Dempsey's strikes. Once, he managed it without getting hurt. The clock was ticking, and both men knew it.

But when Dempsey repeated the move, he seized the opportunity, thrusting himself forward into the Duke's space until their chests pressed close. With a swift grip, his left hand clamped around the Duke's sword wrist, freezing it in place. Before Dempsey could pull his own sword for the killing blow, the Duke's blood-slick hand latched onto his wrist. He tried to wrench free, but the Duke held on with a death grip, knowing that letting go meant his imminent end.

Locked in this brutal embrace, they twisted and swayed, their breaths ragged and growling. The door behind them shuddered under heavy blows, a panel splintering. Across the room, Nancy sat slumped in her chair, watching the savage struggle with wide eyes clouded by terror, barely processing the nightmare unfolding before her.

The two men crashed into the daybed by the window, the Duke falling back onto it, still clutching Dempsey's wrist. Dempsey drove his knee into the Duke's stomach, desperate for the upper hand. The Duke's fingers began to loosen from the strain, inch by inch.

Then, with a final, resounding crack, the door burst apart. The lock gave way and the Duke's grooms poured into the room, racing to their master's aid. Dempsey managed to wrench free his wrist, but it was too little, too late. He threw the Duke's sword hand away and spun around, a guttural sob escaping his throat as he faced the incoming servants. His sword point gleamed menacingly for a fleeting moment before a club smashed into it, shattering the blade and driving the lackeys into a frenzy.

Dempsey lashed out, the hilt of his broken sword connecting with one attacker's skull, dropping him. But another club came down hard on Dempsey's head, sending him staggering against the table. His legs gave out, and he crumpled to the floor in a limp, unconscious heap.

As he lay there, one of the grooms looming over him swung his club with the clear intent to crush his skull. But the Duke halted the descending blow.

"That's enough," the Duke said, his voice low and steady despite the adrenaline surging through him. His face was pale, his breathing labored, and a feverish gleam danced in his eyes, but he still had a tight grip on his composure.

"Your arm, Duke!" cried François, pointing at the blood seeping through his sleeve.

"Just a scratch. I'll deal with it later." He then motioned to the limp figure of Dempsey, blood slowly leaking from his head. "Get a rope, François, and tie him up." François hurried off. "The rest of you, carry Antoine out. Then come back for Bobadil. I might still need him."

The men snapped to action, hefting the fallen Antoine whom Dempsey had knocked out before getting taken down himself. The Duke watched them with a severe frown, dissatisfied. They had almost been too late. To voice this would require an admission of vulnerability he was unwilling to make.

They filed out without protest, and Buckingham, still ghostly pale but with his breathing now more even, turned to Nancy with a strange little smile on lips that now seemed drained of their usual color.

CHAPTER TWENTY

She had reached that edge where sheer endurance numbs you to the core. Slumped in the chair, head pressed against the high back, eyes shut tight, she was suffused with a deep, sickly nausea. But when the Duke's voice, soft yet sinister, broke through, she forced her heavy blue eyes open. They were stained with the kind of pain only misery could etch into them. There he stood, the handsome, twisted figure of a man, his posture all false reverence.

"Dear Sylvia," he began, his voice a careful melody of regret, "I am deeply sorry that you had to witness such an abhorrent spectacle. It was never my intention."

She replied almost mechanically, but her words were sharp, true to her fierce nature. Even in this pitiful state, she couldn't help but deliver a touch of drama.

"That, sir, I believe."

He studied her, a flicker of surprise in his eyes catching that spark of defiance from one so worn down. If anything, it just fueled his twisted admiration for her. He sighed deeply, a weary lover.

"Ah, Sylvia, forgive me for the lengths to which my love has driven me, and this latest foul act with that blustering fool and the chaos it's caused. Try not to think too harshly of me, my dear. Don't place all the blame on me. Blame it on love's fierce longing, your exquisite beauty and charm," he murmured.

She straightened in the chair, masking her terror with a face of searing contempt.

"Love!" she spat, her scorned voice rising like a storm. "You call this violence love?"

His response came quick, steeped in desperate earnestness, a man defending the last shreds of his sanity.

"Not the violence, Sylvia, but what drives it! That force which would make me raze kingdoms if they stood between you and me. I want you, Sylvia, more than I've ever wanted anything in this cursed life."

It's because of the depth and sincerity of my love that I've messed things up so badly, that every time I've tried to show my devotion, I've only made you angry. But, I swear to you, if it were within my power, if I were free to make you my Duchess, that's exactly what I'd be offering you now. I swear it by everything I hold sacred."

She looked at him. Despite the humility in his posture and the raw sincerity vibrating through his voice, feelings that might have moved her once, now only fanned the flames of her disdain.

"Is anything sacred to a man like you?" She rose, swaying slightly as dizziness and cold shivers wrapped around her, astonished that she couldn't command herself more forcefully. But she managed enough composure to give him her answer. "Sir, your relentless pursuit has made you loathsome and abhorrent to me, and nothing you do now can change that. I tell you this in the hope that some shred of dignity or decency will make you stop; so that you understand there's no way you can win by continuing to hound me with your detestable attentions. And now, sir, I beg you to have your men bring the chair in which I was brought here and take me back. Detain me any further, and I promise you, sir, you will be held accountable for tonight's actions."

Her words, laced with venom and dripping with contempt, lashed at him, her eyes filled with a loathing that only ignited a slow-burning fury within him, awakening the beast that lurked just beneath his surface.

The change was immediate, flickering in the sneer that crept across his pale face, accompanied by a nasty, soft chuckle as he met her demand.

"Let you leave so soon? How could you even think that, Sylvia? After all the trouble I went through to trap you, you beautiful bird, just to set you free again!"

"Either you let me go right now," she declared fiercely, her weakness washed away by her indignation, "or the town will buzz with your disgrace. You've committed abduction, and you know the penalty. I will make sure you pay for it. I swear you'll hang, even if you're a Duke of twenty Buckinghams. You have plenty of enemies who'd love to help me, and I'm not entirely without friends, your grace."

He shrugged, sneering. "Enemies!" he scoffed, "Friends!" He waved a dismissive hand toward the unconscious Dempsey. "There lies one of your so-called friends, if what the scoundrel said was true. The others won't be much harder to eliminate."

"Your stable boys won't be enough to save you from the others."

That remark struck a nerve. Blood rushed to his face at the thinly veiled suggestion that it was only his men who had saved him now. But he answered with a deadly smoothness, "So much even that won't be needed. Come on, girl, be sensible. Look at where you stand."

"I see it clearly enough," she replied.

"I'll permit myself to doubt that. You seem to underestimate my cunning as much as you do my appearance. Who's going to accuse me, and of what? You will charge me. You'll accuse me of bringing you here by force and keeping you against your will. Abduction, you say, and you remind me it's a serious crime in the eyes of the law."

"A hanging offense, even for dukes," she said.

"Maybe; maybe. But first, the charge has to be proven. Where are your witnesses? Until you bring them forward, it's just your word against mine."

"The word of an actress, no matter how esteemed, is... well, just that." He flashed a knowing smile. "As for this house, it's not mine. It belongs to a thug named Dempsey. He rented it a few days ago under his own name. He's the one who dragged you here against your will. Now, if a scapegoat is needed, he's as good as any. Besides, he's already facing the noose for other crimes. He grabbed you and brought you here. Agreed? From there, our stories shouldn't conflict. So how did I end up in this brute's lair? To rescue you, of course, and to comfort you in your distress. My staff will vouch for it. Push comes to shove, they'll say you're the one scheming, twisting kindness into malice to gain from my misplaced goodwill. You're smiling? Think the town's rumors will clear you? I doubt it. And I'm ready to risk it. Oh, I'd take bigger risks for you, darling."

She made a gesture of disdain. "You might be a master of lies, as well as all other dark arts. But your deceit won't save you if you try to hold me now."

"Hold you?" He leaned in, his eyes burning with intensity. "If I dare, child? Dare?"

She recoiled in sheer terror. Then, mustering every ounce of her willpower, she stood tall. With the regality of a tragic queen, she threw out her arm, commanding him.

"Stand back, sir! Stand back and let me pass, let me go."

He stepped back, but only a little, so he could better take in the sight of her.

He found her captivating, a vision of elegance in the way she held herself. Her face, pale like ivory, contrasted sharply with the fierce glow of her eyes, eyes that seemed even larger now, set in deep, dark shadows. Suddenly, with an almost inhuman cry, he lunged forward, desperate to pull her into his grasp. He was determined to crush her icy resistance, to melt her disdain until it ran like water. She darted away in a panic before his ferocious attack, knocking over the high-backed chair she'd been using just moments before. The crash of the chair seemed to cut through the fog in Dempsey's mind, stirring him, making him moan faintly. But beyond that, her escape was futile. Only a few paces away, the wall loomed before her. She thought about fleeing around the table, but before she could even turn, the Duke had her. She faced him, wild and cornered, hands raised in self-defense. His arms locked around her, forcing her hands to her sides, crushing her painfully against him. He didn't even register the searing pain in his own torn shoulder, where his wounds opened wider from the effort. She lay helpless in his grip.

"You coward! You beast! You monster!" she gasped. But he silenced her with rough, desperate kisses.

"Call me what you will. I have you, and nothing in this world can tear you from me now. Understand this," he begged, his tone shifting. "Accept it, and you'll see that I've tamed you only to become your servant."

She didn't respond; a wave of dizziness and nausea washed over her again. She moaned softly, trapped in his embrace, which felt as vile and deadly as a serpent's coils, an image that seared into her mind. He kissed her again, pressing his lips to her eyes, her mouth, her throat, the folds of the blue scarf still hanging around her neck.

The cloth offended him, an obstacle in his way. With a rough yank, he tore it aside, exposing the delicate, pale throat and chest that it had so inconveniently hid. He leaned in, his head dipping towards her like a vile vampire. But his feverish lips never made contact. Mid-bend, he froze, his body going rigid. Footsteps echoed behind him—his grooms re-entering the chamber. But it wasn't their arrival that held him back, that made his eyes bulge and turn his cheeks a ghostly white. It wasn't their presence that set him trembling from head to foot in abject terror.

For a moment, he stood paralyzed, his limbs suddenly leaden and useless. He wanted to release her instantly, but his arms moved sluggishly, unwrapping from her sweet body one reluctant muscle at a time. He stumbled back, his posture hunched forward, his eyes locked on her, his jaw slack. He looked like a man staring into the abyss, frozen in the last extremity of horror.

Then, with a shaking hand, he pointed at her throat, his voice cracking and harsh as he spoke.

"The signs! The signs!"

The three grooms, now in the room, halted as if turned to stone. On the floor, Dempsey stirred, slowly raising himself. Blood matted his hair to his brow from a cracked head wound, and he peered around dazedly. He saw the Duke pointing with that trembling hand, heard his quaking voice repeating:

"The signs!"

The Duke staggered back, step by step, each gasp rattling in his chest, until he swung around to face his men.

"Back!" he shrilled. "Back! Get out! She's infected! My God, she has the plague! The signs are all over her!"

For a moment, the men shared his horror, rooted to the spot.

They leaned in, eyes fixed on Miss Shallmont, who stood pale and fragile against the dark wood paneling. Her white neck and shoulders glowed almost unnaturally in contrast to the rich brown backdrop. From where they were, they could clearly see the ominous purple mark on her throat—a sign of the relentless plague. As the Duke approached, fear swept through them like a cold wind. Could he already be carrying the dreaded infection? Panic set in. With frantic cries, they scattered, bolting from the room, rushing out of the house, oblivious to the Duke's desperate shouts as he chased after them.

CHAPTER TWENTY-ONE

The main door crashed shut behind the men fleeing in haste. Their running steps clattered on the cobblestones, fading quickly into the night. Colonel Dempsey stood alone in the room with the woman he had once pursued with desperate longing until despair had ended his quest. Together at last in this house, brought by a cruel twist of fate, surrounded by layers of horror on horror. The very act of finding her had irrevocably lost her to him again. The chance that brought them together after all these years now hurled them apart more than ever before; and that was without even considering that she now bore the shadow of death. Was he not truly Fortune's fool?

The violent slamming of the door snapped him back to a heightened state of awareness. With great effort, he got to his knees, his eyes clouded as he looked around the room. He brushed back the tangled mess of hair from his brow and stared blankly at his hand, wet and smeared with blood. The fog enveloping his mind, blurring and distorting the events that had transpired before he was struck down and during the slow return of consciousness, was now beginning to lift. The clarity of where he was and how he had gotten there finally settled in. He rose shakily to his feet, swaying for a moment, his gaze dull like that of a drunkard.

He saw Nancy, her back to him, gazing into an oblong Venetian mirror on the wall beyond the table. In the mirror's reflection, he saw her face. It was ashen, her eyes wide with a gaping, ghastly horror. That's when memories began to trickle back, incidents from the chaotic scene that had unfolded before his eyes, each piece slotting into place as his mind slowly returned from the abyss.

Once again, he saw Buckingham. The old man crouched and trembled as he backed away from Nancy, his hand shaking violently as he pointed at her. And once again, the Duke's wavering voice echoed in his ears, filled with dread. He understood now. Nancy was safe from Buckingham, but she had been claimed by something far more merciless and infinitely more vile. She was realizing this too, as she looked at her reflection in that tiny mirror and saw the mark of the plague on her pale chest.

Though she had never seen that damning purple blotch before, she had heard it described. She knew exactly what it meant, even without the horrified explanation Buckingham had given her. Whether it was the horror of what she saw or the early signs of the dreadful disease, which might have also been the cause of the dizziness she'd felt earlier and attributed to emotion, she couldn't tell. Her reflection seemed to pulsate before her eyes; the room swayed and rocked, the ground beneath her feet shifting like the unsteady deck of a ship. She staggered back, powerless to stop her fall, when suddenly, she was caught and held upright.

She looked up and saw the ghastly, blood-smeared face of Randal Dempsey, who had instinctively come to her aid. For a long moment, she stared at him with dull eyes, a tiny frown of effort creasing her brow. Then, with a heavy voice, she spoke:

"Don't touch me. Did you not hear? I have the plague."

"Yeah, I heard," he replied.

"You'll catch it," she warned him.

"That's very likely," he said, "but it doesn't matter much."

With that, he lifted her into his arms, just as he had earlier that same night. Despite his own shaky condition, he managed it easily enough; she was very thin and light. Too dazed and weak to resist, she allowed him to carry her to the daybed.

He laid her down gently, positioning the wine-colored cushions to cradle her head and limbs comfortably. He moved to the shuttered windows, unlatched them, and flung the casement open to let in a gust of cool night air that sliced through the suffocating room. Task complete, he turned back and stood by the couch, staring down at her with eyes full of mute suffering. The fresh air revived her a bit, steadying her pulse and clearing some of the fog weighing down her mind. For a while, she lay there, panting slightly, recollecting her situation and condition. Then she lifted her eyes to meet his, seeing the harrowed face above her, registering his anguished gaze. She stared at him, her face blank.

"Why are you still here?" she asked finally, her voice flat. "Go... just go and leave me to die. There's nothing left to do. And... and I think I'd die easier without you here."

He recoiled as if she had slapped him. He seemed about to say something, then closed his mouth, his head dropping until his chin touched his chest. He turned, and dragging his feet, slowly left the room, closing the door gently behind him. She was suddenly seized by a great fear. She strained to catch the sound of his footsteps in the corridor until finally the slam of the street door echoed up to her, confirming that he had really gone. She bolted upright, alarm gripping her, holding her breath, straining to hear his steps as they quickened, almost to a run, up the street. At last, she could hear them no more. Her fear surged, roaring in her ears.

Despite all her brave talk, the thought of dying alone, abandoned in this empty house, filled her with sheer terror. It seemed now that even the company of that despicable scoundrel would have been preferable to this horrifying solitude in the face of death. She tried to get up, to follow, to find the companionship of anyone who might offer her some help, someone to lessen her suffering. But her limbs betrayed her. She rose to her feet only to collapse again, utterly spent. She then threw herself down on the daybed and sobbed uncontrollably until the piercing pain in her chest overwhelmed even her self-pity, contorting her in agony as though she were on a medieval torture rack. Finally, a blessed unconsciousness took hold of her.

Meanwhile, Dempsey moved instinctively and urgently up Sermon Lane toward St. Paul's. Why he chose that direction, he couldn't say. The streets were completely deserted, even at that early hour. It was not a time when people ventured out at night, and besides, the Lord Mayor's orders required all taverns and entertainment houses to shut their doors by nine o'clock. Without a hat or cloak, his empty scabbard swinging uselessly about his legs, he pushed onward, half-crazed, with only a vague sense of purpose and no real idea of the best direction to take.

As he neared Carter Lane, a lantern bobbed like a will-o'-the-wisp around the corner to meet him, and soon the dark outline of the man carrying it became visible. This figure walked with the help of a staff which the lantern light soon revealed to be red. With a gasp of relief, Dempsey rushed forward.

"Stay back, sir! Stay back!" a voice warned from the shadows. "Beware of infection."

But Dempsey charged on heedlessly until the long red wand was lifted and pointed towards him, halting his advance.

"Are you mad, sir?" the man cried sharply.

Dempsey could now make out the pale contour of the man's face, previously obscured by the wide brim of his hat. "I inspect infected houses," the man said.

Dempsey's breath hitched. "I was hoping for someone like you. I need a doctor right away. Someone's got the plague."

The man's demeanor shifted instantly. "Where?" he asked.

"Just down the street, on Knight Ryder."

"Then Dr. Rickels at the corner is your best bet. Follow me."

So it was that Nancy, roused from a fainting swoon that had mercifully dulled her senses, heard footsteps and voices. Her gaze drifted to the doorway and, through a haze that seemed like a rolling mist, she saw Colonel Dempsey enter with two strangers. One was a small, wiry man, somewhere around middle age. The other was younger, broad-shouldered, and round-faced. Both wore black and carried the red wand dictated by law. The younger man, the examiner Dempsey had met on Sermon Lane, stayed by the door. He pressed a cloth soaked in vinegar to his nose and chewed on a stick of snake-root, a preventative measure.

Dr. Rickels, the man the examiner had recommended, approached Nancy. His examination was swift, practiced, and silent. Nancy endured it without protest, too drained to care about what would happen to her next. The doctor's bony fingers gripped her wrist, the middle finger pressed to the pulse point. He then scrutinized a blotch on her throat.

Finally, he lifted one of her arms and then the other, while Dempsey held the candle-branch, illuminating her armpits.

A low grunt escaped him as soon as he found the swelling on the right one.

"This is unusually soon," he muttered. "It's rare for this to show up before the third day."

He pressed the swelling with his forefinger, triggering sharp, fiery streams of pain through her entire body, or so it felt to her. He lowered her arm and stood up straight, lips pursed and eyes thoughtful. At his elbow, Dempsey spoke in a flat voice:

"Does this... does this mean there's no hope for her?"

The doctor looked at him.

"Dum vivimus, speremus," he replied. "While we live, we hope. Her case isn't hopeless—at least, not more than any other. It all depends on how vigorously we fight the disease."

He saw a flash in Dempsey's eyes, as if the Colonel's mind had made a fierce vow right then and there. If it was a fight, he was ready to wage it. He'd battle this plague for her just as relentlessly as he'd fought Buckingham. Seeing this sudden, intense resolve, the doctor, not wanting Dempsey to be overtaken by false hope, added gently:

"Much depends on that. But, ultimately, it all depends on God, my friend." He spoke to Dempsey as though he were her husband, an assumption he figured was accurate. "If we can induce suppuration of that swelling, recovery is possible. That's all I can say. Inducing that suppuration might require infinite effort and tireless work."

"She can count on that," Dempsey replied firmly. The physician nodded. "Nurses," he added slowly, "are scarce and hard to find. I'll do my best to get one for you as soon as possible."

"Until then, you're going to have to rely completely on yourself."

"I'm ready."

"And remember, the law doesn't let you leave this house until you get a health certificate, which won't happen until a month after she recovers or…" He trailed off, leaving the worst unsaid, then continued quickly, "That's Sir John Lawrence's rule to stop the infection from spreading."

"I know, and I understand my position," said Dempsey.

"Good, better for us both. Now there's no time to waste. Speed is everything when it comes to treatments. We need to get her into a full, intense sweat, and she needs to be in bed immediately. If we're going to save her, you need to start now."

"Just tell me what to do, sir."

"More than that, I've brought everything you need."

From his pocket, he pulled out a large, bulky package. He motioned for Dempsey to come to the table, where he carefully opened it, revealing smaller packets and explaining the purpose of each one.

"Here's a stimulating ointment. You'll need to rub this on the swelling in her armpit every two hours. After that, use a poultice made from mallows, linseed, and palm oil. Here's some mithridate; give her a dose as an antidote, then after two hours, give her a posset drink made from Canary wine and spirits of sulfur. This vial here holds the spirits of sulfur. Light a fire using sea-coal in her bedroom and pile all available blankets on her, to sweat out as much of the poison as possible.

"For tonight, if you do all that, you'll have done everything that can be done. I'll come back very early in the morning, and we'll evaluate her condition then."

He turned to the examiner. "You understand?"

The man nodded. "I've already told the constable to send a watchman."

He'll be here by now, and I'll see the house shut tight when we head out."

"Then all that's left," said Dr. Rickels, "is to get the lady to bed. After that, I'll leave you until tomorrow."

To everyone's surprise, the lady managed to handle this herself. When Dempsey, ignoring the doctor's help, had carried her upstairs solo, she recovered enough to insist she be left alone. Despite her obvious weakness, Dr. Rickels agreed that letting her have her way might speed up the recovery. However, the effort of undressing drained her and brought on such searing pain that, once she finally collapsed into bed, she lay there gasping, utterly spent. That's how Dempsey and the doctor found her when they returned. Dr. Rickels placed everything Dempsey would need on a table at the foot of the bed and, after repeating his instructions, finally took his leave. The Colonel escorted him to the door.

The door stood open, and by the light of a lantern held by the watchman, the examiner was finishing a rough inscription: "Lord have mercy upon us," beneath the ominous red cross he had painted above. Wishing Dempsey a good night and courage, the physician and the examiner left together. The watchman, staying to block any unauthorized entry or exit, then closed the door. Dempsey heard the key turn from the outside and realized he was trapped in that plague-ridden house for weeks to come, unless death freed him first.

Quickly now, driven by the urgency of his duty and ignoring the persistent throb in his bruised head, Dempsey headed back up the stairs.

A memory jolted through his mind—those three would-be heroes who had rushed to her cries, ready to save her from his grip. But he had scared them off with a lie, a dark fabrication claiming she had the plague. He once thought it a necessary deceit, but now he wondered—what would have happened if they had succeeded? Would anyone else be ready to fight the battle he was about to face, willing to sacrifice everything, even life itself, to save her?

From the depths of his despair, he found an unexpected gratitude. This fight before him, this fierce resolve, was a strange blessing, bringing good out of evil. He found her sunk in lethargy, aware of everything around her but paralyzed, unable to speak or move. Her head rested against the pillows—reluctantly adjusted by the doctor during his last visit—and her fever- bright eyes tracked every move the Colonel made as he stripped off his jacket and set to work.

His preparations were brisk, methodical, but his touch brought her such pain that she slipped into unconsciousness. When she resurfaced, it was only to be thrust into raving delirium, alternating between frantic ravings and periods of drained, listless sleep for days on end.

CHAPTER TWENTY-TWO

F or five days—each one stretching into eons of torment for Randal Dempsey—Nancy teetered between life and death. It felt like one tiny gust of fate could tip the scales against her, and the slightest drop in vigilance might snap the fragile thread keeping her tied to this world. Hanging by this metaphorical thread, her fever-ravaged body waged a desperate war for survival.

The doctor had performed a small miracle by securing a nurse, bringing her to the house on Knight Ryder Street the day after Nancy fell ill. This nurse, a woman named Mrs. Dallows, was slender yet surprisingly strong, brimming with good nature even at forty. Despite her competence and willingness, had Mrs. Dallows been left solely responsible, Nancy likely wouldn't have made it. No hired help could match the relentless, guilt-ridden devotion of Randal, the man who loved her with every ounce of his soul. No professional could muster the same iron will and single-minded determination that kept Randal's fatigued body moving, driving him ever onward down this self-imposed, punishing path.

Randal never allowed himself a moment's respite in this grim battle with death. Sleep became a foreign concept, an indulgence he couldn't afford. The scant meals he did manage to consume, forced upon him by Mrs. Dallows, were taken at Nancy's bedside, his eyes never leaving her gaunt, feverish face.

Mrs. Dallows did her best, urging Randal to rest while she took over during her shifts. It was a plea that fell on deaf ears. Dr. Rickels, more forceful and authoritative, echoed her calls for him to take a break and follow basic precautions to protect his own health. But Randal disregarded them all. He was a man singularly focused, powered by love and guilt, ready to sacrifice everything for a chance to pull Nancy back from the edge.

The sulfur balm that the small-town doctor had given Dempsey to use as a disinfectant remained untouched; the wormwood, masterwort, and zedoary he insisted on as protective measures were equally ignored.

"Look, my friend," the doctor had said to him on just the second day of her illness, "if you keep going like this, you're going to end up killing yourself."

Dempsey had simply smiled and replied, "If she lives, it's a small price to pay. If she dies, nothing else matters."

The doctor, clueless about who she truly was, had wrongly assumed the two were married. He saw Dempsey's stoic response as a sign of exceptional spousal devotion. But that misconception didn't stop him from trying to talk Dempsey out of his stubbornness.

"What if she survives but you don't?" he had asked, only to be met with a spark of sudden anger in Dempsey's eyes.

"Don't pester me anymore!"

From that point on, Dr. Rickels had given up, figuring that the widespread belief—that the man's apparent lack of fear of the infection served as his best protection—was probably true. Regardless, Dempsey ignored every preventive measure the doctor had earnestly outlined for him. Instead, he smoked a lot, sitting by the open window of her room, letting in the suffocating heat of that dreadful July. The roaring fire, kept going on the doctor's persistent orders despite the oppressive warmth, helped cleanse and purify the air. These efforts might've shielded Dempsey, even against his own carelessness, providing him with some form of disinfection.

It was entirely thanks to his relentless watchfulness and the constant poultices he applied that, on the fourth day, the swelling under her arm began to vent the deadly poison in her veins.

Rickels was both amazed and thrilled.

"Colonel," he said on the evening of the fourth day, "your efforts are paying off. It's already a miracle in the making."

"You mean she'll live?" Dempsey asked, his voice trembling with desperate hope. The doctor hesitated, his satisfaction tempered by caution.

"I can't promise that yet. But the worst seems to be over. With proper care and a bit of luck, we might just save her."

"You can count on the care; just tell me what needs to be done."

Rickels laid out the instructions, and despite his exhaustion, Dempsey listened intently. He banished his weariness and set about doing exactly as he was told. Meanwhile, outside their small haven, the plague was sweeping through London with a vengeance, like some infernal wildfire. Rickels kept Dempsey informed of the virus's deadly march, how the death toll had soared within days, reaching almost a thousand in the past week alone. And even without Rickels' updates, Dempsey could see the chaos unfolding from the narrow confines of his makeshift prison.

From his perch at the first-floor window, he watched Knight Ryder Street, once bustling with life, growing eerily desolate. The daily hum of London's activity, usually as constant and essential as a heartbeat, was fading, growing weaker as the city's lifeblood ebbed away. Across the street, several houses were already marked with the dreaded red cross, each guarded day and night by watchmen standing sentinel at padlocked doors. Supplies reached these quarantined houses through the efforts of those watchmen, who ensured the inhabitants received the necessities while the world outside teetered on the brink of collapse.

Dempsey, still flush with the cash Buckingham had generously provided for this grim endeavor, would lower the money in a basket from the window. The watchman, in turn, would send up the goods, disappearing when necessary but always making sure the door remained locked, taking the key with him. The air, growing more ominously still by the day, was punctuated occasionally by the mournful tolling of bells, marking yet another soul lost to the plague. Every night, just after dusk, and again before dawn, a more chilling sound shattered the silence.

"Bring out your dead!"

Glancing down as he always did, Dempsey could make out the ghastly silhouette of the dead-cart as it lumbered into view, called forth by the marked houses, like a vulture drawn to carrion. It would invariably pause outside Dempsey's door, halting at the sight of the watchman and the faint glow of the lantern revealing the red cross. That voice would then rise again, more insistent, dripping with a vile blend of authority and contempt.

"Bring out your dead!"

Then, following a nod from the watchman, the dreadful cart would trundle away, and Dempsey, shivering, would glance back over his shoulder at the feverish woman, tossing in her sheets. His mind churned with the fear that duty and the merciless hand of fate might soon force him to answer that call, to surrender her lovely body to the festering mass aboard that ghastly vehicle.

So it continued until the morning of the sixth day. From dawn until well past eight, Dempsey paced in a frenzy of impatience, waiting for Rickels. When Rickels finally arrived, Dempsey was there to meet him at the top of the stairs.

The Colonel's face was a pallid mask, his eyes wild and feverish. He was practically vibrating with nervous energy.

"She's sleeping soundly now," he whispered to the doctor, pressing a finger to his lips. They slipped into the dimly lit room, their footsteps barely disturbing the hush. Dempsey, consumed by a desperate hope, positioned himself at the foot of the ornate bed. With a quick look, he verified what Dempsey had already stated. The woman on the bed lay in a serene, dreamless sleep, something she hadn't achieved since being confined to this room. The fever had vanished, an observation the doctor noted even before he checked her pulse. As his fingers closed around her wrist, she stirred, sighed, and opened her eyes, lucid and calm at last. Her gaze met the doctor's kindly, bespectacled face—first in confusion, then in rising comprehension as he spoke.

"The crisis has passed," he said gently. "She's going to recover, thanks be to God and to your unwavering vigilance. But now, it's you I'm worried about. Leave her in Mrs. Dallow's capable hands and get some rest yourself, or I won't be responsible for what happens to you." His stern look shifted from Dempsey to the woman, whose eyes had lost their fevered glaze.

"See, she's awake," he pointed out with relief.

"The crisis has passed?" Dempsey echoed, his voice cracking under the weight of disbelief. "Are you saying the crisis is really over? I am not dreaming, am I, doctor? I haven't just dozed off at my post and imagined this?"

"You are wide awake," the doctor reassured him, looking him squarely in the eyes. "And yes, the danger is truly over."

"Go and rest," the doctor commanded.

She glanced around, curiosity piqued by the harsh, tired voice that had spoken. Her gaze landed on a tall, gaunt figure, a ghost of a man with hollow eyes and pallid, sunken cheeks, shadowed by a scruffy, unkempt beard. He leaned heavily against one of the bedposts, using it for support. When their eyes met, he recoiled and let go of the post, staggering back a step before placing a hand on his brow.

"There's nothing wrong with me, doctor," he mumbled. Recognition dawned on her as she remembered who he was. "I'd rather..."

His words trailed off abruptly. He swayed, then collapsed to the floor, landing face down with a heavy thud. Mrs. Dallows cried out in alarm and dropped to her knees beside him. She managed to turn him over and lift his head onto her lap just as Dr. Rickels rushed over. A shared look passed between the nurse and the doctor.

Nancy, weak and frail herself, struggled to prop herself up to see what was happening beyond the foot of the bed. With swift, practiced hands, Dr. Rickels tore open the Colonel's jacket, but the motion was almost redundant. The reality of the situation was immediately clear. It seemed as if the knowledge that she was now safe had released the iron grip Dempsey had maintained over his exhaustion. Like a dam finally bursting, his body succumbed to the fatigue he had so long denied.

"He's asleep," Dr. Rickels said, a hint of a chuckle in his voice. "That's all. Help me get him onto that couch, Mrs. Dallows. There's no need to move him far or do more for him right now. Believe me, you won't be able to wake him for at least a full day."

They lifted him onto a couch, placing a pillow under his head. Rickels then turned back to his patient's side.

She sank back into the bed, her eyes—now looking enormous in her gaunt, sunken cheeks—fixated on Dempsey's figure. He lay there, utterly motionless, just within the edges of her hazy vision.

"Is he sleeping?" she asked the doctor, bewilderment clear in her frail voice. "Is that what sleep looks like?"

She had never seen sleep claim a man so swiftly, almost as if he had been shot.

"Nothing worse, ma'am. The Colonel hasn't shut his eyes for a whole week. Finally, nature stepped in and gave him what he needed. Don't torment yourself on his account. All he needs now is rest. So, please, save your strength."

She stared at him, searchingly. "I have the plague, don't I?"

"More like you had it, ma'am. It's no longer in you. It's left you weak, but that's all. You're out of danger now. Once you regain your strength, you can go wherever you want without fear. The plague won't come for you again. For that mercy, you ought to thank God, and right after Him, your husband."

Her eyebrows knitted together in confusion.

"My husband?"

"Yes, ma'am. Your husband. And a rare one he is, too. I've seen many husbands lately, and I can tell you, the fear of the plague wipes out all other feelings. I've seen it strip men down to their basest selves. But not Colonel Dempsey. His devotion makes him a hero; his courage kept him safe. As they say, fortune favors the brave, ma'am."

"But... but he isn't my husband."

"Not your husband?" The doctor was flabbergasted. He repeated, "Not your husband?" Then, with a touch of sarcasm that seemed out of place for his normally warm, kindly demeanor, he muttered, "Well, now, perhaps that explains it."

"What kind of man is he, the one who's just about sacrificed his life for you?"

She hesitated, unsure how to put their relationship into words. Finally, she said, "He was my friend once."

"Once?" The doctor raised an eyebrow, his grizzled brows knitting together. "And when exactly did he stop being your friend? This man who stayed with you in this plague-ridden house when he could've easily run? This man who's deprived himself of sleep, so he could always be ready to help you? This man who's fought death head-on for your sake, risking infection a thousand times over just for you?"

"Did he really do all this?" she whispered. Dr. Rickels recounted the acts of bravery and self-sacrifice that Dempsey had shown. When he finished, she lay silent, deep in thought, the details weighing heavily on her. The doctor allowed himself a smile, a hint of mischief in his eyes.

"He may have been your friend once, as you say," he said with a wise grin. "But I don't think he's ever been more of a friend than he is right now. God grant me such a friend when I'm in need!"

She didn't respond, just lay there, silent and contemplative. She stared up at the carved canopy of the grand, foreign bed, her face an unreadable mask. The little doctor tried to decipher the riddle of their relationship, but her expression gave nothing away. If he were a more curious man, he might've asked more questions. But he knew better. Her health came first. She needed nourishment and rest, not an interrogation, and he wasn't about to jeopardize her peace with probing questions.

CHAPTER TWENTY-THREE

That evening, Dr. Rickels showed up again, this time with a public examiner in tow, just like his first visit. This official had come to verify the doctor's claim that the cure had worked, all so he could file a report. If no new outbreak of disease occurred in the next twenty-eight days, the house could finally be opened again. Dempsey woke up from eleven hours of deep, uninterrupted sleep, still feeling utterly exhausted. He stood there, heavy-eyed and detached, as the examiner conducted his formal inspection of not just him, but Mrs. Dallows and the patient too.

Standing gaunt, pale, hair a mess, and face unshaved, Dempsey couldn't bring himself to glance at Nancy, even as her eyes studied him, serious and intent. When the examiner and the doctor finally left the room, Dempsey dragged himself after them, trailing behind with the weariness of a man burdened by unseen chains. He watched them head down the stairs and then stood alone in the oppressive quiet after their departure. Twenty-eight days, he thought, twenty-eight long days of being a prisoner in this house. He set about making his plans.

That night, Dempsey decided to sleep in a small bedroom on the ground floor. Come morning, he cobbled together breakfast in the kitchen, though Mrs. Dallows offered some help. With sustenance, he moved on to clearing out the dining room, intending to use it as his base of operations during this involuntary quarantine. The room was pitch dark, untouched since the night Nancy had first entered it. Stumbling through the blackness, he finally reached the shutters. He remembered closing them on the examiner's orders after carrying Nancy out during that hellish night a week ago. Swinging the shutters open, a flood of daylight rushed in, illuminating a tableau that brought the past screaming back.

There lay the toppled chair, a silent witness to the chaos when Nancy had backed away from Buckingham. Dempsey stood still, imagining the mess of that night—the frantic panic, the sense of doom. Every detail called out to him, like whispers from shadows that refused to stay dead in the light.

The sword, now fractured and gleaming malevolently, lay hidden beneath the table, shielded from Dr. Rickels' probing gaze. Nearby, in a darkened corner, rested the hilt that had slipped from his nerveless grasp when he had been struck down. A ruddy stain marred the polished floor by the table, a silent testimony to his own bloodspill. Similar discolored blotches defiled the daybed and table linens, likely remnants of Buckingham's own blood.

He glanced towards the slender dress rapier, half-hidden between the daybed and the window. Buckingham had abandoned it there, a relic of their fierce confrontation, left behind in his frantic escape. The room was a graveyard of decadent disarray: melted candles, wilted flowers, and rotting fruit cluttered the table, their lustre dulled beneath a blanket of dust. The sideboard bore an array of elegant dishes, once intended for an intimate supper that never was consumed.

Now, they lay decaying, suffusing the room with a sickly, putrid stench that Dempsey could almost taste—it was the exhalation of sinister memories, suffocating him.

Throwing the windows wide, he let in a flood of fresh air, dispelling the morbid miasma. He spent hours setting the room to rights, purging it of refuse, a futile exercise that brought little solace. Weary and hollow, he sprawled on the daybed, a smoke curling from his lips, lost in fragmented thoughts. The days that followed were an echo of this somber inertia, stretching endlessly into a void.

He existed like a ghost, convinced his life had ended in all but the final breath, anticipating death's merciful reprieve. Vaguely, he wished he could pray, but the habit had long since left him. Perhaps the infection he sensed lurking within these walls would finally claim him, finalizing the chapter of a life that felt already concluded.

Morning and night, and intermittently throughout the day, he'd unbutton his shirt to press his hand against his chest and probe his armpits, searching eagerly for any sign of the plague. But the cruel irony that had shadowed him all his life now thwarted his longing for death just as it had dashed every hope he held in life. Surrounded by the pestilence, breathing in its toxic air, he remained inexplicably untouched, as if he were singled out for survival.

The first three days stretched out into a monotonous haze of utter, mind-numbing idleness. Though books lined the shelves of the house, he had no inclination to read. Instead, he simply lay there, smoking and sinking deeper into his own despondence. Each morning, Mrs. Dallows updated him on the patient's condition, noting a steady improvement. The doctor confirmed this during his twice-daily visits over those three days. On the second visit, he lingered, engaging Dempsey in conversation and bringing grim news from the outside world. Whitehall now stood deserted, its once-bustling corridors emptied of all but the solitary figure of the Duke of Northridge. Courageous George Monk had chosen to stay undaunted at his post, acting in the name of the King. While His Majesty was preoccupied in Salisbury, chasing after Miss Frances Stewart, Monk took on the royal duty of alleviating his subjects' suffering in this time of national crisis.

Dempsey, his voice tinged with hope, asked Rickels if he had any news of Buckingham, with the unspoken desire to hear that the Duke had fallen victim to the plague.

"He's gone with the rest," the doctor replied. "A week ago, he fled to the North, suddenly awakened to his responsibilities as Lord Lieutenant of York, thanks to a French servant in his household who came down with the plague. He'll be safe enough in York, I reckon."

"A French servant, huh?"

"Just a lackey," the Colonel muttered, his face etched with disappointment. "The devil looks after his own," he grumbled. "A miserable lackey pays for his master's sins. Well, I guess there is a God after all."

"Don't you have any reason to know it, sir, and to give thanks?" Rickels admonished him. Dempsey turned away, sighing and shrugging, leaving the doctor even more perplexed about the strange behavior of this odd household. It was clear that things were far from right.

Acting on a sudden impulse, Dr. Rickels left the room and headed back up the stairs, even though his schedule was packed and his patients were many. He sent Mrs. Dallows on a trivial errand to the kitchen and then spent five minutes alone with Miss Russell. That was the name she'd chosen to go by with both the doctor and the nurse.

Whether it was something he said to her in those five minutes or some other influence at play, within an hour of the doctor's departure, Mrs. Dallows found Dempsey with a message: Miss Russell was up and wanted to speak with him. The nurse, her eyes sharpened by concern, noticed as Dempsey turned pale and trembled at the news.

His first impulse was to ignore it. But before he could respond, he paced the dark, wood-paneled room, then, with a sigh of resignation, agreed to see her.

Mrs. Dallows opened the door and let him walk out, tactfully holding back from following him. He was cleaned up, shaven, and tolerably dressed. His long, well- combed golden-brown hair hung in smooth ringlets to the freshly laundered, snowy collar that Mrs. Dallows had found time to wash and iron for him. Gone was the wild, scruffy man Miss Russell had last seen. But the lines of his mouth were drawn with haggard dejection, and a haunting sadness lingered in his eyes that no amount of grooming could hide.

He found Miss Russell seated by the open window, the same one where he had spent practically every hour of those five relentless days and six sleepless nights, fighting to fend off death's hungry grip. She was in a large chair placed there by Mrs. Dallows, a rug draped over her lap. Although she looked frail and ghostly pale, her weakened state somehow added to her ethereal beauty. She wore the same ivory-white gown in which she had been brought to this cursed house, her chestnut hair meticulously styled with a strand of pearls woven through it. Her long-lashed eyes, now a deeper, darker blue, seemed even more striking thanks to the shadows left by her illness. There were other, subtler changes, too, that lent her an almost otherworldly aura, so much so that to Dempsey, she seemed to have reclaimed a piece of her lost innocence, her youthful vigor. She looked less like Sylvia Shallmont, the worshipped actress, and more like Nancy Russell, the cherished woman he had once loved with all his heart.

She glanced up at him wistfully as he entered, then turned her gaze back out to the blazing sunlight that scorched the nearly deserted street. He shut the door, took a few strides forward, and hesitated.

"You sent for me," he said, almost reverently, "otherwise I wouldn't have dared to intrude." He stood there, uneasy, a man awaiting orders. A blush crept over her pale cheeks. One of her delicate, almost translucent hands nervously tugged at the rug over her knees.

Claire's voice wavered with her unease, adopting an almost formal tone despite her best efforts.

"I asked you here, sir, to acknowledge the immense debt I owe you; to thank you for your care, for risking your life to save mine; to express my gratitude for my life, which would have been lost without you."

She met his eyes suddenly, forcing him to shift his gaze toward the sunlight filtering through the window, evading the intensity of her eyes that shimmered like wet sapphires.

"You don't owe me any thanks," he said, his voice edged with a roughness that hinted at deeper turmoil. "I was just trying to make amends for what I did."

"That was before the plague intervened. You risked everything to save me from the malicious man you unwittingly delivered me to. The plague, though—catching that was beyond your control. It was already upon me when you brought me here."

"Regardless," he replied. "I had a duty to repair the damage. I owed it to myself."

"You didn't owe it to yourself to risk your life for me."

"My life, madam, isn't worth much. A wasted, misused existence holds little value. It was the least I could do."

"Perhaps," she said softly. "But also the most. And far more than you owed."

"I disagree. But it's not worth debating."

She fell silent, and he didn't offer any further help. He was convinced her words, however kind, were laced with a subtle disdain—for he believed he deserved nothing more. Her expressions of gratitude felt like pity, and it stung. Overwhelmed by a sense of unworthiness, he sank into a state of abject humility. Yet without realizing it, this humility was fortified by an underlying pride.

His deepest wish was to avoid a conversation that could only bring more pain. But she stopped him, insistent with what he saw as a harsh kindness.

"At least you've made amends," she said. "And that's more than enough."

"I'd find some comfort in your words, if I could believe them," he replied, a grim look on his face as he turned to leave. But she wasn't letting him go that easily.

"Why don't you believe me? Why wouldn't I be sincere in wanting to thank you?"

At last, he met her gaze, and in his eyes, she saw the reflection of his agony.

"Oh, I believe you mean it," he said. "You want to thank me. I get that. It's natural, I suppose. You're grateful. But you can't stand the sight of me. Your gratitude won't take away your contempt. It's impossible."

"Are you so sure?" she asked softly, her eyes full of compassion.

"Sure? What else could it be? How could it be any different? I despise myself. Am I so out of touch with my own vileness that I'd imagine any part of it escapes you?"

"Don't," she whispered. "Please, don't." But the sorrow in her eyes only confirmed what she was trying so weakly to deny.

"Is there any point in denying something so obvious?" he cried out. "I searched for you for years, Nan, as a man with a spotless reputation, only to finally find you now when I'm so tainted I can barely stand your gaze. The same cruel twist of fate that brought us together was also the moment I hit rock bottom. That horrible night, you looked at me with utter disgust, and now you look at me with pity because there's nothing but filth left in me."

Out of a strange sense of pity, you throw me thanks that I don't deserve. Everything I did was simply to atone for my mistakes. What more can I say? If this place wasn't locked up and I weren't a prisoner here, I would have left already. I would have taken off the second Rickels said you were safe. I'd have made sure our paths would never cross again, so you wouldn't have to put up with my repulsiveness or feel the need to thank me for anything. You despise me, and rightly so."

"You think that's all there is to say?" she asked him, her voice laced with sad disbelief. "It's not over. There's still more to be said."

"Spare me that," he pleaded passionately. "From the same charity that made you thank me, just spare me the rest." Then, more briskly, with a certain finality, he added, "If you have any commands, madam, I'll be downstairs until this place reopens. Then we can go our separate ways."

He bowed stiffly and turned to leave.

"Randal!" she called out when he reached the door. He stopped, his firm resolve crushed by the desperate utterance of his name. "Randal, won't you tell me how...how you ended up in the state where I found you? Won't you let me know everything so I can judge for myself?"

He stood there for a moment, pale and trembling, wrestling with his pride—a pride that hid behind a mask of humility, deceiving him into letting it win.

"Judge me, madam, based on what you already know. That's enough to decide my fate. Nothing from my chaotic past can excuse what you've discovered about me. I'm a scoundrel, a loathsome creature, an offense, and you know that. Yet, I wanted you to see me as a man of honor. God, have mercy! Don't you see?"

"Don't you see?"

Her eyes glistened with sudden tears, their raw emotion piercing through the gloom.

"I think you're being too hard on yourself. Let me decide for myself, Randal. Can't you see I'm desperate to forgive you? Doesn't my forgiveness mean anything to you?"

"It means everything," he replied, voice trembling. "But I could never believe it. Never. You say you're aching to forgive. Those blessed, healing words! But why? Because you're thankful I helped save a life. That's the real reason for your pity, for this deformed soul of mine, for making you want to offer forgiveness. But behind that gratitude, behind that forgiveness, there must always be contempt, a loathing for what I am. It must be so. I know it, or I know nothing. Because of that …" He broke off, leaving the sentence unfinished, his face twisting into a bitter smile before he shrugged in resignation. But she saw neither. Her gaze had turned away again, lost in the sunlight streaming through the window, blurring the black-timbered, yellow houses across the street.

Quietly, he left, closing the door with care. She heard him go, felt the weight of his departure but made no move to stop him, lost in her own turmoil, unable to counter his bleak certainties.

His feet felt heavy as he descended the stairs, heading back to the room that had come to define his existence. And with each step, his thoughts cemented his conviction. They had met at last, only to part again. Their paths could never truly converge. Looming over their lives was that dreadful memory of what he had done, an irreversible stain. Even if he wasn't the broken man he had become, even if he had something to offer the woman of his dreams, the specter of his betrayal—the time when he acted as Buckingham's pawn—would always stand between them, making any genuine tenderness impossible.

He was trapped in a mood from which there was no escape.

Pride weighed on his soul, boxing it in with walls of false humility and gnawing shame, leaving no escape except perhaps through the doorway that the plague might swing open. But even the plague turned its back on him.

Chapter Twenty-four

As the weeks dragged on, August drew near. Soon, the quarantine would be over, and the house on Knight Ryder Street would open its doors again, freeing its inhabitants. Time moved forward, but Dempsey's mood remained unchanged. He kept his distance from Nancy, and she did the same. Each day, he inquired about her progress and was relieved to hear she was regaining her strength. Yet, Mrs. Dallows, the bearer of this news, made sure he also knew that Nancy's spirits showed no sign of recovery.

"She's very sad and lonely, poor dear," Mrs. Dallows said, a worried frown settling on her face. "It would break your heart to see her, sir."

"Aye," Dempsey would reply in his usual grim tone. And that was that. Mrs. Dallows grew more afflicted each day, her concern making her look even more like a flustered hen. She saw there was something between Dempsey and Nancy, a barrier keeping them apart, though it was clear they were meant to be together. More than once, she tried to get one or the other to open up, her intentions purely charitable. She wanted to help them reach a better understanding. But her efforts came to nothing, and she could only share in their sorrow.

It vexed her deeply, especially since both showed such care for each other in the questions they asked daily.

Dempsey stayed in his quarters downstairs, chain-smoking and drinking heavily until he drained the house's meager supply of wine. Without even the comfort of a drink, his despair deepened. Over and over, he told himself his life was over, that he was merely a ghost haunting the world aboveground.

By the time August rolled around, they could almost taste the desperation hanging in the London air. The watchman filled their nights with tales so harrowing they felt surreal. Each evening, as he peered out of his window, the comet scorched the sky—a fiery menace, the watchman called it the flaming sword of wrath, stretching ominously from Whitehall to the Tower. Just three days before they were set to reopen the house, Mrs. Dallows came to him, her breath ragged, trembling with urgent excitement.

"Miss Russell, sir, asks if you could kindly go upstairs to see her."

He felt a jolt of terror.

"No, no!" he blurted out, panic overtaking him. Then, fighting to regain his composure, he grasped at a delay, anything to buy some time. "Tell Miss Russell ... tell her I can't tonight. I'm exhausted ... the heat ..." he babbled. The nurse tilted her head thoughtfully, her sharp little eyes studying him keenly. "If not tonight, then when? Tomorrow morning?"

"Yes, yes," he eagerly responded, desperate to push away the immediate threat. "In the morning. Tell her I'll come to her then."

Mrs. Dallows left, and he found himself shaken to his core, gripped by a fear that gnawed at him from within. It was himself he feared, himself he no longer trusted. The boy who had worshipped blindly had grown into a man wrestling with a love so intense it felt like a curse, a love that stoked the flames of shame inside him until they nearly consumed him. During his one meeting with Nancy, he had bared his soul. He had been strong then, but he knew he might not be strong again. The gentleness she showed him—a gentleness rooted in her damned gratitude—threatened to weaken his resolve, to make him play the coward. He feared he'd give her the complete honesty she sought, that he'd conflate her pity with absolution, banking on her compassion for full forgiveness.

And then, if it came to pass that he was so weak as to collapse at her feet and spill out the tale of his longing and love, out of her sense of debt, pity, and gratitude, she might take him in. This shattered wreck of a man might drag her down with him into the pit where his future lay. The threat of a wrong far greater than any he had already committed loomed, even though he might have tried to make amends.

He couldn't trust himself to face her again, knowing he couldn't keep the silence his honor demanded. He was tortured by the thought that tomorrow, he must see her because it was her wish, and she was determined enough to come find him if he refused to go. He sat, smoked, and pondered, deciding at all costs that the meeting must not happen. There was a way to avoid it and definitively end its threat. He could break out of the sealed house immediately, not waiting for the legal term to expire. It was a desperate move, one that might have severe consequences for him. But nothing else seemed possible, and the consequences were of no importance anymore.

This line of thought solidified into a resolve, and with that decision, his mind found peace. This, more than the pain and risks he had taken to save her from the plague, was true reparation. When she would later reflect on his actions, she might understand their true significance and purpose. Perhaps this understanding would finally erase the contempt she surely harbored, even if she tried to cover it with charity. An idea seized him, grew into a purpose, and exalted him.

He reached for a pen and paper, pulling a chair up to the table where he sat down, driven by a sudden bout of inspiration.

"You've asked," he began, diving right in, "to know how I sank into the pit of disgrace where you found me. I held back from answering you, fearing it would stir more of your kind, self-deluding sympathy. But now, as I stand on the brink of leaving your life for good, with no chance of us ever meeting again, I'm compelled to tell you everything. Maybe then you'll remember me with a pity stripped of any lingering disdain.

"The tale of the misfortune that's dogged my steps begins on a May morning, many years ago. I rode into Charmouth, full of hope and excitement, a young man with some means and more pride. My feet were set firmly on an honorable path. I came to claim you, to lay my modest successes and the promise of greater things to come at your beloved feet."

He wrote on as daylight dwindled. When darkness crept in, he lit candles and continued, his words flowing effortlessly like a man with a clear story to tell and a heart brimming with unspent emotions. The night breeze wafted through the open window, causing the flames to flicker and cast eerie shadows on the walls. The candles burned down, wax dripping to form twisted shapes, but he did not stop. He heard the changing of the watchman below but paid no mind. The distant clanging of the dead-cart's bell broke the stillness, but it was just a faint echo in his single-minded focus. Only once did he pause, to light new candles, and then resumed writing. Not until long after midnight, not until dawn's first light, did he finally stop.

He leaned back in his tall chair, staring ahead, a man lost in thought, contemplating the weight of the words he'd just committed to paper. And there he sat, enveloped by the quiet, pondering his next move.

From the depths of his worn leather jacket, he pulled out a yellow glove, long and slim, with fringed edges that had seen better days. As he held it in his hand, memories of that early morning years ago flooded back, when it had fluttered down from her window, a token he had placed in his hat as a symbol of her favor. He sighed deeply, a tear—a rare trespass from his hardened adventurer's heart—slipping onto his hand. With a sudden movement, he leaned forward, grabbed the pen with a resolve that stung, and wrote with feverish speed at the bottom of the last page:

"Here is the glove you gave me so long ago. I wore it as your knight, a proud emblem of your favor in life's battles, marked by both your gift and my clean honor. For years, it served as my talisman, keeping that honor intact against countless tests and temptations. Now that I have failed in my duty through my own cowardice and shortcomings, you may not want me to keep it any longer."

That manuscript—though one could hardly call it a mere letter—still exists. Its faded ink sprawls across thirty pages, the paper aged to a dull yellow by centuries. As you might deduce, it has remained in my possession. It provided me with more than just the basic elements of this history; without it, this tale could never have been written. He didn't pause to read it over when he was done. There wasn't time for that. He left it as it had poured from his heart. He folded the sheets, enclosing the glove within, wrapped a strand of silk around the bundle, and secured it with a wax seal pressed with his thumb. He addressed it simply, "To Miss Nancy Russell," and propped it up against the base of the candleholder, ready for the first person to enter that room to find.

Dempsey reached for his hefty wallet and emptied its contents onto the table. He set aside half, making two piles from the rest, labeling one for Dr. Rickels and the other for Mrs. Dallows. Quietly, he pushed his chair back and stood. He tiptoed over to the window, peering down into the shadowy corners where the watchman leaned lazily against the padlocked door, his snores cutting through the silence. Just as Dempsey had guessed, the man was asleep. Why shouldn't he be? No one in their right mind would try to escape a place slated to open in three days.

Dempsey returned to the table, grabbed his hat and cloak, and then, on impulse, fetched his baldric. He fitted the empty scabbard with the slender rapier Buckingham had left behind. The blade was a bit loose, but he managed to secure it. Slinging the baldric over his head and situating it on his shoulder, he blew out the candles and moved back to the window. Barely a whisper of sound escaped as he swung a leg over the sill, lowering himself until his toes dangled three feet above the rough cobblestones of the deserted street below. For a heartbeat, he hung there, steadying himself before letting go. He landed lightly, the absence of spurs making his descent nearly soundless.

He set off toward Sermon Lane, his footsteps muffled in the stillness. The watchman stirred, momentarily roused by the nearby movements, but he drowsily dismissed the fleeting echoes of retreating footsteps. He settled back into his cozy niche and returned to his dreams.

Yet, Dempsey's escape hadn't gone completely unnoticed.

Despite the small noise he made, it was enough to reach the window of the room just above - Nancy's room. Nancy, kept awake by thoughts that refused her sleep, sat by the window, driven to a nocturnal vigil. The faint sound below caught her attention, and she leaned out, peering into the darkness. She heard the soft thud as Dempsey landed on the street, followed by the fading patter of his retreating footsteps. Straining her eyes, she thought she might've seen his shadowy figure slipping away, blending with the night.

Her instinct was to cry out, but caution silenced her; rousing the watchman could set off a chase that might have dire consequences for Dempsey if it succeeded. Fear gave her the strength to stifle the impulse to call him back. She steadied herself with a deep breath. Maybe she was wrong. Perhaps her mind, fraught with anxiety, was playing tricks on her. But the uncertainty gnawed at her. She needed to know, now.

With trembling hands, she lit a lamp. Wrapping herself in a rug over her nightgown, she descended the stairs for the first time that night, cursing herself for not having done so sooner. Each step deepened her conviction that she would find what she feared: a confirmation that, by her delay, she had failed him.

The following morning, Mrs. Dallows entered the dining room with a heart full of dread, searching for her charge. To her immense relief and simultaneous distress, she found Nancy there. The rug had slipped from Nancy's bare shoulders, and she sat in her nightgown on the daybed beneath the open window, looking haunted and lost.

Her face was an ashen mask, dry eyes holding a well of agony so deep that tears would have felt like a blessing. A burned-out candle stood silently on the table beside her, just a waxy stub now. The floor around her was littered with the scattered pages of Dempsey's letter, dropped helplessly from her lifeless grip. That letter had wrought exactly what Dempsey intended. It stamped out the last flickers of her anger, replacing them with compassion, a resurgence of old love, and, ultimately, despair. By his own will, he had severed their bonds once more. Dempsey was gone, forever, as he had announced. His departure branded him an outlaw, unreachable and lost to her, permanently.

CHAPTER TWENTY-FIVE

Worried sick about her charge, Mrs. Dallows immediately sent the watchman to fetch Dr. Rickels. When the doctor arrived a short while later, she filled him in on the Colonel's escape and the dazed, almost dreamlike state Miss Russell was now in. Dr. Rickels, who had developed a fondness for the two—rooted perhaps in a mix of pity and the gnawing puzzle of their obviously troubled relationship—headed straight upstairs to find Miss Russell.

In her room, he found her, eerily composed despite the turmoil that must have been raging inside her. Her calm was unnatural, and it troubled him deeply.

"This is awful, my dear," he said gently, taking her hands. "What could have driven that poor man to such a desperate measure?"

"He has to be found. You'll organize a search, won't you?" she pleaded. He sighed deeply, shaking his head with sorrow. "I don't even need to order it. My duty requires me to report his escape. They'll search for him, but if they find him, it could go very badly for him. There are severe consequences."

His words weighed down her already burdened heart, pushing her toward the edge of despair. She was torn between two terrible outcomes. If no one searched for him, she might never see him again. Yet, if they did find him, he would face the full force of the law, and there was no guarantee she'd see him even then. Trying to help, Dr. Rickels encouraged her to open up. He saw in this a case of stubborn, human pride that threatened to break two hearts. Because of the affection he had for both of them, he was willing to do whatever he could to help—if only she would show him the way.

But despite her intense desire to unburden herself, Miss Russell found she couldn't reveal the sordid secret that tethered her to Dempsey. The abhorrent act that had landed her in this house remained a cross too heavy to lift with mere confession. A fierce, inexplicable loyalty to him shackled her, making any disclosure impossible. So, clutching her silent torment, she continued to drift like a ghost through the days that followed, her face pale, movements devoid of life. The doctor didn't approach her again until the third morning, this time with the examiner. They handed her and her nurse-keeper certificates of health, granting them freedom. Dempsey was still missing, news that left her in a vexing limbo—uncertain whether to celebrate or mourn.

Bearers were arranged for her departure, the watchman even offering his services. Her chair, tucked away within the house since her arrival, was fetched at her request to carry her once more.

"Where will you go now?" the doctor asked with genuine concern, standing with her in the doorway. She pulled a light hooded cloak of blue taffetas over her white gown, while the chair awaited under the morning sun.

"Home. Back to my lodging," she replied softly.

"Home?" he repeated, bewilderment lacing his voice. "But... this house?"

Her brow furrowed slightly at his confusion before she managed a faint smile. "This house? It's not mine. I was... I was just here by chance when I fell ill."

The weight of her admission hit him all at once, filling him with a sudden, cold dread for her fate.

The recent weeks had turned the city into a wasteland. Abandoned houses stood wide open, like gaping mouths, letting the gusts of wind howl through their empty halls. Dr. Rickels knew that her home might be just another of these spectral shells, lost to the encroaching desolation. The odds were grim that she'd find it as she'd left it.

"Where are you staying?" he asked her softly.

She told him, her voice steady but resigned. She mentioned that once she got there, she'd figure out her next steps. Maybe she would find solace and quiet in the country for a while. Perhaps she'd return to London once this living nightmare was over, or maybe she wouldn't. That's what she said, but her eyes revealed a deeper, unspoken dread. Her words, far from easing his concern, only deepened his anguish for her.

Escaping to the countryside was a nice thought, easier fantasized than achieved unless you had serious influence or cash. All those with the means had fled a long time ago. The recent mass exodus from London had hit a wall. There wasn't a village or hamlet for miles that would take in refugees from the city, too scared of the invisible death they might bring along. In some places, the villagers had even taken up arms to fend them off. So, to prevent more violence and as a desperate attempt to keep the plague from spreading further across England, the Lord Mayor had stopped issuing health certificates. Without one, no one could leave.

For those trapped in the infected zones, where the plague claimed thousands of lives every week, escape was a cruel illusion. In this nightmarish reality, Dr. Rickels realized that she needed him now more than ever.

Both practical and spiritual help might be just as crucial for her right now as the doctor's treatments had been recently.

"Come with me," he said suddenly, "I'll walk you to your place and make sure you get there safely—if you allow it, that is."

"Allow it? Oh, my friend!" She reached out her hand to him. "Shall I let you do me this last kindness? I would be more grateful than I could ever express."

He smiled through his round spectacles, gently patting her small hand. Without saying a word, he started to lead her to her chair. But there was one last thing she needed to do. In the dimly lit hall behind them stood Mrs. Dallows, almost in tears at the thought of parting from the young woman she'd grown so fond of. Miss Russell hurried back to her.

"Please remember me as someone who will never forget her debt to you and will always think of you fondly." She pressed a brilliant clasp, taken from her bodice, into Mrs. Dallows's hand—a piece far more valuable than the gold Dempsey had left to pay the nurse. As Mrs. Dallows began to simultaneously thank her and protest the extravagant gift, Nancy enveloped the kind woman in a hug and kissed her. Both were in tears when Nancy turned away and ran out to the waiting sedan. The bearers—the watchman and his helper—hoisted the chair and began their journey toward Paul's Chains. The doctor, a small black-clad figure, strutted beside it, swinging the long red staff he used as a cane. Mrs. Dallows, standing at the door of the house on Knight Ryder Street, watched them disappear through a blur of tears.

And within the chair, Miss Russell found herself finally giving in to tears as well.

The tears that streamed down her face were the first she'd shed since she received the Colonel's letter. That letter was the only tangible thing she took with her from that cursed house. Consumed by her own thoughts, she paid no attention to the eerie silence that enveloped the streets, nor the desolate and furtive air that seemed to cling to the sparse figures they occasionally passed, or to the very buildings themselves.

Eventually, they arrived at Salisbury Court and the house Nancy had pointed out. Immediately, Dr. Rickels' heart sank; his worst fears were confirmed. The door was ajar, dust coated the grimy window panes, two of which gaped with shattered glass like hollow eyes. After stepping out from her chair, Miss Russell paused, unnerved by the house's ominous appearance. An unshakable sense of dread gnawed at her. She scanned the empty court, every corner echoing the same sense of abandonment. From a window in the house opposite—a window smeared with dirt and barred—a wrinkled face peered out, with eyes radiating a sinister curiosity. That malevolent gaze was the only hint of life in the entire court.

"What does it mean?" she asked Dr. Rickels, her voice dripping with unease. He shook his head somberly.

"Can't you guess? The plague and the fear of it have ravaged this place in your absence." He let out a heavy sigh. "Let's go inside."

They stepped into the dark vestibule, where the ground was littered with dried leaves that rustled under their feet. The narrow staircase loomed ahead, its handrail shrouded in a thick layer of dust. Miss Russell called out a few times as they advanced, but the only reply was the dismal echo bouncing off the empty walls. Her home had been on the first floor, all three rooms. As they reached the landing, the doors stood wide open, mirroring the desolation that gripped her heart.

Two of the rooms were shut tight, shrouded in darkness, but the living room, right at the top of the stairs, was bathed in sunlight. As they reached it, the full extent of the chaos hit them like a freight train. Furniture wasn't just thrown around; it had been violently upended, some pieces broken, others simply vanished. Drawers hung open, their contents scattered on the floor like the aftermath of a ransacking. A glass cabinet that once stood proudly in a corner now lay smashed, shards glinting in the light.

The secrétaire stood agape, its lock busted, papers littering its surface and the floor around it. Curtains had been ripped from their poles, one dangling pitifully over a broken window. The luxurious Eastern rug that had graced a portion of the floor had disappeared completely. Dr. Rickels and Miss Russell stood frozen in the doorway, the sheer magnitude of the destruction rendering them speechless.

Eventually, Miss Russell broke free of her trance and hurried to the secrétaire, her heart hammering in her chest. She had stashed a significant sum of money in an inner drawer, her lifeline in these desperate times. That drawer had been pried open; the money was gone. She turned to Dr. Rickels, her face a mask of despair, pale as death.

Her lips quivered as she tried to speak, tears welling up anew. To survive so much only to come home to this? The doctor, moved by her silent plea, stepped forward and offered her a chair, one of the few that remained intact. He urged her to sit, as though rest could mend her shattered spirit. She complied, folding her hands in her lap, her eyes darting helplessly over the wreckage.

"What am I supposed to do? Where can I go?" she whispered. Barely giving herself a chance to breathe, she answered her own question, her voice tinged with bitter resolve. "I must leave this cursed place at once. I have an old aunt living in Charmouth."

"I'll go back to her."

She mentioned she had some money with a banker near Charing Cross. Once she withdrew those funds, there wouldn't be anything keeping her in London. She stood up as if to act on it immediately, but the doctor gently stopped her, revealing just how desperate her situation was—more desperate than she had realized. Most likely, the banker she named had already shut down and left a city where panic and chaos had halted all business. Even if he were still there and able to give her the money, her journey to the countryside was practically impossible. True, surviving the plague had given her a certificate of health. With that, no one could stop her from leaving. But given where she was coming from, finding someone outside London willing to shelter her was nearly impossible. She would probably be forced back by sheer necessity or even physical force before she got more than a day's journey away.

Facing the brutal truth that she was trapped in this dreadful city, seemingly abandoned by both God and man, a place filled with the unfortunate and unclean, the dead and dying, drove her to the brink of despair. For a moment, she was stunned into silence. Then came a wild, frantic outburst.

"What now? What's left? What am I supposed to do? How can I live? Dear God, I wish I had died of the plague! I see it now... the worst thing Randal Dempsey ever did was save my wretched life."

"Hush, hush!"

"What are you saying, child?" The doctor placed a comforting arm around her shoulders. "You're not completely alone," he assured softly. "I'm still here to support you, dear, and I am your friend."

"Forgive me," she pleaded. He gave her shoulder a gentle pat. "I understand. It's tough, I know. But you have to be brave. As long as we have our health and strength, no misfortune in life is beyond fixing. I'm old, my dear; I know things. Now, let's talk about your situation."

"My friend, it's beyond discussion. Who can possibly help me now?"

"I can, for one, and that's exactly what I intend to do."

"But how?"

"In several ways, depending on what's needed. But first, I can show you how to help yourself."

"Help myself?" She looked up at him, confusion knitting her brows.

"Helping others is the best way to help yourself," he explained. "Living only for yourself leads to an empty life, much like an unfaithful steward wasting his talents. True happiness comes from working for the good of others. It's a double reward. You get satisfaction from your efforts and joy from the accomplishments. And by focusing on others' needs and miseries, you forget your own sorrows."

"Yes, yes. But how can I possibly do that now?"

"Several ways, my dear. Here's one. By God's grace and another's heroic love, you were cured of the plague. This cure has made you what we call a 'safe woman' – you're immune to the infection and can move among the sick without fear. Right now, nurse-keepers are incredibly scarce. Their ranks are thinning daily, and they can't meet the rising tide of this sorrowful epidemic."

Most of the women who do it are incredibly brave. They go into the thick of it without even the safety nets you have now. And many of them, unfortunately, don't make it out," he said, pausing to adjust his glasses, squinting at her through them like he was trying to decode a message she wasn't even aware she was broadcasting. She met his gaze with wide-eyed amusement, her lips curling into a slight smile.

"And you're suggesting that I should...?" Her voice trailed off, the full weight of his suggestion sinking in and stopping her cold.

"You might consider it a debt to God and humanity for your own survival. Or perhaps, in helping to heal others, you might find a way to heal yourself. No matter your reason, it would be an act of great nobility and would surely be rewarded in ways you can't even fathom now."

She got up slowly, her thoughts clearly racing, visible in the furrow of her brow. She let out a small laugh, tinged with a trace of bitterness. "And if I don't do this, what then? What's left for me?"

"No, no," he quickly reassured her, his voice tinged with concern. "I would never push you into something you're not ready for. I completely understand if this idea feels absolutely unbearable to you. And let's be clear—I'm not abandoning you. You won't be left alone to face anything. Trust that."

She looked at him and allowed herself a small, resigned smile.

"Of course it's unbearable," she admitted candidly. "How could it be otherwise? My life has been nothing but comfort and indulgence. Maybe that's why it's so important for me to do this—maybe because it costs me more, it means more. As you said, it's a debt I owe." She reached out and placed her hand on his arm, a gesture both of resolution and of seeking strength. "I'm ready, my friend. Ready to start making things right."

CHAPTER TWENTY-SIX

I f you'd asked Colonel Dempsey later about how he spent the week after his harrowing escape from the house on Knight Ryder Street, his account would've been a fuzz-filled blur. His memories were a tangled mess, dotted with a few sharp points of clarity. The harsh truth—there's no way to sugarcoat it—is that during that entire week, he was rarely sober.

It kicked off the very night—no, rather, morning—of his evasion. With no clear destination and only the goal of putting as much distance as he could between himself and Knight Ryder Street, Dempsey found himself wandering through Carter Lane into Paul's Yard. He lingered there, hesitating, because when you're that aimless, any direction seems just as good—or bad—as the next. Finally, he veered east down Watling Street, eventually losing himself in a maze of narrow alleys.

He might've roamed there until dawn, but fate tugged him toward sounds of revelry leaking from a narrow door, beneath which a slice of light cut through the cobblestones. The unlikeliness of those sounds—so out of place in plague- ridden London, as if they'd sprung from the depths of a tomb—made him pause. He stood on that meager threshold, scrutinizing the sign above, barely able to make out its flagon shape. That alone was enough to tell him it was a tavern. And knowing that the law required such places to close at nine, it didn't take long for him to figure out that someone here was breaking the rules flagrantly.

Drawn by the idea of escaping into a void of forgetfulness, yet repulsed by the sleazy grime of the place and the certain disdain Nancy would harbor if she saw him surrender to such despicable temptation, he decided to walk on. But just as he turned, the door suddenly swung open, and a blazing shaft of yellow light cut across the street, catching him in its glare. Two staggering drunks, reeling out, paused in surprise at the sight of him standing there. Without a second thought, they descended on him, each grabbing an arm, and dragged him, weakly resisting, over the threshold of that filthy dive. The inhabitants, a motley crew, welcomed him with raucous, mindless joy.

Dempsey found himself squinting in the harsh, foul-smelling light cast by a half-dozen fish-oil lamps hanging from the low, grimy ceiling. The taverner cursed vehemently at the idiots who'd left the door open, then hurried to shut it, desperately trying to block out the noise and sight of their law-breaking revelry. As Dempsey's eyes adjusted, he surveyed the room. It was filled with a ragged assembly of seedy men and equally disreputable women. There were about thirty of them cramped into the oppressive space. The men were rogues and scoundrels, their faces etched with vice; the women, painted with garish makeup, had eyes that glittered with a mix of malice and amusement.

Some of the women were laughing hysterically, others slumped in drunken stupor, their bodies as lifeless as logs. The air was heavy with the stench of sweat and booze. The only ones not completely in their cups were a few miscreants gathered around a table, snarling over a pack of greasy cards, their eyes flashing with greedy intent.

They were the dregs of society, the men and women consigned to the city's dark corners, trapped there as if the plague itself had locked the gates. No new health certificates were being issued; there was no way out. The desperation gnawed at them, and in their usual fashion, they turned to excess, a brief escape from the perpetual terror that shrouded their lives in that necropolis.

It was a grotesque assembly, the kind of damnable congregation Asmodeus himself might have spied beneath the eaves of London on any suffocating August night. Dempsey's gaze swept over them, cold and hard like a winter's blade, while they stared back, eyes full of uncertainty and fear. The room fell silent, except for one drunken fool in the corner who continued to croak out a lewd song, oblivious to the new tension rippling through the room at the Colonel's entrance.

"Gads my life!" Dempsey eventually barked. "If I didn't know the Court's scuttled off to Salisbury, I might think I'd stumbled into Whitehall."

The acidic humor broke the tension, sending ripples of ragged laughter through the room. They soon hailed him as one of their own, a wit among degenerates, and the two drunkards who had yanked him in from the street now dragged him to a table where space was grudgingly made. Dempsey relented to his fate. He dug a few coins from his pocket and traded one for a mug of scorched wine. They caroused until the small hours, scattering like vermin at the break of dawn, each slithering to a miserable den.

Later, he bought a bed from the tavern keeper and collapsed until nearly noon. Rising bleary-eyed, he broke his fast with a bowl of salty herring and drifted back into the labyrinthine streets. Aimlessly, he wandered through the fetid, narrow alleys until he emerged at the eastern fringe of Cheapside. He stood there, thunderstruck by the transformation that had taken place over the past month. Usually bustling with life, the street was now empty and dead silent, a ghostly testament to the plague's unyielding grip.

The streets once thrived with life, bustling with the daily grind—carriages and pedestrians, horseback riders navigating the chaos, merchants shouting from their shopfronts, "What do you need?" enticing every passerby with deals too good to resist. Now, the street stretched out in eerie silence, deserted but for a few stragglers like him. One man, face turned away, pushed a wheelbarrow—its grim cargo concealed beneath a dark cloak. No coaches, no horses, no vibrant calls from merchants, not even the desperate lilt of a beggar's plea. Some shops stood open, forlorn and unvisited; a sale meant nothing without buyers. Here and there, houses were tightly shuttered, marked with the ominous red cross and guarded by stern watchmen, while others lay abandoned, forgotten by time.

The most unnerving sight, the one that drove home the depth of desolation, were the blades of grass forcing their way through the cobblestones, suggesting that but for the silent, grim rows of houses, he might forgotten he was in the heart of the city. He turned towards St. Paul's, his footsteps echoing through the empty street like the lonely tread of a late-night reveler.

Following him through those aimless meanderings would serve no purpose, for his days were spent wandering in a daze. At one point, he ventured towards Whitehall, driven by a burning desire to confirm the Duke of Buckingham had indeed fled, as Dr. Rickels had relayed. A flicker of rage pushed through the fog of his dulled mind, surfacing like oil on water. But Wallingford House greeted him with closed gates and tightly shut windows, a scene mirrored in the majority of homes along that now desolate, once grand thoroughfare.

Northridge, he learned from a chatty sailor, was still at the Cockpit. True to form, Honest George Monk remained grimly stationed,
untouched by the looming danger; indeed, he roamed freely, scoffing
at peril, absorbed in the noble task of alleviating the general suffering.
Dempsey felt a brief urge to seek him out, but it was weak, and he
resisted. A visit would only squander the time of a man who had none
to spare; consequently, Northridge was unlikely to welcome him.

Dempsey's nights were habitually spent at the Flagon, a seedy inn
tucked away in a bleak alley off Watling Street—a borough he stumbled into by pure chance. Why the place captivated him, he could
scarcely say in hindsight. It was likely his crushing loneliness that drove
him there, seeking the only company he knew he could find—a motley
crew of lost souls, similarly adrift, who sought solace in the bottom of
a wine glass and wild revelry, to temporarily forget their misery and
desolation.

Though Dempsey had fallen far, this wasn't his usual haunt, and
neither were the thieves and harlots his typical choice of companions.
Nevertheless, fate had cast him among these human wrecks, and there
he stayed, finding in the place the only thing he craved—numbing
oblivion—until death, which he hoped would mercifully bring final
peace.

The end came suddenly. It was the seventh night he spent in that
den of debauchery, and he drank even more than his usual deep habit.
Consequently, when the innkeeper finally shoved him out into the
pitch-dark alley, the last of the night's revelers, Dempsey's mind was
muddled to the brink of blackout. He staggered like a puppet, his legs
moving on autopilot, disconnected from conscious thought.

Staggering, he lurched down the lane like some flimsy mannequin,
swayed by the whims of the wind. Directionless and unconcerned, he
stumbled onto Watling Street, crossed it, and stumbled into a narrow

alley on the southern side. He moved blindly forward until his feet struck something unseen, sending him sprawling onto his face. Lacking the will and strength to rise, he lay where he fell and sank into a deep, lethargic sleep.

Half an hour passed. It was the half-hour before dawn, the darkest part of the night. A bell began to tinkle in the distance, slowly drawing nearer. A repeated cry echoed through the silence, a sound Dempsey might have understood if he'd been conscious. Joining the cry came other sounds: the mournful creak of an axle in need of grease, and the slow clank and thud of hooves on cobblestones. Closer and closer came the cry through the quiet night:

"Bring out your dead!"

The cart halted at the mouth of the alley where the Colonel lay, and a man stepped forward, holding a flaming torch above his head. Its ruddy glare cast long, wavering shadows in the dark corners of the alley. The man saw two bodies stretched out on the ground: the Colonel's and the one over which he had tripped. Shouting over his shoulder, he moved forward again. He was joined moments later by his partner, who guided the horse and puffed on a short pipe.

The torchbearer stood to light the area while his companion stooped to inspect the first body. Satisfied with his grim work, he stepped forward to the Colonel. Rolling him over, he saw that the Colonel's face was as pallid as the corpse that had felled him, his breath barely perceptible.

They barely glanced at him, their faces blank with the cold familiarity that comes from doing the job too long, and turned back to the other body. The man with the chain hooked it onto a holder fixed to the front of the death cart. Then, kneeling, they began inspecting the corpse's clothes.

"Not much to fuss over here, Larry," one of them muttered.

"Yeah," growled Larry. "Pretty sad rags. Come on, Nick. Let's get her on board."

They picked up their hooks and, with practiced ease, swung the body onto the cart.

"Bring the horse closer," Nick instructed, stepping towards Dempsey. The horse moved forward a few steps, and the cart's light fell more fully on the Colonel's sprawled figure. Nick knelt beside him, a pleased grunt escaping his lips. "This is better."

His partner peered over his shoulder.

"A real gentleman, damn it!" he swore with a twisted sense of satisfaction. Their ghoulish fingers moved swiftly over Dempsey, and they chuckled darkly at the sight of the half-dozen gold pieces now clutched in Larry's grubby hand.

"Not much else," grumbled one after another search.

"Look at his sword, a fancy hilt; see, Larry."

"And those boots are top-notch," added Larry, who was already busying himself at the Colonel's feet. "Give me a hand, Nick."

They pulled off the boots and bundled them together with the Colonel's hat and cloak. Larry dumped the bundle into a basket hung behind the cart, while Nick stayed behind to strip Dempsey of his doublet. Suddenly, he stopped.

"He's still warm, Larry," he said petulantly. Larry sauntered over, puffing on his pipe. He cursed crudely, drenched in contempt and indifference.

"So what?" he added cynically. "He'll be cold enough by the time we reach Aldgate." He laughed as he took the doublet Nick tossed to him.

The next moment, their grimy hooks snagged the clothes that still clung to Dempsey, and they threw him onto the horrific heap already half-filling their cart. They reversed the creaking vehicle out of the alley and lumbered eastward, heading to the dreaded pit at Aldgate. Periodically, their sluggish journey was interrupted, either by the shout of a watchman or by something wretched they stumbled upon themselves. At each stop, they added to their grisly load, hauling away more bodies for a hasty burial in the Aldgate plague pit. Over that forsaken place, corpse-candles flickered tirelessly in the stifling nights, feeding the belief that tortured souls wandered restlessly among the shallow graves, their decaying bodies scarcely covered by loose earth.

They were almost there, the pit drawing nearer as the first light of dawn crept into the sky—pallid, cold, and devoid of color like a lifeless stone. The cart's relentless jolting, or perhaps the persistent flow of blood from a gouge on his thigh, or maybe the instinctual surge of self-preservation, jolted Colonel Dempsey awake. With a sudden rush of panic, he fought for breath, struggling to push off the heavy weight smothering his face. At first, his attempts were feeble, befitting his alcohol-soaked state; brief snatches of air were all he could manage, like a drowning man breaking the surface only to be dragged under again.

But as each effort brought sharper waves of suffocating terror, clarity cut through his drunken haze. Driven by a primal fear, he mustered his strength and heaved forcefully until his head finally broke free. Above him, the stars were fading, and for the first time in what felt like an eternity, he could draw a full breath, the foul stench around him be damned.

The weight he thought he'd pushed from his mind now lay heavy on his chest, a suffocating presence that hurt with every breath. Reaching out, he felt the distinct shape of a human arm beneath his fingers. He shook it hard, frustration building as there was no response.

"Hey, you drunk fool," he growled, voice slurred and rough. "Get up. I'm not your bed. Get off me! Get up!" His anger flared with each word, the lack of response only feeding his rage. "Get up, or I'll—"

His words were cut short when a sudden light blazed across his eyes. The torchlight had pierced the darkness, casting eerie shadows that danced wildly in his blurred vision. The cart had come to a halt, and over its tall sides appeared the ghastly figures of the carters, drawn by the sound of his voice. The hellish glow of the torch revealed their vile, almost demonic faces, bringing him closer to a sobering clarity. He struggled to sit up, his mind reeling, desperately trying to piece together where he was. Through the crimson haze came the nasal whine of one of those ghouls.

"Told you he was still warm, Larry."

"Yeah, so what?" the other snapped irritably.

"Dump him out, obviously."

"Leave him. If he's not stiff yet, he will be soon enough. What's it to us?"

"And what about the plague examiner, you idiot? He'll see it's just a drunk passed out and ask us questions. Just dump him! Lend a hand!"

But Dempsey no longer needed their help. Their words and the grim reality of his surroundings had driven home the horror of his situation.

The sheer terror of it all didn't just sober him up; it injected him with a raw, almost inhuman strength. He hauled himself free, gasping for air as he fought to his knees. He gripped the side of the cart, pulling himself to his feet, swinging a leg over, and leaping to the ground, nearly face-planting in the process. By the time he managed to stand, the cart was already rolling away, the rough, throaty laughter of the carters echoing through the eerie silence of the street.

Dempsey bolted away from the sinister sound, retracing his steps. It wasn't until he had put some distance between himself and the obnoxious cackling, until the cursed cart's clatter had faded into the night, that he began to process his situation. Cloak, hat, doublet, boots—gone. His sword and the few coins he had left? Somehow, that seemed like a minor detail. Mostly, he was cold, shivering uncontrollably, and his head throbbed like a molten lead weight. He reassured himself that he was sober—his thoughts were clear, and he could piece together not only what had happened to him but the sequence of events.

Mechanically, he lurched forward, like a man adrift in a waking nightmare. The sky shifted slowly from the ghostly pallor of pre-dawn to the fiery hues of morning. Without realizing it, he stumbled to a stop, drained of all energy. He collapsed into the doorway of a deserted house, seeking shelter, and his exhaustion claimed him instantly.

When he awoke, sunlight was blazing down from a high noon sky.

Dempsey blinked his eyes open, finding himself in a place he didn't recognize, the surroundings unfamiliarly foreign, like he'd stumbled into someone else's dream. Right in the middle of the street, there stood a man, his black attire stark against the dusk. Leaning on a crimson cane, the man in the steeple hat watched him carefully.

"You okay?" the man asked, noting Dempsey's dazed expression. Irritated, Dempsey shot back, "Seeing you," he snarled, forcing his aching body upright. "That's what's wrong."

But as he rose, a wave of dizziness tried to pull him back down. He steadied himself against a nearby doorpost, but soon, the strength seeped out of him like sand in an hourglass, and he collapsed back onto the step that had served as his bed. For a few moments, he sat there, addled and confused, wondering what had brought him to this state. Suddenly, a thought struck him with the force of a hammer.

Ripping open his shirt, he yelled, "I lied!" His voice rang out wildly in the empty street. When he next looked up, he was laughing, a manic, triumphant sound. "I lied! There is something else. Look!" He yanked his shirt further apart, revealing what he had discovered.

That was when everything faded to black. The last thing he saw was the man's eyes widening in horror as he set eyes on Dempsey's chest, where the grotesque flower of the plague had bloomed while he had slept.

CHAPTER TWENTY-SEVEN

For Colonel Dempsey, life had crawled into some dark corner of his mind, leaving him to wrestle with demons on an otherworldly plane. There, he faced twisted visions and haunting battles, relentless clashes against an opponent draped in black and white satin. This phantom wore the face of His Grace of Buckingham, ever poised to bring death yet tortuously holding back. The duels always unfolded in a somber, wood-paneled room, lit only by a cluster of candles in a silver candelabrum, witnessed by a ghostlike woman clad in white. Her face was pallid, her eyes a cold sea-green, her hair a heavy cascade of chestnut. She giggled and clapped her hands, reveling in every brutal twist of the encounter.

Occasionally, the scenes shifted. One moment, they battled in a cherry orchard, the next inside a modest peasant's cottage near Worcester. But no matter where his fevered mind took him, the players remained steadfast: Dempsey, the Duke, and the eerie woman. Reality blurred as Dempsey lived through these nightmares, perpetually fighting, relentlessly restless.

Dempsey finally broke free from his delirium, waking to sanity just to think he was about to die. As he pulled together his fragmented memories, he took stock of his surroundings. He lay on a rough pallet near a window. Through it, he saw the restless dance of leaves and a strip of indigo sky. Above him stretched bare rafters, the ceiling long gone.

He turned his head, eyes sweeping over a long, barn-like room dotted with others like him, each lying on similarly crude pallets. Some were deathly still, others writhed and groaned, while one soul fought violently against those trying to restrain him. It was a grim scene for anyone, let alone a man as frail as Dempsey. He turned back toward the window, locking his gaze onto that thin slice of sky.

A profound calm blanketed his battered soul. Clarity washed over him—he understood his dire situation all too well.

He was ravaged by the plague, hanging on by this slender thread of awareness—the kind that often heralds the end. It was a final gift, this consciousness, allowing him to thank God that his wretched life was finally running its course and that peace awaited him just beyond the veil. The thought alone was enough to erase the shame that had shadowed him, the ever-present specter of disgust he knew he had kindled in her, the one he had wronged so deeply. He remembered the exhaustive confession he had left for her. And it brought him solace, a bitter kind of sweetness before he slipped into the cold embrace of death, that its words—laying bare the twists of fate that had forged him into a villain—might soften her inevitable scorn.

Tears welled up, brimming over and tracing hollow paths down his gaunt cheeks. These were not tears of self-pity but of physical frailty and a strange, aching gratitude. He heard footsteps approaching, soft and deliberate. Someone was there, bending over him. He turned his head and looked up, and in that instant, fear gripped him tight, making his heart seem to contract into a cold, hard knot.

"I'm dreaming again," he whispered, the sound barely more than a breath.

Standing by his bedside was a young woman, her figure neat in the plain grey homespun, accented by the white bands, bib, and coif of the Puritans. Her face was small, pale, and delicately oval, and her eyes—an arresting blend of blue and green—held a wistful look. A few heavy chestnut curls had escaped the confines of her coif, resting softly against her white neck. A fine, cool hand reached for his where it lay weakly on the coverlet, and a voice, gentle and mournfully melodic, broke the silence.

"No, Randal, you're awake."

"You're awake! Thank God!"

He finally noticed her eyes, glistening with tears, longing and relieved.

"Where am I?" he asked, his confusion genuine for the first time since waking up. He almost believed all those memories from before his delirium had just been dreams.

"You're in the pest-house at Bunhill Fields," she said, which only added to his bewilderment.

"That makes sense... I know I have the plague. I remember getting sick. But you? How did you end up in a pest-house?"

"There was nowhere else for me to go after I left that house on Knight Ryder Street." She briefly recounted her circumstances. "Dr. Rickels brought me here. I've been tending to the plague victims ever since, by the grace of Providence," she concluded.

"And you looked after me? You?" His voice, weakened but filled with astonishment.

"Didn't you care for me once?" she replied. He shook his frail, pallid hand in disagreement, then sighed and smiled, a contentment softening his features.

"God is merciful to a sinner like me. As I lay here, all I desired was for you, knowing the truth of my wrongdoings and the temptations that led me astray, to offer a word of pity and forgiveness... to ease my passing."

"Your passing? Why speak of death?"

"Because it's coming, by God's mercy. Dying from the plague is the fate I deserve. I sought it, but it eluded me. Yet, by chance, it found me. My whole life has been like that. What I desire always slips away. When I stop chasing, it finds me unexpectedly."

In every part of my life, I've been Fortune's plaything, and it seems my death is no different."

She wanted to interrupt, but he pressed on, fooled by his own frailty.

"Just listen for a moment, in case I don't make it through. There's something I need to add to the letter I left for you. I swear, with my last flicker of faith, that I had no idea it was you the Duke wanted me to kidnap. If I had known, I would have died before agreeing to his scheme. Do you believe me?"

"You don't need to convince me, Randal. I never questioned it. How could I?"

"How could you, indeed? Yes. That's true. You couldn't have. At least that much wouldn't have been possible, no matter how low I might have fallen." He looked at her, his eyes full of sorrow. "I hardly dare to hope you'll forgive me for everything..."

"But I do, Randal. I do. I forgave you long ago. When I realized the lengths you went to for my sake, how you risked your life to make things right, I couldn't hold anything against you. I forgave you then, knowing the full story only reinforces that. I forgive you completely and unconditionally, dear Randal."

"Say it again," he pleaded softly. She repeated it, tears streaming down her face.

"Then I can be at peace. What do all my unfulfilled dreams of knighthood and grand ambitions matter? This was my inevitable end. I was foolish not to embrace the simple good I was born into. We could have been happy, Nan. Neither of us would have had to chase the hollow triumphs of the world."

"You talk like you're about to die," she said through her sobs. "But you'll get better."

"That would be the final folly, to survive when I could die so contentedly."

And then the doctor entered, cutting them off, and confirmed her words, assuring her that Dempsey was now out of danger.

The reality was stark and undeniable. What he had done for her when she was racked with the plague, she had now done for him. Through relentless care during the endless hours of his feverish delirium, heedless of the toll it took on her own strength, she had guided him back from the brink. Even as he spoke of dying, his voice fragile and weakened, convinced he hovered at death's door, his recovery was already taking root. In less than a week, he was up and moving, the infection banished from his system. But before he could re-enter the world, he had to endure the mandated period of isolation to ensure he posed no risk of spreading the disease. They planned to move him from the pest-house to a nearby convalescence home.

When the time came to leave, he sought out Nancy. She was waiting for him on the lawn beneath towering old cedar trees that lent a solemn grace to the converted farmhouse hospital. She stood there, slender and elegant, while he struggled to steady his voice to deliver the words of a final goodbye. This was far from what she had been expecting, and the pallor of dismay that washed over her face made that plain.

There was a stone bench nearby in the shade, and she sank down onto it, her strength ebbing, as he stood beside her, waiting for her to release him. He was dressed in simple clothes that she had secretly arranged for him, though he believed them to be a parting gift from the compassionate pest-house staff. She composed herself enough to ask in a steady voice:

"What are you going to do? Where will you go when... when the month is over?"

He smiled faintly and shrugged. "I haven't really thought about it," he replied, his words telling her one thing, but his tone revealing he hadn't given their future or his a moment's contemplation.

Fate, some might say, had favored him; it had given him back his life when it was on the brink of being snatched away. But Fate, ever the trickster, teased him with gifts when he could no longer make use of them. "Maybe," he mused, meeting her unblinking gaze, "I should head to France. A soldier can always find work there."

She lowered her eyes, and a heavy silence settled between them. When she finally spoke again, her voice was calm and deliberate, as if laying out an argument she'd pondered endlessly.

"Do you remember that day we talked in the house on Knight Ryder Street, right after I'd recovered? I wanted to thank you for saving my life, but you rejected my gratitude just as you turned down the forgiveness I offered. You thought my thanks were born only out of the debt I owed you."

"That's right," he said. "And it's still true. It can't be any other way."

"Are you so certain?" Her eyes flickered up to his, seeking something.

"I am as certain as I am that you're lying to yourself out of your own kindness," he replied.

"Am I? Let's say I was. But if you claim I still am, you're missing a crucial point. I'm no longer in your debt. I've repaid you in a fuller way. Just as you saved my life, I have saved yours. I thanked God for the chance to do it because it cleared the debt that seemed to separate us. We're even now, Randal. I don't owe you anything more. I've repaid you, so I'm no longer obligated to feel grateful. You can't deny that."

"I wouldn't if I could."

"Then don't you see? With no debts between us, with no obligations to you, I've forgiven you freely, sincerely, and completely."

"Your offense wasn't really against me…"

"It was, it was," he cut in with fierce intensity. "Against you and my own honor. It made me undeserving."

"Even so, from the moment I learned how you were cruelly driven, I forgave you entirely. In fact, I think I forgave you long before that. My heart told me, my senses told me when you tried to save me from the Duke of Buckingham, that some misfortune must be behind your actions."

A faint blush broke through the pallor his illness had left on his cheeks. He bowed his head.

"Bless you for those words. They'll give me the courage to face whatever's coming. I'll cherish the memory of your kindness always."

"But you still don't believe me!" she cried. "You think there are still traces of resentment in my heart!"

"No, Nan. I believe you."

"And yet you're still leaving?"

"What else can I do? Knowing all you do now, you must see there's no place for me in England."

A quick reply was on her lips, but she couldn't bring herself to say it. Not yet. So she hung her head again, searching desperately for another way to break through his stubborn pride. Failing to reason with him, she turned to sentiment. From her gown's bodice, she pulled a worn, tasselled glove. Holding it out to him, she looked up, and he saw her eyes glistening with tears.

"Here's something that belongs to you, Randal. Take it."

"Take it; it's all you'll have of me."

Hesitant, almost not daring to believe, he took the small, delicate glove, still warm and sweet from her touch, and held onto her offered hand as well.

"It... it will be a talisman again," he whispered, "to keep me worthy as... as it failed to once." He bowed over her hand, pressing it gently to his lips. "Goodbye, Nan. May God always protect you."

He tried to let go, but she held on tightly.

"Randal!" she cried, her voice sharp and desperate, a plea from a heart that wanted more than he dared to give. In sorrowful reproach, she added, "Can you really think of leaving me again?"

His face turned as pale as death, and he trembled.

"What else can I do?" he asked, his voice filled with anguish.

"That's something you need to decide for yourself."

"What answer can I give?" His usually steady and commanding grey eyes now looked at her almost fearfully. He moistened his lips before continuing. "Am I supposed to let you gather up the shattered pieces of my wretched life with hands full of pity?"

"Pity?" she cried out, rejecting the notion. Then, shaking her head slightly, she asked, "And what if it is pity? What then? Oh, Randal, if I pity you, do you have none for me?"

"Pity for you? I thank God you don't need pity."

"Don't I? What else can you call my situation? I've waited years with as much patience and fortitude as I could muster for the one I believed I belonged to, and when he finally comes, he rejects me."

He laughed at that, but it was a bitter, humorless sound.

"No, no," he said. "I'm not so easily fooled by your charitable acts. Admit it, out of pity you're just playing a part."

"I get it. You think because I was once an actress, I must always be acting."

Do you believe me, I wonder? When I swear to you that in all those years of agonizing waiting, I resisted every temptation that came my way, keeping myself pure for you? Do you believe that? And if you do believe it, will you betray me now?

"Believe it! Oh God! If I didn't, perhaps I could relent more easily. The distance between us would feel less overwhelming."

"There's no distance between us, Randal. It's been crossed and crossed again."

Finally, he pulled his hand away from her grasp. "Why do you test me, Nan?" he cried, his voice raw with pain. "God knows you can't need me. What do I have to offer? I'm as bankrupt of fortune as I am of honor."

"Do women love men for what they bring?" she asked him. "Is that what a mercenary life has taught you? Oh, Randal, you spoke of Chance and how it dictated your whole life, and yet you've learned nothing from it. A world lay between us, and we were lost to each other. Yet Chance brought us back together. And if the way of it was dark, it was still the way of Chance. Again we parted. You left me driven by shame and wounded pride—yes, pride, Randal—thinking the separation would be forever. And here we are together once more. Will you demand that Chance perform this miracle for a third time?"

He looked at her with a steady gaze now, a man who had found his honor again, despite all the scourges that had befallen him.

"If I've been Chance's victim my whole life, that's no reason why you should be too. Out there, there's the great world, your art, life, and joy when this pestilence finally ends. I have nothing to offer you in exchange for all that. Nothing, Nan. My entire worth is the clothes on my back. If it were anything else..."

Oh, but why waste words and spiral into torturous thoughts about what might be? We have to deal with what is. Goodbye!"

Abruptly, he turned on his heel and left her. So sudden was his departure that it took her by surprise, leaving her speechless, unable to stop him. Like a dream, she watched his tall, lean, soldierly figure stride away through the trees towards the avenue.

At last, she half-rose, a little fluttering cry escaping her lips.

"Randal! Randal!"

But he was already too far away to hear her, even if he would have listened.

Chapter Twenty-eight

F ate hadn't finished with Colonel Dempsey just yet. By the middle of September, a month after his last encounter, he was finally free from quarantine, clutching a certificate of health like a prisoner handed his release papers. He hadn't seen Nancy since they last met—such a meeting would have been impossible, prohibited by the strict isolation protocols that had kept him from anyone and anything tainted. Now, cleared and healthy, he was a man set loose into a city that scarcely resembled the one he had known.

In the days leading up to his release, Dempsey had mulled over his next move. Freedom didn't come with directions, and he needed a plan. He settled on his old notion of joining a ship bound for France, thinking it the quickest route to a new life. But he had one pressing problem: he was utterly broke. His possessions amounted to the threadbare clothes on his back. Taking alms from the pest-house authorities wasn't an option—his pride revolted at the thought of accepting charity from those who had already done more for him than he could repay.

So, within an hour of being discharged, he hit the nearly deserted streets, heading for Wapping on foot. He didn't have a choice; his pockets were empty, and the usual riverboats and hackney-coaches had long since ceased operations. London was now more like a city of the dead than a bustling metropolis.

As Dempsey trudged along, he couldn't ignore the massive bonfires of sea-coal burning in the streets. At first, the sight confused him. What purpose did they serve in a city devoid of life? It wasn't until he crossed paths with a lone traveler that he understood. The fires were the Lord Mayor's desperate attempt, sanctioned by His Grace of Northridge, to purge the air of lingering contagion. Yet the week-old fires seemed to mock such efforts, as the reek of death still clung to the air like an unwelcome guest refusing to leave.

The city's lifeless streets stretched out before him, lined with the futile flames that neither warmed the soul nor cleansed the air. Dempsey's steps echoed in the eerie silence, a lone man navigating through a landscape that felt more like a graveyard than the London he once knew.

The death toll that week was staggering—higher than anyone had ever seen. Eight thousand souls, a number that seemed almost too monstrous to grasp. Dempsey marveled that anyone was still alive in London to die. Trudging through the oppressive heat of that unrelenting summer, he made his way through the empty, desolate streets until he arrived at the Fleet Ditch.

It was there that he remembered The Harp on Wood Street, where he'd once lodged, and its owner, the ever-friendly Banks. Banks had risked a lot to warn him that the law was on his tail. Now, it was his total desperation that shaped his path. If not for his dire state, he might not have recalled that he'd left some of his belongings behind in his hasty departure—a set of fine clothes among them.

He chuckled darkly at the thought of snakeskin suits in his current predicament. The rough homespun garb he wore now was more suitable for someone looking for work on a ship. But if he could retrieve those clothes, he might be able to sell them for a bit of money to tide him over. The absurd idea that Lady Luck would be so generous as to let him find The Harp still in business, or Banks still alive, brought a bitter laugh to his lips. Feeble though it was, hope was all he had left.

So, he angled his footsteps towards Wood Street. Most of the city looked the same—three out of four shops were shut tight, and the few that remained open had hardly any trade. Even Proctor's famed eatery, The Mitre, known to be the most illustrious dining spot in London, was boarded up. To Dempsey, this felt like a bad omen.

But he pressed on and, to his astonishment, found himself standing before the modest Harp. Its windows were clean and open, the door swinging wide.

Dempsey stepped over the threshold into the dimly lit common room on his left. The floor was swept clean, and the long wooden tables scrubbed to a bright sheen. Yet, business was as dead as the night outside; there was just one patron—a man in a stained apron, jerking awake from a hard wooden armchair with a startled exclamation:

"By God, a customer!"

Dempsey glared at the man who'd roused himself from his slumber. It was Banks, the vintner himself. But this Banks was a shadow of his former self, his once ample belly now hollowed, and his rosy cheeks faded and gaunt.

"Colonel Dempsey!" he hollered, eyes wide with surprise. "Or is it your ghost we're seeing? More ghosts than living souls in this cursed city now."

"We're both just specters, I think, Banks," Dempsey replied, his voice a dry rasp.

"Maybe so, but our throats are still flesh and blood, thank the Lord! And there's some sack left at The Harp. Dr. Hodges swears by it, says a good sack with plenty of nutmeg will ward off the sweat. That's been my lifeline. What do you say, Colonel? Shall we partake in some of this liquid medicine?"

"I'd say yes with all my heart. But, alas! I'm flat broke."

"Broke?" Banks scoffed. "Take a seat, Colonel."

Banks fetched a dusty bottle of wine and poured dark, swirling liquid into two glasses.

"A plague on the plague, is the toast," he declared. They clinked glasses and drank deeply. "Good God, Colonel, I am glad to see you alive. Feared the plague had taken you. And you dodged not just the plague but those bloodhounds that were on your trail." Without waiting for a response, he added in a low voice, "Heard how Danvers got caught and then slipped away—good for him! But that conspiracy's old news now, not even the government cares. They're too busy with other nightmares. But what of you, Colonel?"

"My story's quickly told. I haven't fared as well as you might think. I've had the plague."

"Damnation! You've had it?"

"So, you made it through!" Banks looked at him with newfound respect. "Guess you were born under a lucky star, sir."

"Quite the revelation," said the Colonel dryly.

"Not many make it out," the vintner said with a shake of his head. "And having survived the plague makes you a rare bird. You can come and go without worry."

"And your remedy is wasted on me. But while I'm safe, I'm flat broke. That's why I'm here—to see if you've still got any of my stuff that I can turn into coin."

"Sure thing, it's all here," Banks assured him. "A fine suit, boots, a hat, a baldric, and some other odds and ends. They're upstairs, ready whenever you need them. But what's on your mind, Colonel, if you don't mind me asking?"

Dempsey mentioned his plan to work his way to France on a ship. The vintner frowned, studying him from under furrowed brows.

"Sir," he said, "there's no French ships or any headed that way at Wapping, and barely any ships at all. The plague's killed all that. London's port is as empty as an old grave. No foreign ship's coming in, and no English ship's leaving because no port will take them, fearing the plague."

The Colonel's face fell in dismay. It felt like the final blow of his relentless bad luck.

"I'll have to get to Portsmouth, then," he said gloomily. "God knows how I'll manage that."

"You won't. Portsmouth won't have you, nor will any other town in England, coming as you do from London."

"I'm telling you, sir, the whole countryside is gripped with fear of the plague."

"But I've got a health certificate."

"You'd better get it signed by a high-ranking official before Portsmouth lets you through their gates."

Dempsey stared at him for a moment, then let out a bitter laugh.

"In that case, I'm not sure what's left to do. I suppose you don't need a drawer these days?"

The vintner frowned, pondering the first question more deeply.

"Well, you say you're a clean man. Haven't you seen the Duke of Northridge's announcement for clean men?"

"For clean men? For what purpose?"

"The announcement doesn't specify. Maybe you'll find out in Whitehall. But there's some kind of service the Duke is offering to those who are safe. Given your situation, it might be worth looking into. Could be something useful for you, at least for now."

"Maybe," Dempsey said. "And it seems that's my only option. They probably need scavengers or drivers for the death carts."

"No, no, it's bound to be better than that," Banks said, taking him literally. Dempsey stood up. "Whatever it is, when a man faces starvation, he needs to remember that pride won't fill an empty stomach."

"No, it won't," Banks agreed, glancing at the Colonel's shabby clothes. "But if you're planning to visit Whitehall, you should change into the other suit upstairs. You won't get past the guards in those rags."

So you see, emerging from The Harp, a Colonel Dempsey quite different from the one who entered it an hour earlier. Dressed in a dark blue camlet suit adorned with a touch of gold lace, black Spanish boots, and a black beaver hat with a royal blue plume, he cut an exceptional figure rarely seen on the London streets at that time. Though without a sword, he carried a long cane, projecting an air of something almost lost in the city's fearful climate.

Maybe it was because of this that his sudden appearance at the Cockpit startled the few remaining, mostly idle ushers into action. They scrambled to announce him immediately. He waited for just a moment in the empty anteroom, where three months ago, he had overheard Mr. Pepys of the Navy Office loudly declaring England's desperate need for experienced soldiers. The usher who went to announce him returned almost immediately and led him into that delightful chamber overlooking the park. Here, the Duke of Northridge was standing in for the pleasure-seeking libertine prince who had abandoned his plague-stricken capital. The Duke heaved himself up as the Colonel entered the room.

"So you finally decided to show up, Randal!" he greeted him with a startling grin. "I swear, I thought the plague had claimed you, given how long you took to respond to my letter."

"Your letter?" Dempsey replied, staring blankly at the Duke while shaking his offered hand.

"Yes, my letter. The one I sent you nearly a month ago to the Paul's Head?"

"No," said Dempsey. "I never received any letter."

"But..." Northridge looked like he couldn't believe it. "The landlady there kept it for you. She mentioned you were away at the time but would return in a day or two and that you'd get the letter as soon as you were back."

"A month ago, you say? But it's been over two months since I left the Paul's Head!"

"What are you telling me? Wait. My messenger can explain this." And he moved swiftly toward the bell-rope, but Dempsey stopped him.

"No, no," he said with a wry smile. "There's no need. I think I understand. Mrs. Quinn must have let her malice run wild. Your messenger likely announced where he came from, and Mrs. Quinn, fearing the news might benefit me, made sure he couldn't find me."

"Seems the plague spared that wretched woman."

The Duke's face turned a dangerous shade of red. "What's this? Are you accusing her of hiding a message from a state office? By God, if she's alive, I'll have her locked up."

"Leave her be," Dempsey said, gripping his arm. "To hell with her! Tell me about the letter. You don't mean you found a job for me after all, do you?"

"Do you doubt it, Randal? Did you question my effort on your behalf?"

"It's not your effort I doubted, but the possibility of you helping someone in my position."

"True, but Buckingham vouched for your loyalty before the Justices. I heard all about that. And when the opportunity arose, the chance for this Bombay command that I'd intended for you from the start..."

"Bombay command?" Dempsey was starting to wonder if he was dreaming. "But I thought Buckingham reserved that for a friend of his."

"Sir Henry Stanhope, yes. He did, and Stanhope left for the Indies with the commission. But he was already carrying the plague when he set sail. He died of it on the voyage. Providence, though—poor devil—for he was no more suited for the command than to be Archbishop of Canterbury. I wrote to you right away, asking you to meet me here. I waited a fortnight for your reply. When you didn't respond, I figured either you had the plague or no longer wanted the position, so I appointed another gentleman of promise."

Dempsey felt the wings of his soaring hopes collapse, and he fell back into despair with a groan.

"But that's not the end of it," Northridge interrupted. "No sooner had I appointed this other man than he, too, caught the plague and died a week ago. I've found another suitable candidate—not an easy task these days—and I had planned to appoint him to the vacant office tomorrow."

"But if you're not afraid that this commission carries the plague's curse, it's yours, and we'll have it drawn up immediately."

Dempsey struggled to catch his breath. "You ... you mean ... I'm actually going to get the command?" It seemed impossible. He couldn't
bring himself to believe it.

"That's exactly what I'm saying. The commission is ..." Northridge
suddenly stopped, stepping back. "What's wrong with you, man?
You're pale as death. You're not sick, are you?" He pulled out a handkerchief, its pungent scent of myrrh and ginger filling the air, making
it clear to Dempsey what the Duke feared. Northridge thought the
plague, which he hinted at being tied to this commission, was already
taking hold of the man he intended to honor. The irony hit Dempsey
hard, and he burst into laughter, startling the Duke further.

"No need to worry about me," he reassured the Duke. "I'm perfectly healthy and carry no disease. I left Bunhill Fields just this morning."

"What?" Northridge was taken aback. "You mean you've had the
plague?"

"That's exactly why I'm here. I'm immune now. I came because
your proclamation asked for immune men."

Northridge continued to stare at him, his amazement growing.

"So that's what brought you here?" he finally asked, comprehension dawning.

"Without that, I wouldn't have come."

"Good God!" Northridge exclaimed, repeating himself with a
laugh, finding the situation almost humorous in its complexity.
"Good God! The ways of Fate!"

"Fate," Dempsey echoed, suddenly grave, as he realized how this
unexpected twist of fortune had altered the entire course of his life.
"It seems Fate has finally favored me, though it waited until I hit
rock bottom. Without your proclamation, and without Mrs. Quinn,
I would have been a fool to miss out on this commission once again."

It would have been here waiting for me, and I never would have known. The very spite Mrs. Quinn used to try to harm me has actually worked out in my favor. If she had told your messenger the truth—that I had disappeared and that she had no idea where I was—you would have never tracked me down, and you wouldn't have waited those two weeks. Everything might have changed." He paused, lost in a sense of awe that Northridge did not share.

"Maybe, maybe," said Northridge briskly. "But what matters now is that you're here, and the position is yours if you still want it. The fear of the plague won't deter you, since you're in the clear now. It's an important role, as I told you, and if you handle its responsibilities well, as I know you will, it could be a stepping-stone to bigger things. What do you say?"

"Say?" Dempsey exclaimed, his cheeks flushed, his gray eyes shimmering. "I thank you with all my heart."

"Then you accept. Good! I believe you're exactly the right man for the job." Northridge moved to his writing desk, picked a parchment with a heavy seal from a pile of documents, and sat down to write swiftly. After a few seconds, he dusted the writing, then handed over the document. "Here, then, is your commission. How soon can you set sail?"

"In a month," Dempsey replied without hesitation.

"A month!" Northridge was taken aback. He frowned. "Why, man, you should be ready in a week."

"I could be ready in a day myself. But I mean to seize this new tide of fortune fully, and—"

But Northridge interrupted him, impatient.

"Don't you realize the time that's already been lost? The position has been vacant for four months now."

"Which means there's a capable lieutenant handling things. Let him continue a bit longer. Once I'm there, I'll make up for lost time quickly. That I can promise you."

"You see, I might actually need a partner, someone who's going to take at least a month to be ready."

With a wild confidence that made his heart race, he added, "You've said I'm the perfect man for the job. Well, the government can wait a month, or you can choose someone who's less likely to do the job as well as I can."

Northridge gave him a wry smile from across the table, his eyes sharp and probing. "You're full of surprises today, Master Randal. This one really throws me."

"Want me to explain?"

"It would be a revelation."

Dempsey spilled his story, and Northridge listened with a keen, almost empathetic interest. When Dempsey finished, the Duke sighed, turning aside to flip through the pages of a notebook at his elbow.

"Well, well," he said finally, his finger trailing down an entry. "The English Lass is prepping for her voyage at Portsmouth. She's supposed to be ready in two weeks, but delays are pretty much a given these days. Odds are, she won't be ready in less than three weeks. I'll make sure she's not set to sail under a month."

With a rush of emotion, the Colonel reached out both hands to the Duke.

"You're a true friend!" he exclaimed. Northridge clasped his hands firmly. "You're damnably like your father, God rest him," he said. Then, almost abruptly, "Off with you now, and good luck. I won't ask you to stay and see her grace right now since you're in a rush. You can kiss her hands before you sail. Now go!"

Dempsey turned to leave but paused at the door, his face revealing a mix of gratitude and concern.

"Even though I have the King's commission and hold an important position, I'm flat broke," he admitted. "Not a single shilling to my name."

Without hesitation, Northridge produced a purse and counted out twenty pounds. There wasn't the slightest hint of reluctance.

"Consider it a loan," Dempsey said, gathering the gold coins.

"No, no," Northridge corrected him firmly. "An advance. Don't worry about it."

"The Treasury better give me my money back immediately."

CHAPTER TWENTY-NINE

C olonel Dempsey tore away from Whitehall, the green expanse of Islington in his sights. His heart pounded with a vigor it hadn't felt in years, surging through his chest with the energy of a younger man. His legs churned the ground beneath him as his mind raced even further ahead, locked on the destination and the hope it promised. But hope has a way of souring quickly when misfortune has been a constant companion.

A chill twisted through him as dread crept into his thoughts. Fortune had played him for a fool so many times that trusting her now felt like inviting disaster. It had been four long weeks since he'd last seen Nancy. The house of rest where he'd been confined offered no news, its occupants isolated from those trapped in the pest-houses. A month is more than enough time for calamity to strike. She could have been harmed or worse, and even if she had left, she wouldn't have been released until she completed the mandatory quarantine.

The dread began to suffocate him, curling around his thoughts like a snake. His entire life seemed a series of near-misses and cruel twists of fate, setting him up for one last, grand disappointment. Even now, with fortune seemingly favoring him, he couldn't shake the feeling that it might already be too late—that the universe was toying with him one final time.

By the time he reached the sprawling fields leading to the lazaretto's spiked gates, he was breathless and drenched in sweat. The sight of the stout gates brought a mix of desperation and determination crashing over him. A stern, solitary figure stood guard, eyes hard as flint.

"You can't come in, sir. What's your business here?" The man's voice was like iron.

"Happiness," Dempsey replied, with a note of conviction that startled even the guard. The word hung in the air like a madman's rant, but there was no mistaking the authority in his stance, a forcefulness that transcended sanity, demanding to be reckoned with.

He radiated that old mix of friendly arrogance, now cloaked in a heavy shroud of despair and soul-weariness. His command to open the gate came with a gravity that couldn't be easily brushed off.

"You understand, sir," the gatekeeper asked, "that once you go in, you can't come back out for at least twenty-eight days, right?"

"I understand," Dempsey said firmly. "I'm ready to pay the price. So, in the name of God, open up, my friend."

The gatekeeper shrugged, a gesture filled with the resignation of someone who thought he was watching a fool rush toward his undoing. "You've been warned," he said, lifting the bar and clearing the way. Colonel Dempsey stepped through. The gates clanked shut behind him, and he moved briskly, almost at a run, down the long, shaded avenue, the beech trees and elms casting a flickering pattern of light and shadow along his path. He headed straight for the closest red-brick outhouse, the one he had occupied during his illness.

An elderly woman, stout and formidable, spotted him from the doorway. Surprise and alarm crossed her features as she hurried toward him, shouting for him to stop. But he kept coming, heedless and breathless, until they stood face to face.

"How did you get in here, you foolish man?" she exclaimed.

"Don't you recognize me, Mrs. Barlow?" he asked.

Her eyes widened with renewed shock at the sound of that familiar voice. She looked him over again, squinting at the transformation. Beneath the robust energy and finer clothes that almost made him unrecognizable, she finally recognized the man she remembered as haggard and poorly dressed just a month ago.

"Good heavens! It's Colonel Dempsey!" she gasped, her voice tinged with distress. "But you were supposed to leave the house of rest today. What in the world brought you back here, risking everything again?"

"Not to undo anything, Mrs. Barlow. To get things done, by God's help. But you've got a remarkable memory to recall I was leaving today!"

She shook her head, a sad smile tugging at her lips. "It wasn't just me who remembered, sir."

"It was Miss Russell," she said, shaking her head again.

"She's here, then! Is she okay?"

"Well enough, poor dear. But she's so terribly sad. She's over there, resting under the cedars, where she's been a lot this past month."

Without another word, he turned and hurried across the lawn towards the cluster of cedars. In the shadow of their gnarled trunks, he could see the faint flutter of a gray gown. This was where she had spent much of her time recently, Mrs. Barlow had told him. It was also where they'd said their farewells. Surely, this time, Fortune wouldn't be so cruel. Not again would she snatch away hope just as it was within his grasp.

As he drew nearer, the soft turf muffling his footsteps, he saw her sitting on the stone bench where he had left her a month ago, convinced he would never see her again. Her back was turned to him, but he could sense the heavy gloom weighing her down. He paused, heart pounding, uncertain if he should go on. He didn't want to startle her, but there was no way to avoid it.

He stood there, breathless, not knowing what to do. Then, as if she sensed him, she slowly turned around. Her eyes met his, wide with shock, her face pale.

"Randal!" She jumped to her feet, facing him. He stepped forward, urgency and longing propelling him.

"Oh, Randal, why have you come here?"

"You should have gone today..."

"I went, and I've come back, Nan," he said, now standing beside her.

"You've come back!" She eyed him carefully now, taking in the brave suit of dark blue camlet that suited his tall, lean frame so well, and the fine Spanish boots now caked with dust. "You've come back!" she repeated.

"Nan," he said, "a miracle has happened." From his breast, he pulled out a parchment with a grand seal. "A month ago, I was a beggar. Today, I am Colonel Dempsey in more than just name, commanding more than just a regiment. I've come back, Nan, because now I can finally offer you something worthy of all you'll sacrifice by being with me."

She sank slowly, almost weakly, into the seat, him standing over her, the scene reminiscent of a month ago. But how different everything was now! She leaned her elbows on her knees, pressing her hands to her throbbing temples.

"Is this real? Is it... is it true? True?" she asked aloud, though not directly to him. Then, she sat back and looked up into his face.

"It may not seem like much, but today it feels like everything to me. And with you by my side, I know I can make it more. Still, for now, it's all I have to offer." He tossed the parchment into her lap. She looked at the white cylinder without touching it, then back at him. A small smile crept around the corners of her sweet mouth and trembled there. The memory of his grand promises of conquest for her sake from long ago surged into her mind.

"Is this the world you promised me, Randal?" she asked, and his heart soared at the familiar, teasing note, banishing his last doubt.

"It's as much of it as I can get my hands on," he said.

"Then it will be enough for me," she replied.

Her voice now lacked any trace of teasing, replaced by an infinite tenderness. She stood up, moving closer to him, holding out the parchment, still unfolded.

"You haven't even looked," he protested.

"Why should I? It's your kingdom, as you've told me. And I'll share your kingdom, no matter where it is."

"It's in the Indies... in Bombay," he said, his voice carrying a hint of hesitation. She considered it carefully.

"I've always had a thirst for adventure," she replied, with a deliberate calmness. He felt compelled to explain the appointment and how it had come to be. As he told the tale, tears welled up in her eyes.

"Why? Why? What now?" he exclaimed, distressed. "Do you regret it?"

"Regret it? Oh, Randal! How could you think that? These are tears of relief. I've endured a month of such hopeless anguish, and now..."

He wrapped an arm around her shoulders, drawing her head to his chest. "My dear," he whispered. He sighed, holding her close in a silence that felt like a prayer, until finally, she lifted her face to his.

"Do you realize, Randal, how many years it's been since you last kissed me? And back then, you angered me by stealing what is now yours to take freely."

He felt a strange awe, but courage had always been his companion, despite his many flaws. They married the next day and spent their honeymoon in the isolation imposed by the law. Once they were declared free of infection, they stepped into the world to claim the honors that Fortune had stored up for Randal Dempsey, making amends for all the suffering she had caused him.

THE END.

Printed in Great Britain
by Amazon

60540945R00167